A NOVEL BY...

DENIS CRONIN

The Stain

ISBN 978-1-914488-60-3

This edition printed and bound in the Republic of Ireland by

Lettertec Publishing

Springhill House,

Carrigtwohill

Co. Cork

Republic of Ireland

www.selfpublishbooks.ie

29.01.'23

To Mags, Julie, Ian, Colin and Abbie,
with love

TO ED,

THANKS SO MUCH FOR YOUR SUPPORT —

BEST WISHES

Denis

Nadir

(Arabic Origin)

The worst moment or the moment of least hope and least achievement

PART 1

* * * * *

He had done most bitter wrong
To some who are near my heart,
Yet I number him in the song;
He, too, has resigned his part
In the casual comedy;
He, too, has been changed in his turn,
Transformed utterly:
A terrible beauty is born.

William Butler Yeats, Easter 1916

1

Dublin, Wednesday 10th May *(24 days to Nadir)*

We were sitting in the back of the taxi, not talking but each of us fuming for different reasons. I thought that he'd gone too far, whereas he thought that I hadn't gone far enough. Either way, the meeting had come to an abrupt end when the other side walked out, and we were left sitting there twiddling our thumbs. No one had spoken for a minute and then Anthony hit the table hard with the palm of his hand and exclaimed rhetorically; 'For Christ's sake Jack, how can you get any business done in this town.'

I turned to our advisors and asked them to go work on a recovery plan and that we'd get back at six in the morning. I knew I had two things to do that evening: manage my American colleague and get the other side back to the table tomorrow.

'Come on Anthony, let's get to our hotel and we'll get a bite to eat, all's not yet lost. I'll talk to Harry tonight and we'll get them back talking in the morning.'

Anthony looked at me with a strained expression. 'I need a drink, a strong one … and I need to call my boss, you know they expected this thing to be closed out tonight, they were planning to announce it on Friday.'

'Get another twenty-four hours from them; I know you can do that. We'll close it out tomorrow, I promise.' Anthony's call to the States didn't particularly worry me; there was absolutely nothing they could do about it anyway. They needed the acquisition and they needed union buy-in to close the deal. Anthony had hoped to be on a plane tomorrow heading home, and it was precisely because the finish line felt so close to him that he couldn't take the pantomime of the negotiations any longer. I could feel him next to me twitching restlessly all afternoon, looking at his watch, like a volcano about to erupt. And eventually, of course, he exploded in an outburst, telling Harry and friends to 'either take the fucking deal or leave it.' (Even I was thrown, I had rarely heard Anthony use *that* expletive).

Harry was well used to dealing with Americans and would easily have weathered the outburst, but O'Donoghue, from the electrical and drama brigade, had been goading Anthony throughout the entire meeting, and saw an opportunity for some self-aggrandisement and promotion. In a classic coup, he seized the high moral ground and pronounced with great indignation: 'Well, mister Castelletto' - he deliberately mispronounced his name as Ca-*stiletto,* to the grins and smirks of his colleagues - 'you might threaten your other minions, while slipping that dagger through their hearts but us Paddies certainly aren't going to take it.' And with that he stood up and proclaimed, 'Ok lads, we're out of here.' End of meeting!

The taxi ride through Dublin didn't take very long as it was evening time, midweek and the town was quiet. The driver turned up the radio to hear Trump saying that America was being screwed by Obama's Paris Climate Agreement and he wasn't going to commit to it. And, to add insult to injury, neither was he going to commit a budget to NATO because they were paying too much and Europe, who was screwing the US, needed to pony up. Anthony grunted. 'What have we done to our children in electing this moron? It doesn't bode well for the future, Jack.' As we got close to the Westin Hotel, I suggested that we have a quick freshen-up and meet in the bar for an aperitif in thirty minutes. I needed time to call Harry, but first I needed space to figure out how we could get out of this.

Harry vented on our call; 'You told me you'd keep your American on a tether, Jack, how the fuck am I supposed to get my people over the line if we have to listen to fucking threats like that?'

'I can't legislate for everything Harry, you know that, and you could've done something to stop O'Donoghue getting on his high horse and walking out. Doesn't he get the bigger picture here? I thought you'd got him between the ditches … I've just had to listen to Anthony-fucking-Castelletto tell me that he's out of here and fuck the deal.'

'Jack, listen, you know O'Donoghue's not my union, and you know he's trying to make a name for himself on the council, and you, my friend, let the American give him a free ride. And I'll tell you something for nothing, you're gonna have a problem getting him back to the table.'

'I won't have that problem, Harry, you will. My problem will be getting Castelletto to reschedule his ticket, 'cause right now he's on a flight at eleven thirty tomorrow. And if he goes you know he ain't coming back and the whole deal is off. Picture the headlines, Harry, three hundred of your members signing the dole on Monday, because we both know there's no other show in town.'

Harry said nothing for a long while, but I could almost hear him swearing under his breath. He'd been doing this work for close to thirty years, but recently, in a confessional moment, he'd admitted that each year was becoming harder and certainly less rewarding for him. 'Idealism being traded for pragmatism,' he'd said, 'and it's your fault Jack, and people like you. With you people, everything is material, everything is profit. When I was a young organiser, I thought that I could help stop the incoming tide of globalisation, but I was like King-fucking-Canute trying to hold back the waves. I thought I could stop its appalling rush to the bottom for cheap labour. But now all I can do is watch helplessly as the unions get strangled with every fucking year. I suddenly feel old and tired at the wheel.'

We knew each other well, sat across many tables from one another over the years, and although we may have had different ideologies, different masters, we shared a respect for each other and shared a trust in each other to deliver our side of a handshake.

I also knew that, although Harry wasn't quite sure how much the Americans needed this deal, he couldn't take the risk of a stand-off.

'I'll get O'Donoghue back to the table, Jack, but the American will need to lead with an apology, in front of my team.'

'I'll do all the apologising, Harry. I'll say whatever needs to be said.'

'The American, Jack, it has to be Castelletto.'

When I arrived at the hotel bar, Anthony was already there nursing his usual double gin and tonic. He nodded to the bartender to mix the same for me.

'Jessie is asking after your health Jack, she's wondering when we're gonna see you again in Framingham. You know she's got a soft spot for you, my friend.'

'Ah, that's nice to hear Anthony. Tell her that I promise the three of us will get dinner when I'm over in a couple of weeks.'

'Great, I'll hold you to that. I presume I'll change my ticket to Friday?'

'Yep, if you don't mind. I've had a call with Harry and we're back at the table in the morning at nine bells. Paul and his team will run the numbers tonight and we'll have something to look at over breakfast. I reckon if we tweak one or two of the actuarial assumptions, and if we can find a little cash to top up the pension pot, we'll nail it. As you know, most of those guys are well into their fifties so pensions are *the* hot item for them. It won't cost us much more and we'll still be within our approval space.'

'Yeah, ok, you know 'em better than I do, I'll move my flight to Friday.'

I played with my drink and then sipped it slowly.

Anthony read the silence; 'There's something else, is there?'

'Yep, you know me too well, my friend. There's just one other thing we need to do at the meeting, first thing in fact.'

'Which is?'

'Well, we need to untangle some of the language from earlier, you know, before they walked out.'

'Untangle the language? I've heard that one before, Jack, that's a euphemism for taking it back.'

'Well yes, in a way, or just say it differently, you know, something that sounds like an apology but actually isn't.'

'No fucking way Jack, there's no way that you or I are going to apologise.'

'Well, not me Anthony, you.'

'You gotta be joking man, do you actually believe that I'm gonna apologise to those cretins? I'd sooner eat my bloody hand off.' Anthony threw back the remainder of his drink and signalled to the barman for a refill.

'Don't think of it as an apology, Anthony. Think of it as a few well-chosen words to get you on a plane on Friday. Park your pride and keep your eye on the prize. You've spent almost two weeks here closing this deal, working your ass off on due diligence, and you know as well as I that the hardest part was always gonna be the unions. You get this group over the line in the morning and you go back to Boston a hero, with this big fat deal in your back pocket. I promise you, my friend, if you're prepared to open tomorrow's meeting with a few choice but meaningless words I'll have us out of there before eleven.'

'Sorry, Jack, but I'm not apologising to that prick O'Donoghue.'

'You're right, Anthony, not to O'Donoghue, to Harry. We need to give Harry due respect.'

Anthony sipped his fresh gin, and without looking at me he said, 'Do you ever get fed up with this game? Do you ever just want to walk away and not come back, you know, wonder what the hell we're actually doing with our lives? I'm three thousand miles from home, from my family, and do you think this company gives a shit?'

'My friend, let's at least be honest with each other, we're not in this for anyone else except ourselves. I've often thought about what drives us, and I realise that it's the risk, the thrill of closing the deal, the win. And yes, there's collateral. It's given Bea and me and the kids a good lifestyle, but like you right now, I'm not at home with them. I remember the family events I've missed for so-called essential work reasons, but I can't remember any of those reasons now. We're in it, Anthony, because we want to be in it.'

'Well, if that's the case, Jack, then it's time for me to get off the bloody ride. I'll do what I need to do in the morning to close this deal, but it'll be my last one. I've lost the hunger for it, my friend. It's time for me to go home.'

We sipped our drinks in silence, lost in our respective reveries. I could tell that Anthony was yearning to be at home in the bosom of his family, whereas I was visualising three or four chess moves ahead, until checkmate was in sight.

* * * * *

We finished our drinks at the bar and moved to the Michelin star restaurant, *La Gourmandise*. In the ten years that we were with the Boston-based Jackson and Associates we'd overlapped on a dozen or so deals, Anthony managing the US interests and I running the European side. We had found ourselves in the trenches many times together, always having each other's back. We admired each other's professional integrity and work ethic, understood and played on each other's respective but very different strengths, but mostly we enjoyed each other's company. Anthony and his wife Jessie had often stayed at our place in Spiddal on the Connemara coastline outside of Galway, and Bea and I in turn had stayed at Anthony's large log house in the woodlands in Framingham on the outskirts of Boston.

Our progression in the firm had followed similar trajectories, both of us making senior partners five years previously, when I was forty-nine and Anthony fifty-two. We spent most of our workweeks away from home, generally catching early flights on a Monday morning and arriving home late Friday evening, or Saturday morning, depending on flight alignments. It was a bonus for me when work projects anchored me in the Dublin office as I was only a two-hour drive to my Connemara home; however, my main office was in London, in the

City, from where I could be in any European capital within a couple of hours.

The restaurant was unusually busy for mid-week. As we made our way to our table, we surreptitiously scanned the room with the sole intention of recognising, but then avoiding any familiar business faces. There were mostly tables of three to four business diners, generally male. In the corner, a group of women who were boisterously celebrating some occasion or other, one guy on his own working his laptop and a table of four tourists, easily identified as Americans, by their accents and volume. We smiled at each other as we reached our table; we were in the clear. We ordered fillet steak rare and an Argentinian Malbec.

The staff was always attentive as they knew us pretty well and probably saw us as easy-going and uncomplicated diners and, more importantly, we tipped on the generous side, the benefit of business dining. I suspect that they saw Anthony as the quieter one, always courteous and respectful, mannerly to a fault, speaking English in a broad Boston accent. He sometimes seemed embarrassed by my gregariousness, my outgoing, chatty personality (Anthony: *You're over-chatty*), it stung his conservative sensibilities. For instance, I loved chatting with staff *en français* whenever I could, to excerise my French, and so he once described me as '*over-the-top and loud, in any language*.' I had laughed and pleaded that I was just being engaging. Physically we were both about the same height at slightly over six feet, but there the resemblance ended. Anthony was big-featured and broad, dark sallow skin, jet black hair harshly combed back, with greying at the temples. His eyes too were black and darted in his face when he became animated. Dressed American-style in his dark sports jacket and grey pants, he filled the clothes with his bulk, and filled the room with his quiet presence. A very clever but naturally cautious operator.

I guess I'm a different kettle of fish. Leaner than my American friend, my mother used to say that we got it from my father's side, the greyhound breed. My problem is nervous energy, never at rest, always gesticulating, tactile. Not satisfied with wearing myself out, I naturally wear everyone else out in the process. And my colouring comes from my mother; fair reddish hair, blue eyes, pale skin, freckles; yes, and burn to a cinder under the summer sun. If Anthony devoured the detail, then I relished solving the problem. I believed in the power of compromise, on the presumption of course that the prize was worth it and in sight. And I was grateful to have arrived at a point in my life where I could simply order my business apparel without ever again having the need to work out sizes, colours, styles or labels. I had successfully and proudly arrived at middle age.

Our meals arrived and our conversation moved easily from the business at hand to family matters, the stresses, the hopes and the future. I manoeuvred the conversation to bring us back to the point earlier in the evening when Anthony had said that he'd wanted out. Although we'd both been here before there seemed to be a determination and finality in his mood.

'You're not really thinking of moving on, are you?'

Anthony considered the question. 'I've been thinking about it for a good while Jack, but especially these last six months, in fact I think I probably came to a decision when getting on that flight on my way out here a couple of weeks ago.'

'Why, what triggered it, anything in particular?

'Ah nothing, and it's probably my imagination anyway, something Jessie said before I left, or maybe it was something that she didn't say.'

'Like what?'

'Nothing, nothing really, like I say, probably my imagination. Too much time away Jack, too much travelling, it plays with your mind you know, you lose the threads and anyway, neither of us is getting any younger, it's time to reprioritise I guess.'

'Hm, ok, well I'm not quite sure what's got to you bud but it sounds like you're fairly serious, and you're a stubborn old bollix. But you know, deciding to leave the firm now is a seismic move. What would you do with yourself, and as a matter of interest, what does Jessie have to say about it?'

'Well, I haven't mentioned it to her yet ...'

But as Anthony was talking, I saw that his line of sight was attracted to something over my shoulder. I turned around to see what had caught his eye. Directly behind me but at the far end of the restaurant I could see the table with the celebrating women, and one of them had left her seat and was making her way towards us. I was struck by her elegance, her confident almost catwalk-like stride, tall in a black figure-hugging dress, set off with a simple, single string of pearls. Her shoulder-length hair was dark and full. She was a beautiful woman, but there was something ... something about her ... something familiar.

Anthony whispered, 'Stop staring for fuck's sake,' and so I quickly turned back. Then I felt a hand on my shoulder, and she was saying: 'I'm sorry to interrupt you gentlemen, but I think I know this man; Jack Sommers, isn't it?' Startled, I turned my head to look at her. She was smiling mischievously with her mouth and her wide eyes. I studied her for a few seconds and then couldn't help myself from smiling too, and stumbled: 'Yes indeed, I am Jack ... and you are ... unbelievably ... Marianne.'

'Phew, well done Jack, I was afraid that you wouldn't remember or recognise me, it's such a long time.'

'Well, I was nineteen, or twenty - well over thirty years ago I guess, but Christ you look the same, I'd recognise you anywhere.'

'It was thirty-five years ago,' Marianne said definitively, 'you were nineteen, I was twenty-one and blonde, remember? You used to call me ol' gal.'

Anthony coughed to get our attention. 'Aren't you going to introduce me to the lovely lady, Jack?'

'Oh, I'm so sorry.' I jumped to my feet. 'This is an old friend of mine; Marianne, Marianne Gordon, and this is Anthony Castelletto, a colleague and a very good friend.'

Marianne laughed. 'I'm an old friend, Jack? You mean an old *girl*friend, surely.'

'Em, yes, yes of course, an old girlfriend.'

Anthony rose and offered his hand. 'Delighted to meet you Marianne, and my condolences to you for however long you were stuck with him.'

Now the three of us were standing, a little awkwardly.

Marianne and I went to say something simultaneously, I apologised; 'Sorry, you go ahead.'

'No, no', she said, 'I was just going to say that you look great, you men definitely have it over us when it comes to ageing.'

'Ha, not so sure about that, but were you over at that table the whole time? I didn't see you.'

'Well, I saw you the minute you came in, Jack.'

'Let's get you a chair,' offered Anthony, 'join us in a glass of wine.'

'No, no, thanks, even though I'd love to, but I need to get back to the girls. It's my friend Susan's half century and they're about to bring the cake in shortly, wait for the screams.'

'Ah, go on,' insisted Anthony, 'I'm sure they wouldn't mind you going on the missing list for fifteen minutes.'

'No, no, really, I can't, but thanks. Are you guys in town for a while?'

'Well, I'm here until Friday afternoon, and Anthony is on the 11.00 Boston flight Friday morning.'

'Well, I'd love to catch up for a coffee Jack, before you disappear again for another thirty-five years.' We laughed. 'Have you any free time tomorrow?'

'Em, not sure, but give me your mobile number and I'll call you in the afternoon, I'll know how I'm fixed by then.'

Marianne called out her number and I tapped it into my phone.

'Ok, well, I'd better get back to the party, lovely to meet you Anthony and safe travels. I love Boston, by the way … and it's so great to see you again, Jack, and hopefully we'll get that coffee before you leave town.'

'Same here Marianne, really good to see you. I'll buzz you tomorrow.'

She turned to leave, then hesitated, and about to say something she stopped herself and said instead; 'never mind.'

In that moment of awkwardness, she reached across and kissed my cheek, she mumbled bye-bye and turned and hurried back to her table and friends, just as a large cake with fizzing lighted candles like mini fireworks came from the kitchen, and an uncoordinated chorus of 'happy-birthdays' filled the restaurant.

We resumed our seats and sipped some wine until the shrieks and choruses died down and then smiling, Anthony said, 'Wow, beautiful woman, Jack. Haven't ever seen you tongue-tied like that before, tell me all, what's the back-story?'

'Ah, no story really, she was my first girlfriend way back when. She arrived as I was stumbling from the darkness after five years of boarding school up in Donegal, she kinda ran away with my innocence. She was over from Dublin for the holidays, staying with an aunt of hers in Salthill. We were only together for a month or so, you know one of those summer things, and then she, well, she dumped me, I guess. I assumed that she'd just left and gone back to Dublin and college, but I found out later that she'd met another guy, a Dublin guy over for the summer too. And that's the story in a nutshell, and I haven't laid eyes on her since.'

'But it must have been something special, the fact that you recognised her after thirty-five years, it looked to me like you were a little misty-eyed there, bud?' Anthony prodded mischievously.

'Well, it was first love, Anthony, for me anyway, not for her though. And she really was a great girl, great craic. But she was a lifetime more mature than I was, she seemed so sophisticated and knowing, and I was really clumsy and gauche in every possible way. And when I say she took my innocence, I promise you, I was so naïve I didn't even know it was gone. The truth is I probably didn't give her what she needed, and …'

'Go on, and?'

'Well, that's it.'

We continued with our dinner until the noise and sounds from the birthday table suggested that their celebrations were coming to an end, chairs were scraping, presents and balloons were being gathered, and friends were standing and kissing their goodbyes. Anthony indicated for me to turn around, and when I did, I could see Marianne looking over in our direction, waving her goodbyes and indicating with her hand to her ear for me to call her as promised. I waved back, nodding my commitment.

Soon after the party had dispersed, we rose to leave. 'Ok, Jack, I'd better call Boston and get them over the line on this.'

'Right, text me if there's any issue, although I'm sure they'll be fine. I need to call home anyway and catch up on other stuff.'

When I was back in my bedroom I checked in with Bea. She seemed tired from her day's labours, so the call was short, but warm:

'How're you doing, darling?'

'I'm good but a little tired, the shop was manic today and Helen was out sick again.'

'Ouch, poor baby. Maybe you need a new partner, Helen's out a lot these days.'

'Ah she's ok, you know she's got her own problems.'

'Yeah, don't we all, but you shouldn't be carrying all the pressure on your own shoulders.'

'I'm fine, really, anyway how was your day? How's Anthony?'

'Anthony's fine, can't wait to get home, we had a little wrinkle at the meeting today and he's now stuck here until Friday. But if we can wrap up by midday tomorrow, we'll get him to Heathrow in the afternoon and he can get a flight home tomorrow night. Obviously, he was asking for you; "now make show you give Bea ma regaads."' (I mimicked my friend's broad Boston accent).

Bea laughed. 'Any other news?'

'No not really, nothing else to report. Go on, I'll let you get some sleep, give Sadie a kiss for me.'

'Ok mon amour, bonne nuit et je t'aime.'

'Oui, bonne nuit ma chérie et je t'aime aussi.'

I sat on the edge of the bed and gently swirled the glass of Jameson I had poured earlier. I thought about Bea and the fact that I hadn't mentioned my chance meeting with Marianne. It's not that it slipped my mind, but I suppose I thought that it would have been inappropriate at this late hour, a place and a time for everything, I guess! Anyway, I knew Bea better than to introduce something like this out of the blue and away from home, even though it was just bumping into an old friend. But I knew that she'd have had a sleepless night if I told her that it was an old *girl*friend, and her almost pathological jealousy and insecurity would project all kinds of illogical and irrational fears and could actually lead her to be physically ill.

Indeed, Bea was somewhat of a paradox. She was supremely confident and successful in running her gallery business, with that French arrogance which could leave all adversaries, guilty or innocent, pleading for mercy. And in most cases, for a crime that they didn't even know they had committed. Yet, behind it all she would admit to her very closest and intimate circle that she was troubled with a deep sense of uncertainty and insecurity. *Mes demons,* she called them. On those occasions, Bea needed a magnified level of reassurance of her value and worth. She needed to hear that she was liked and loved by those whose respect she craved, and who incidentally were likely to be the very same people she'd left in a pool of tears earlier.

I sipped my whiskey and thought about tomorrow, but not the business end of it. Although I'd promised to call Marianne at some point during the day, I knew already that that would never happen. Although I couldn't quite grasp it then, I sensed a cloud gathering, a shadow blowing from the past, a chill. Anyway, I knew that I'd awaken in the morning to a new sobriety; after all, it's what every new day brings. Night-time either darkens the conscience or clears it, sandcastle issues get washed away by the new tide. Yes, I knew well that in the clarity of the morning the thought of calling Marianne would seem out of place, inappropriate, even silly.

It was midnight. I finished my whiskey, set my alarm for five thirty, and turned onto my side and into my clear conscience.

2

We had met in Lyon when I was twenty-seven and attached to the local Accenture office. She too was twenty-seven and she worked as a teacher in a high school which was quite close to my office on Rue Avignon. Nearby was a little park close to Pont du Morand on the Rhone. On the corner of the park and under the canopies of the ancient plane trees there were a few shops and a café, and outside the café there were benches which faced the river and which sometimes offered a cool breeze against the heat of the day. I had seen her on a number of occasions buying coffee and a sandwich during lunchtime. She was always alone, and she'd take her purchase to one of the faraway benches and read her book. I thought she was so beautiful and elegant and a little mysterious. She wasn't tall and model-like but petite, perfectly proportioned, with a mass of rusty auburn hair, large hazel eyes, high cheekbones, and a full wide luscious mouth. I saluted her one day and, although she nodded in acknowledgement, she didn't engage in conversation, and didn't seem to want to. But this was the French way - brusque, stand-offish - and then she hurried from the café and sat on her bench in the park. When she was out of earshot one of my colleagues elbowed me and laughingly said, 'No joy there, Jack, you must be losing your touch.'

A couple of weeks later I found myself in front of her in the queue in the café (I had engineered the circumstances, staying out of sight while waiting for her to appear and then hurrying in before she arrived and before other customers were in sight). I dallied at the service counter looking at the various deli offerings, and then casually turned and apologised for my indecision, which was causing her delay, and asked if she would recommend something nice. This very un-French approach took her by surprise, and she mumbled no and shook her head. I apologised for intruding on her but continued to look for her help. Flustered and annoyed, she reluctantly pointed to the first thing she saw behind the glass which was a ham and cheese croissant (which happened to be the least appealing lunch on offer). Of course, there was no going back and so appreciatively I said yes, ordering it along with a coffee. I waited outside the café until she came out and, with the brashness and doggedness only an Irishman could enjoy, I walked alongside her, uninvited, as she headed to her bench, commenting on the weather and asking that tragic one-liner, 'Do you come here often?' When she sat strategically on the centre of the bench, allowing little room on either side, I asked if maybe I could join her, and with no option other than to be downright rude, she acquiesced and moved to give me room to sit beside her. I introduced myself and offered my hand, she said her name was Beatrice and, in attempting to free up her hand, she fumbled and almost dropped her sandwich and coffee. I moved quickly to help her recover and prevent a disaster. Then, when a level of calmness and composure was restored and formalities were over, I asked if we could speak informally, such being the protocol.

As we lunched, we chatted, awkwardly at first but then more easily. We traded our working histories, swapped a little of our life circumstances, and then too quickly her lunchtime was up, and, in a little panic, she said goodbye and hurried away. I was surprised at how disappointed I felt when she was gone. I returned each lunchtime of that week but sadly, she didn't show. However, on Wednesday of the following week she arrived at her usual time, and after a few minutes, I, having given up on the loitering strategy, sheepishly made my way to her bench once she had settled. Interestingly though, this time she sat to one side, which seemed to me like an open invitation to join her, and, having asked and received her permission, I duly did. And it was from these small moments over the following few weeks I realised that I spent my time in excited anticipation of lunchtimes, and more and more my distracted thoughts were of her. I was sure that she felt the same way by her expression and enthusiasm each time we met. So, one day I walked her back to her school and asked if she would have dinner with me that weekend.

'Do you believe in destiny?' she asked as we sipped our wine and waited for our meals to arrive.

'Hm, how do you mean?'

'You know, like that the events in our lives are predetermined, that they're outside our control.'

'Hm, not generally, but why do you ask?'

'Oh, just wondering. You don't think that it was fated that we should have met, or was it just the randomness of life?'

'Uh, don't know really; but I guess that it's about timing and circumstance; and in our case the timing was perfect and the circumstance was pure romance' I smiled, well-pleased with my response.

'So, you don't think that we were destined to bump into each other in the café?' I knew full well that the 'bumping into' had been choreographed but I didn't want to give away the ruse.

'Hm, well maybe a little Bea, maybe destiny had indeed a small part to play in it.'

'Ah, so you weren't waiting for me to go into the café then, before you made your move?'

'What, how do you mean?' I was shocked.

'Jack Sommers, I saw you hiding from me at the side of the café, and then when I got closer you jumped in ahead of me,' and she laughed.

'But how did you know that I was waiting for you?'

'Because I saw you looking at me lots of times before then. You and your work friends, giggling like school boys, and thinking that you're not at all obvious. I wondered in fact how you were going to talk to me. And it took you long enough,' and she laughed again, a little triumphantly.

'What! That's manipulation, in fact entrapment' I cried. But Bea just laughed.

'Aha, it's clever when you do it but it's manipulation when I do it.'

I laughed, acknowledging her superiority in the game of cat and mouse;

'You're a smooth operator Beatrice; I'll have to have my wits about me with you.'

That first date started a relationship which led us to becoming inseparable. She met my friends and I met hers and everyone agreed that we were made for one another. My job regularly took me out of town for days or weeks at a time and when I returned, we would hide away for twenty-four hours and drown in each other's presence and passions, and devour each other in our hunger as if emerging from a long famine of intimacy.

Over dinner one evening early that August, Bea suggested that we should take a trip to Paris some time soon.

'Jaysas. Bea, are you mad? Paris in August, I'll suffocate in that heat. Anyway, I hate Paris.'

'Ah yes, you told me already, you hate all capital cities.'

'Well, it's not so much that I hate capital cities, it's just that I prefer second or third cities. Less pandering to tourists, less forced grandiose architecture, less attitudes of superiority, less government. You know what I mean, sure, isn't that why you live in Lyon?'

'Ok, well what about early October then, it'll be cooler?'

'But I hate Paris any time, darling. I'll tell you what, let's go to Florence some weekend, how about that?'

'But I don't want to go to Florence, I want to go to Paris, I love Paris.'

'Ha, now I know you're winding me up, sure you hate Paris too.'

'Ok, then I'll get them to come here to meet you.'

'Who?'

'Maman and Papa, of course. They really want to meet you, Jack. They keep asking when they will get to see you.'

'Aaah, you she-devil, I was wondering what you were up to. But for you, my darling, anything. *Shine your shoes, get rid of your blues, take you under my wing, anything.'* I sang the words as I leaned over and kissed her lovely lips. 'Anything, *except* meeting your parents.'

'Ah, Jack Sommers, you're mean, I hate you, I hate you.'

'Don't be silly, you love me, my little sexy mademoiselle.' Then I theatrically clapped my hands and announced, 'Ok, let's go to Paris, let's meet the parents, and God help us all.'

And so, the first weekend in September we travelled to Paris to meet Madame et Monsieur Dufort. Lydia and Tomas Dufort had been separated for a number of years but remained good friends, if intensely competitive. Lydia had reserved a table at the two Michelin star restaurant, L'oie D'or on Rue Saint-Paul overlooking the Seine and Pont Marie, and once the introductions were over, we settled into informal chat.

'I haven't been to this place before, Jack, but Lydia assures me that it has excellent fish - if you like fish of course. I'm an animal flesh man myself, you know. My preference was for a lovely little informal place over by the Sorbonne, but I'm sure that this will be just fine, if a little ostentatious. Tell me, do you like Paris?'

But before I had a chance to answer Lydia jumped in, 'Apparently Georges Pompidou - he's our president, Jack - was seen here eating lobster only last month.'

'Pompidou is a pompous ass, Lydia, and Jack knows full well who our president is, he's living in Lyon for God's sake. Isn't that right, Jack?'

I went to answer again but Lydia jumped in again, 'Pompidou is a good man, Jack, don't mind Tomas, he's old fashioned and conservative and Pompidou is the future for France.'

Bea moved her hand under the table and squeezed my thigh, I responded by squeezing her hand in mine, as if to signal: *fortify ourselves!* But I steered the conversation in a different direction.

'I hear you've been to Ireland; how did you like it?' As soon as I asked the question of them, I knew it was a mistake, because of course they both answered together.

'We loved it. We went in June.' Tomas' voice, being the louder, crushed Lydia's.

'July, I think Tomas. Remember, your grandmother passed away in June and we went the following month.'

'My grandmother didn't *pass* anywhere, darling, she bloody *died*, in May.' Tomas encouraged us to laugh with him, and I thought: poor little Lydia, 'and so it was in June that we went. Anyway, we loved it, Jack, but it rained for the first three days.'

'No darling, it was the *last* three days. Remember, we landed in Dublin and the fields were so green and the sky was clear blue, and the air was so clean and fresh.'

'Not fresh, Jack, cold. Christ, your country is bloody cold. But we loved it, didn't we, Lydi?'

'Yes, Tomi, we loved it, one of the best holidays we ever had together. We were like children discovering a fairy-tale land, everything was so different from Paris, small and funny and colourful and music in every bar.'

'Pubs, Lydi, they call them pubs. Isn't that right, Jack? But you're right there, it was the most romantic place we'd ever visited. Of course, we were only kids then, in our twenties. But you know the strangest thing about the place, Beatrice? Well, I'll tell you, the people - never stopped talking, that right, Lydi?' (*Pot calling kettle black,* I thought).

'And you didn't even have to know them, they'd just come up to you and talk to you, they were so full of curiosity.' (*Hm, that'd be foolishness and nosiness*, I thought).

'Remember when it happened first you thought that they were going to rob you, Tomi.'

'Christ, no I didn't, woman. I swear I never thought that, Jack. It might be different nowadays but back then you could trust the Irish with your wallet.'

'Beatrice tells us that you're from Galway, Jack, is that right? (I knew at this stage that there was no point in attempting to answer). 'We stayed in Galway the second time we visited, a gorgeous place, little fields and walls made of stones and rocks, and oh my god, the Atlantic Ocean was so beautiful and frightening.'

'But cold, Jack, that water was so cold it'd freeze the balls off a brass monkey. That right, Lydi?'

'Really, Tomas, there's no need to be crude.'

And so, the meal continued as it had started, with neither Lydia nor Tomas conceding anything and neither Beatrice nor I contributing anything except our nodding, smiling presence. Long after the meal was finished and the restaurant was emptying, the waiter was hovering for someone to request the bill and to avoid further awkwardness, I 'insisted' on paying and, unsurprisingly, on this I got no dissention. When I was handed the bill I could feel the blood drain from my face - a pasty white is how Bea later described my colour when we were on our own and she actually had a stitch in her side from laughing. *Jesus Christ it's a fucking month's salary* I thought, and when I handed the waiter my credit card there was a definite disappointed glance between Lydia and Tomas and disdain from the waiter: *he doesn't have a gold card!*

'Christ, Bea. He's a handful, isn't he? Poor Lydia.'

'Papa? Yeah, the surprise is that they stayed together for so long. Maman told me after they split up that they only stayed together for me, which made me feel guilty. But only for a little while, because then it dawned on me that seeing as they fucked each other to have me, they deserved to fuck *with* each other for a few more years to keep me.'

'Hm, interesting perspective on your parents, Freud would love you. Remind me never to introduce you to Martha and Uncle Marty.'

But it wasn't long before I did indeed introduce her to my Mam and step dad, Martha and Uncle Marty, when we spent some time in Ireland later that October. Only this time it was up to Bea and I to do all the talking at dinner at the aptly named Galway Hooker, as Martha and Uncle Marty hardly opened the locks of their jaws (except to eat everything that was put on their plates before turning their appetite and their cutlery in the direction of what was left in the serving dishes), and seemed in awe of Bea, this French exotica. And they continued their silence when the bill was produced (in case there could be any doubt, Uncle Marty actually parked his hands in his pants pockets), and after a little awkwardness I 'insisted' on picking it up.

And of course, Bea met the wonderful and colourful Lizzie, my twin sister, and Lizzie's girlfriend Bella, and the four of us spent a glorious week exploring and introducing her to the Irish way of life. She experienced what she later called *Irishness,* the casual and informal way of people, the conversations that spontaneously erupted with strangers on the street and in the cafes and pubs. Bea told me later that she now understood my personality better in the context of my own people. She suggested that my gregarious, open, outgoing, and friendly way weren't just traits of me, the individual - they were national traits. She was particularly taken with the West of Ireland where people seemed to be made of their environment, the rugged but beautiful landscapes of Clare and Connemara and further up the coast to Donegal. She loved that the wild Atlantic seemed to be battling with the jagged coastline, and the small fields with their stone walls protecting their little crops, and the lazy grazing sheep (who were surprisingly agile when spooked). Everywhere the colourful houses like confetti were scattered randomly across the countryside or squashed tightly together in little villages.

And she laughed too at the national twin obsessions with the weather and the pub. Every conversation started with a commentary on the weather conditions, 'Are we going to get rain?' 'Sure it might hold off.' Worst October that I can remember.' 'Sure the farmers will be happy anyway' and so on. In France, or it seemed anywhere else in the world, the weather generally stayed stable and predictable for at least a few hours or days or weeks, but in Ireland there could be four seasons in one day, and this was especially the case by the Atlantic coast. The second obsession, the pub (and for the pub read alcohol, the essential Irish social lubricant), wherein it seemed every social experience had to take place and which appeared to legitimise the country's affliction and dependence on the demon drink. She discovered that the Irish had a strange unconditional love affair with alcohol. The paradoxical nature of the pub: the chat, the music, the craic, the silken glove masking the iron fist, but the fist did all the damage. Even though I had of course warned her, nothing could have prepared her for the tragic comedy of the ubiquitous Irish pub. Every village had two or three and they all seemed to be busy every night.

The following year saw dramatic changes in our circumstances. As Bea was spending most weekends in my apartment, we decided that it would be easier if we moved in together. Anyway, I had a two-bed on Rue Foch which was convenient to both our workplaces as opposed to her one-bed on the Confluence which required a metro change. Bea de-personalised her place to rent, and personalised my place to live. And then, just as we were getting used to playing house together, Bea became pregnant - unplanned but certainly not unwanted. Ben was born with red hair and blue eyes and of course we adored him, and the noise and energy and chaos that ensued in 25 Rue Foch gave testament to the expansion of our little independent family. When Ben was a toddler, we upped sticks and moved to London to follow my career and Bea took up a teaching post at a local primary school. Ben was three when his brother Sean came along. Sean, a quieter and a more laid-back creature than his brother, had a smile that seemed to have been painted across his face, and which nothing could shift even when he was being used as a punching bag by Ben. And then just twenty-three months later, Sadie appeared, and if Ben and Sean were the head of me then Sadie, with her rusty auburn hair and hazel eyes and sallow skin, was born in the image of her mother.

My job kept me busy and I found myself travelling regularly, but that was the path that I had chosen. My career in London seemed supercharged and Bea had agreed to take time from her teaching and look after the kids. Then, in bed one night, as I slept, I slowly became aware of Bea whispering in my ear; 'Darling, are you awake?' and when I gave no response, she shook me a little. 'Darling, are you asleep?' I squeezed my eyelids tighter, hoping she'd go back to sleep, but then I felt her shake me with more determination; 'Darling, are you awake?'

Resistance was useless, I roused myself, looked at my watch and moaned. 'Jesus, Bea, it's two in the morning.'

'I know Jack, I'm sorry, but I'd like to talk about something.'

'But can't it wait till the morning?'

'Well, I suppose so, but I'd like to talk about it now, will I make you a cup of tea?'

'Christ no, no tea.' I forced my eyes open and my brain to park the dream that I had been enjoying. 'Go on.'

'We can't stay in London forever, you know.'

'Yes, I know that, Bea, we've known that since we arrived five years ago.'

'But we can't stay here much longer really.'

'Why not? And what's much longer anyway?'

'Oh, a few months maybe.'

'A few *months*?'

'Well, a year at the most.'

'Why, for God's sake? What's the rush to move?'

'The kids, of course. They need to settle somewhere.'

'But they're settled here, aren't they?'

'No, of course they're not, we have no family here, and they really have no friends either, just themselves. No, we need to move soon.'

I moaned; 'Back to Lyon you mean, or sweet Jesus, don't say to your parents in Paris.'

'No, silly, to Ireland of course! We need to move to Ireland, that's where our gorgeous children must live, that's where they belong. Will you talk to your boss tomorrow?'

'Christ, Bea, are you out of your mind? Talk to my manager tomorrow? Oh sure, of course I will, and we can move to Ireland over the weekend.' My sarcasm went straight over her beautiful head, deliberately or otherwise.

'Good, that's settled then. Ok mon amour, dors un peu, te reposer et t'aimer, you're such a sweetie.'

She turned on her side with her back to me and within a few minutes was sleeping soundly. I lay on my back and considered the deal that I'd just been craftily hustled into, in my half-asleep state. *She's clever,* I thought, *but now, where-to my career? London to Dublin, not exactly the trajectory I'd planned.*

3

Dublin, Thursday 11th May *(23 days to Nadir)*

I awoke as normal, five minutes before my alarm was due to bleep. I lay in the hotel bed for a few minutes and quickly processed the stuff of the night before and the agenda for the day ahead. Such was my waking routine. I met Paul and his team at six and reviewed their pension numbers. Yes, with a few tweaks of the actuarial assumptions, we could present a healthier fund without committing too much more cash to the pot.

I met Anthony at seven for breakfast and brought him through the figures and we agreed on our strategy for the union meeting. I again promised to have it concluded by eleven and offered to have him rerouted on an afternoon flight through Heathrow so he could be on an evening flight to Boston and be home early in the morning. After breakfast, I went for a stroll down towards the docklands for some fresh air and called Harry to put the offer of the pension top-up on the table, conditional of course - as Harry himself would say - on everything else being agreed.

Without putting the actual words in his head, I hinted that the offer would blindside O'Donoghue and should bring the other union reps over. Harry, of course, reminded me of the apology and that I'd better prepare my side to listen to a lot of noisy rhetoric, but he indicated that with the pension top-up, he could carry his side. So, we did a virtual handshake and the deal was struck. To further appease the unions, I suggested that the meeting would take place in the boardroom on the sixteenth floor at the union offices in Liberty Hall, just across the river from the Westin.

Once everyone had gathered in the boardroom and taken up their respective positions, both physically and ideologically, Anthony opened the meeting, directing his well-chosen words to Harry:

'Mr. Boylan; I'd firstly like to thank you and your colleagues for the tremendous amount of work which you have invested in these discussions. I appreciate that they have been very arduous at times and they have tested the resolve and patience of both sides. However, after my untimely outburst yesterday, I have to say that I hugely admire your magnanimity and professionalism in recommencing our negotiations this morning.'

O'Donoghue went to speak but Harry firmly interjected:

'Before I accept your apology Mr. Castelletto (*what apology?* I thought), I'd like to remind you of a few truths.'

His voice began low and calm and authoritative:

'You've only been around here for a wet week, sir, but this company has been in existence for over sixty-six years and during that time it has made enormous profits for its shareholders - some might even say immoral profits. You see, these gains have been made on the backs of my members, the downtrodden and unappreciated workforce. This company, sir, has been propped up by its lowly-paid employees, who through their pain and suffering and tribulations have given the best years of their lives, nay, who in some cases have given their *actual* lives for this place. The very same company that has wrung from them their sweat and energy and taken the best years of their lives …'

'Hear, hear,' and 'you tell em, Harry' his colleagues rumbled. Even I was impressed. *I mean, they weren't exactly coal mining, they were just assembling components in an ultra-modern factory with a first-class canteen … and even a gym*. But warming to his theme and building to a crescendo, Harry continued to rasp eloquently:

'... and don't you doubt for one minute, Mr. Castelletto, that this company would have been nothing but for the blood and tears that have been shed by my brothers and sisters, whose inalienable rights of justice and fairness, that you so casually trample on, have been handed down by the spirits of Larkin and Connolly, and if I may be so bold to say sir, even Marx himself …'

This brought louder 'hear hears' and a few misty eyes, and table-slapping in shows of noisy agreement from his cronies. And then, with an exaggerated show of weariness, which seemed to alight on him as if from the dust and rust of all the old factories that ever were, and from the burden of years of industrial fatigue, Harry finished his monologue by expunging all the hurt and injustices of what he called his *broken classes,* and following a theatrical pause, he eventually exclaimed:

'... and therefore, sir, I accept your apology.'

In the meantime, I watched O'Donoghue, anxiously twitching on the side-lines, eager to get on the pitch, and just when he was about to say something, Anthony pulled from his notes his trump card, the pension sweetener. And now that pride had been restored and, for a price, principles jettisoned, Harry asked that his side be given time to consider the proposal, stressing: '... but remember, gentlemen, nothing's agreed til everything's agreed.' Naturally, on the resumption of the meeting, Harry advised that the proposal had been accepted by the majority of the representatives.

Harry had won back the power. O'Donoghue was left pouting.

And me? Well, I had a self-satisfied inner smile; *checkmate.*

'Good stuff, Jack, another one in the bag, well done. This is the bit I enjoy the most, closing the deal and heading for the airport.'

Everyone else had left the room and we were left tidying up our papers and occasionally stopping to admire the panoramic view of the city of Dublin with the Wicklow Mountains in the distance, glinting in the late morning sunshine.

'Well done you, Anthony, that was the sincerest non-apology I ever heard, ha, I actually thought Harry was gonna shed a tear.'

'Hm, he's a good man, though mind you he looks like he's getting tired of the game too, and he's not going to be able to hold that prick O'Donoghue back for too much longer.'

'Yeah, I agree, although he was outstanding today, I rarely see that mischievous twinkle in his eye much these days, the spark seems to be fading. And speaking about twinkles and sparks, what about you, were you serious about what you said last evening over dinner - about yourself, I mean?'

'I was as serious about it as I'll ever be about anything, Jack, it's time for me to reprioritise. But I'll pick my moment to talk to people, and I value your council so I might give you a buzz in advance, if that's ok.'

'I'll happily talk it through with you, bud. In fact, as you know we'll both be in Boston the week after next and we could catch up then if you're ready to chat.'

We embraced warmly and as we were walking towards the door Anthony asked, 'By the way, I meant to ask, are you going to give that lady a call - what was her name again?'

'Ah, the dinner lady, Marianne? Nah, some things are best left in the past. Anyway, I've too much to do this evening if I want to get away early tomorrow.'

'Finally getting some sense, Sommers, sounds to me like you're getting old.'

I laughed, slapping him on the back, and we did small talk as we descended to the lobby and out into the bright sunshine. There we said our goodbyes as Anthony climbed into his waiting cab to take him to the airport.

It was now 12.30 as I grabbed a sandwich and walked back to my office on the Grand Canal. I was thinking about Anthony and what life would be like without him at the firm. We'd been through so much together, good times, difficult times, but never bad times. Rightly or wrongly, I'd actually come to depend on him, and the thought of him not being around on future projects made me feel uneasy, sad, and even isolated for some reason. And for the first time a fleeting thought crossed my mind, a thought about my own future with the firm, my own endurance.

But right then I needed to get through a mountain of work if I wanted to get away from the office and be on the road by 3.00

pm tomorrow, before the Friday traffic clogged the city. I worked methodically through the afternoon, taking meetings and conference calls, signing off plan updates on this and that project, and suddenly it was 7.00pm as I collected my papers and laptop, threw on my jacket and started the fifteen minutes' walk back to the Westin. I'd planned to change into my running gear and get in a few circuits of Stephens Green before dinner. But so much for plans; I was greeted by Reno, one of the regular hotel receptionists.

'Ah, Mr. Sommers, you have a visitor waiting for you in the lounge.'

Jesus, I thought, as I remembered that I'd had a missed call from Harry, and this was a classic Harry stunt: catch a guy completely unawares and unprepared. That means there's obviously a problem with the deal.

I went straight to the lounge and looked for where he'd most likely be, in one of the booths, out of sight from the main thoroughfare. The lounge was quiet at this time of evening with a few people scattered here and there, but there was no sign of Harry. Then, from one of the alcoves, 'Over here, Jack.'

I turned in the direction of the female voice, and when my eyes adjusted to the artificial lighting I realised, with a start, who was sitting there.

'Marianne? Wow, sorry, I didn't see you when I came in, I was looking for one of my colleagues.'

'Yes Jack, it's me, you look surprised to see me?'

'Well, yes, I haven't seen you in over thirty years and then I bump into you two nights in a row,' I said as light-heartedly as I could muster even as my antenna was now on high alert. 'Are you meeting someone?'

'Well, yes,' she said, 'you!'

'Ah, I'm not losing it, am I? We didn't agree on anything last night, did we?'

'Well, we actually did. You promised to call me today, remember? I gave you my number and everything.'

'Yeah, I'm really sorry about that, the day just ran away from me. The best laid plans of mice and men, I guess.'

Marianne gave a warm, easy laugh and said, 'Hey relax, Jack, you have a look of terror in your eyes. Here, come on, join me for a drink, let's chat for a while, I was looking forward to seeing you all day.'

I don't like surprises, then or now. You see, I don't trust surprises, in my world they're generally delivered by people with agendas. But I couldn't find an easy exit, so I quickly thought the best approach was to acquiesce and so, as I sat alongside her in the booth, I enthused, 'Yes, of course, that'd be great, hey, good to see you again, girl.'

Marianne signalled for bar service and she refreshed her sauvignon and I took a Bombay and tonic.

'Hey, you're looking fantastic,' I said, 'you really have discovered the secret of youth, have you sold your soul or something?'

'Aha, no, nothing like that, and you're too kind, and so is the lighting in here. I just take care of myself these days, nothing extreme. You know the usual, a balanced diet and plenty of exercise. At least that's the plan, but the plan rarely works. But my god, look at you, you look really great, you've kept yourself in shape, you look better now than when you were nineteen.'

'Jaysas, nineteen, that was a long, long time ago, Marianne. So, how've you been keeping?'

'Yeah, I've been good. I've two beautiful children, Freddie and Ellen. Ellen is still here in Dublin, she's got an apartment in town and Freddie works in London, with Cox's, you know, the law firm. He's married with a little girl, Fabeena, a gorgeous little girl. Her mother, Saahira, is Syrian. Muslim. East meets West and all that. It's a strange one. To be honest with you, we were all more than a little surprised (*I heard 'disappointed'*). You'd be amazed how different their culture is. Anyway, I get over to London to see them very regularly … and you, what about you?'

'Yeah, well we've three kids, Ben, Sean, and Sadie. Ben is in Lyon, cutting his teeth in consultancy, Sean is studying here in Trinity and

Sadie is still finding herself in Galway - finding herself at our expense, ha - but they're good kids I guess.'

'And what about their mother, are you guys still together?'

'Yeah, Beatrice, Bea, she's French and we're still together after 27 years, give or take one or two little breaks in between.'

'Ah, you took time out from each other, then?'

'Hm, you could say the pressure cooker blew once or twice, neither one of us was at fault, really. I'm away from home a lot and that puts different pressures on each of us, but we're ok, we're good … and you, are you in a relationship, you didn't mention a partner?'

'No, Rob and I separated about ten years ago. Ah, it became a struggle when the kids were growing up, whatever romance we had at the start seemed to disappear. Eventually the kids were feeling the tension instead of the love, and so we agreed to split. We meet when there's a kids' crisis or celebration, but beyond that we keep our distance. He's been with someone for the last few years, and good luck to them.'

'Oh, I'm sorry to hear that. These things can be difficult, particularly on the kids. And is there anyone special in your life now?'

'No, not really. I mean I've had a few relationships, but I haven't met anyone that I'd see myself spending the rest of my life with, and anyway, that's not really my goal anymore.'

'Ok, so what is your goal these days?'

'Ah you know, live for the here and now, enjoy myself a bit more, pamper myself now and again. Stay healthy in body and mind, ha-ha. Not exactly Maoism, more *carpe diem*.'

'Hey, not a bad philosophy, I should borrow some of that for myself.'

We both laughed. That was followed by an awkward silence, and I felt the mood shifting, Marianne seeming to get a little serious.

'Listen, there's something that I need to ask you, well, to talk to you about.'

Ah, my instincts were right; like all surprises, this one too had an agenda.

'Oh, really? I thought we were just having a drink for old time's sake, no?'

'Well, we are, and trust me, Jack, you don't know how much it means to me to have you sitting here.'

'Ok, go on, let's talk.'

Silence.

Marianne stared into her drink and seemed to think long and hard to find the right words.

I let the silence continue.

Finally, she said, 'There's actually no easy way of saying this, and I often thought about what I'd say if I ever met you, but whatever I planned seems silly now … this is such a big thing … ok Jack, here goes,' she lowered her head, took a deep breath and closed her eyes. 'You and I have a son together; my son, Freddie, is *our* son!'

Silence.

Ah, a joke obviously. And so, I laughed.

Silence.

'I'm not joking, Jack, we have a son together.'

I didn't understand what she was saying. I thought I was generally quick on the uptake, but right then I was completely lost.

'I don't understand, what do you mean?'

'Freddie, my son, is our son. You're his birth father.'

I was speechless. I thought, *she's crazy. What's she up to? She must be mad. I know that we couldn't have had a child together.*

As calmly and as lightly as I could, I said, 'Listen, Marianne, I'm not too sure where you're coming from but …'

Marianne injected urgency; 'No, no, listen to me, Jack, please just hear me out … I know this is a huge shock to you and I know you're not going to believe me and you probably think I'm fucking crazy but, please, let me show you … here, look at this.'

Her hands were shaking as she fumbled in her bag for something, then she pulled out a photograph. She held it up for me to see but I looked straight at her face and wouldn't look at the image. Whatever game she was playing, I wasn't going to be part of it. But she was entreating, insisting, demanding. 'Please Jack, please, just look at it.' She held the picture up in front of my face. I was powerless to avoid looking at it, my eyes involuntarily brought it into focus. It was a photograph of a young man, possibly in his early twenties, laughing, animated; he had a shock of red-tinged blonde hair, pale freckled skin, clear bright blue smiling eyes, wide mouth, high cheekbones. And I recognised the likeness immediately. It was a likeness of Ben, my eldest, but not quite him. It was me as a young man in the picture, but not quite me.

I took the photograph from her, studied it.

This made no sense to me. I felt giddy, lightheaded, disorientated, *what the fuck was going on.* I searched my memory, back, back and deep, deep into my past. Back to then. With her. But there was nothing. There had been some opportunity for fumbling yes, ejaculation yes, but no intercourse, and no knowledge, no worry, no talk, ever. Yet in spite of the sureness of my memory, and the clearness of my conscience, the picture now in my hand told me there was a problem, and the worry cells deep in my consciousness told me it was a big fucking problem.

I put the picture face-down on the table, and slid it towards her. 'Ok, Marianne, to be honest with you I'm a little fucking confused here, what's going on? What's this about?' My voice was hard, had an edge to it, accusatory.

'Jack, Jack, I'm so sorry. I'm so sorry I didn't tell you back then, before now …' She was crying, losing her composure, fumbling for a tissue in her bag. 'But I promise you, I swear before God as my judge that this is our child, this is your son.'

I needed time to think, needed time to consider my options, and needed to put some sense into this ridiculous situation, and Marianne being emotional, genuine or otherwise, wasn't going to be of any help.

'Ok, ok, Marianne, calm down. Here, take some water.' I handed her a glass.

Her hand shook as she accepted it, and breathing slowly and deeply she calmed herself, and drank some water. 'Thanks, I'm sorry, I swore that I wouldn't cry.'

Nothing was said for a long while as I took stock. She stayed quiet; it felt calculating. The ball was in my court, but I had no idea how to move forward, how to deal with this. Asking her to explain everything would seem to be moving to some form of implicit acknowledgement, even psychologically. Yet I needed to know why she thought this stranger to be my son, if only to prove her wrong. I sipped my drink, thinking, *Jesus Christ, where the hell do I go with this. There's no point in getting up and walking out because I'll just be kicking the can down the road. Deal with it now, Jack! If I've learned anything in life, it's to deal with it now. But fuck!*

I picked up the picture and looked at it again.

'This guy looks like he's in his early twenties, if as you say he's my son he should be in his thirties now.'

'Freddie will be thirty-five on April 18th Jack. I picked this photograph because it so reminds me of you. Here, here's a recent shot of him.' She opened her mobile and showed me the screen. Clearly it was the same guy, a little older now but still astonishingly like Ben. She was in the frame too, both of them laughing, enjoying each other's company. But now I also saw her in his face, across the eyes, yes, and their foreheads.

'Show me a picture of his sister.' I returned her phone.

Marianne scrolled through her album and selected one that she obviously liked and presumably showed her daughter in her best light. 'Here, this was taken over Christmas.'

I studied the image of a young woman, probably in her late twenties, early thirties, very beautiful, looking very different to the image in the photograph, and very like her mother. The only similarity between the brother and sister was around the eyes. But then the thought struck me that Ben and Sean and Sadie are very different, like from different parents. But no, not really from different parents because the kids have parts of Bea and me in them. Their features, expressions, mannerisms, not to mention their personalities, nailed them to Bea and me.

I handed her the phone. I needed fresh air, some time to think clearly. I couldn't comprehend the situation. *Photographs can be manipulated and digital images can be made to look like whatever you want*, I thought, although my belief and confidence was shaken, and the previously unmovable ground now felt unsteady. I far from believed her story, but I knew I had to find out more. I checked my watch, *crap, it was eight thirty.*

'Listen, I don't know where we go with this, but I'm going to need to clear a few things and get some fresh air, I'll need thirty or forty minutes. What do you want to do?'

'Well, I want to stay and wait for you, I'm happy to do that. I can get a bite to eat or something.'

'Why don't you hold off eating till I get back and we can get something. Do you want to get a coffee in the meantime, maybe?'

She readily agreed and I ordered her a coffee as I left the lounge.

As I headed for my room I wondered: what the hell do I do now. If for whatever reason it's a stitch-up, then it was a problem that I could deal with, maybe with some difficulty, but deal with all the same. Calmness was required, but not procrastination. But I could undoubtedly find a solution. If, however, it was true, and if I was the father of this person, then this was a problem that I wouldn't be able to contain. I had this vision of a stone, no, not a stone, a boulder, being dropped into the lake of my marriage equilibrium and causing serious fucking waves and threatening the very fabric of my relationship.

Once in my room, I ran the cold water for a while before splashing it on my face a number of times. Then I sat on the edge of the bed and made a couple of phone calls. I had a short call with Bea, told her that I was under work time pressure but that I was looking forward to seeing her the following evening, and we traded our usual good nights. Hearing her voice made me feel anxious already. I called Jo, my PA, and asked her to rearrange my schedule for tomorrow, cancelling anything that wasn't urgent. And then I needed to get some fresh air. I left the hotel and took a walk by the river under a light rain and called Alex, my long-time friend. Al's philosophy in life, when confronted with unwanted surprises, was to '*do nothing*'. Although he was as sharp as a blade, he was as risk averse as a pensioner, and he did nothing that wasn't thought-out or planned. He called it the *science of planned spontaneity*. I filled him in and, unsurprisingly, Al's advice was 'invoke the *do-nothing* principle, Jack.' We agreed to chat again in the morning.

I made my way back into the lounge where Marianne was sipping coffee. She looked like she'd freshened up too, reapplied her makeup and lipstick, and I caught the fresh scent of perfume. She smiled anxiously but said nothing.

'Ok, I've ordered something light from the restaurant and we can have it here, if that's ok?' She nodded, still smiling nervously. I called the bartender to bring us two sauvignons and waited until they arrived before starting the conversation. I had decided that calmness was the best approach, at least for now, there was no point in getting her upset and nothing could be gained from drama.

'So, first question,' I asked her evenly, almost gently, 'tell me, when and how were we supposed to have conceived this child?'

'Well, I know that we never had full intercourse, Jack, I know we never fucked as such. When I met you, you were so innocent. I know I'm not telling you anything you don't already know but, Christ, you came out of that boarding school with no idea of how life worked. But part of that was incredibly exciting for me, I was mad about you, you know. But it was also hugely frustrating, if you know what I mean.' Marianne sipped some wine. 'Anyway, remember we were hanging out for maybe five or six weeks and making out whenever or wherever we could, but we never got beyond kissing and groping. You'd go so far and then either orgasm or pull away, leaving me hugely frustrated. Jesus, Jack, you were so fucking frustrating. Anyway, sure we had nowhere really to go. But then your parents were away for the night and for the first time we had a free house.'

She paused for breath. But even after all the years, I remembered that night like it was yesterday. We'd had a few drinks in O'Donnabhain's with our friends and then she'd given me a signal, and we slipped away quietly and headed back to my house. Once we were there, we opened a couple of beers and then, without much preamble, started kissing, and with the excitement of having the house to ourselves we got incredibly horny, and I remember fumbling our way to my bedroom, pulling off our clothes on the way. Then we were on the bed naked, and I swear to this day, I remember the overpowering sensuality of feeling a totally naked woman in my arms for the first time. Flesh to flesh. God, the exhilaration. Every inch of her. That softness and sexiness and sensuality, and her hands, all over me, and almost instantly I was at the point of coming, before we had barely time to enjoy each other. I remember the feeling of it building quickly and, in an attempt, to stop myself, I pulled back and away, but unfortunately, I'd gone too far. I had no control, and I came involuntarily, helplessly in no-man's land - *the fucking humiliation!*

She continued now, 'I remember we had a few drinks somewhere in town and then we ended up back in your house. I was so fucking horny, Jack, so incredibly aroused. I remember you were nervous about your parents coming back and catching us, but either way we were naked by the time we got to the bedroom. And I remember thinking, *oh god it'll be so good this time.* Then you were on top of me and you were pushing it between my thighs, I didn't know what you were doing, you didn't know what you were doing, and even before we could put on a condom you came on me, on my thighs for Christ's sake - *the fucking frustration!*'

She took a breath and sipped some wine. 'Then you mumbled sorry and got off me and went to the bathroom and left me lying there. I must have laid there for ten, fifteen minutes. I started to feel a chill, and I knew you weren't going to come back to the bedroom. I couldn't be bothered looking for you at that stage because I was so frustrated and pissed off. I remember shouting, '*fuck you, Jack*'. So, I cleaned myself with tissues as best I could, got dressed and I left and walked until I found a taxi back to Salthill.'

I was listening to her version, racking my memory, searching back, back; I don't remember it being between her thighs, was it between her thighs? I thought I came in no-mans-land, that's always been my memory of it ... *but hang on a second, where the fuck is no-mans-land? I* ***must*** *have been lying on her; I* ***had*** *to be lying on her because I remember that feeling of being naked, body to body. Jaysas, if I was lying on her there's no room for no-mans-land ... why the hell have I believed that, all this time, how could my memory be so wrong?*

My mouth was drying up and it felt like a noose was tightening around my neck. 'I remember it differently,' I lied.

'But I rang your house the next day and left a message with your mother, but you didn't contact me. I remember it was a Saturday and I went into town and searched a few of our pubs but I couldn't find you. I knew you were embarrassed at what had happened, but I must have rung your house ten times that week. In the end your mother told me to stop ringing.'

But my mother never told me that she had rung, or did she? Christ, I didn't remember her telling me ... until now, shouting up the stairs to me in my bedroom; 'That poor girl has rung again, Jack, you need to contact her for God's sake.' How the fuck could I have forgotten that, for all this time?

The meal arrived and we stopped talking for a while. We both played with our food, ate a few bits and pieces, but neither of us had any appetite. We sipped our wines. Marianne picked up the conversation. 'A week or two later a guy who I knew from Dublin, Robert Barry, who I'd previously briefly dated, turned up in Galway, we literally bumped into each other on Shop Street. We met a few times for drinks and hung out, I guess.' She looked pleadingly at me. 'I didn't hear from you, Jack, I assumed you'd dumped me. Well, you *had* dumped me for God's sake!'

Once again, my memory was different. *I dumped her? Surely it was the other way round? Why did I think that she dumped me? Christ I'm a fool … of course it was me, I went into hiding, hoping that she wouldn't find me, and she didn't, she couldn't find me … but why have I lied to myself all these years? Christ, I was so cowardly, spineless, pathetic.*

I could feel the heat rising in my cheeks; I knew my face was flushed. She continued her story. 'Anyway, the summer was up, and I headed back home. I was still seeing Rob, but in a matter of a couple weeks I knew there was something wrong. I missed my periods, but I didn't need any proof, I knew instinctively that I was pregnant.' She lifted her eyes from the table and looked at me, directly at me, unflinchingly, for the first time that evening; 'It was your baby, Jack, and it wasn't just the timing, I knew to my core it was your baby.'

'But if you were so sure that it was mine, why didn't you contact me?'

'Well, I did contact you, or tried to contact you. I called your house loads of times, but you never answered, and I hung up each time your mother came on. I even went down to Galway one Saturday to see if I could find you. I tried the usual haunts and asked around, but I only had a few hours before I had to get the train back to Dublin. And then there was another side of me which wanted to protect you, which of course was stupid, stupid for everybody. I thought about everything, Jack. I was sick with worry. I was scared of what my parents would say. I thought about abortion, or maybe going to London or Liverpool to have the baby and get it adopted. A friend of mine had done that, but I guess an easier solution emerged, and to my shame I grabbed it. And I've lived to regret it, Jack, every day since I've regretted it. I led Rob to believe that it was his. You see, he adored me, and when I told him I was pregnant he promised he'd stand by me and we'd get married and he'd get a mortgage from the bank where he worked and we'd buy a house. He had my parents' backing. He was three years older than me and, from my parent's point of view at least, he had a respectable job in Bank of Ireland, which seemed to tick their boxes.'

My steadfastness was slipping. Although I knew that the chances of her becoming pregnant the way she described were probably only one in a million, it was still possible, even without penetration. *Fuck! Yep, fuck is right!*

I could feel the noose tightening.

'But I didn't love him, Jack. I liked him, a lot actually, and I thought I could grow to love him. He was kind and generous and loving, and in fairness he was a good husband and father while it lasted. But I never did come to love him. Ellen came along three years after Freddie was born …'

'Wow, wow, surely after the child was born, he must have known that it wasn't his, I mean did it look like him? His colouring? You said he had red hair when he was born, did your husband have red hair?'

'No, Rob's colouring is like mine, and we joked about it at the start. You know, the usual, the milkman or the postman. But then my grandmother saw him and proclaimed that he was the image of her brother when he was born, red hair, same features, and she claimed him as an O'Regan, and it satisfied everyone. In fact, the relief for me was that once my grandmother claimed him, then everyone saw the O'Regan line in him.'

We sipped our wines. The waiter came and cleared our plates of uneaten food. I was partly aware of people coming and going in the lounge, some couple laughing in another booth, two men standing at the bar, arguing animatedly about some sports result, and I could hear other voices out of sight. I checked the time: it was ten thirty. *Fuck,* it was getting late and I needed one more question answered tonight: motivation.

'Let's say everything you say is true, then why now?'

'Well, why now is because I saw you last night. But to be honest with you I knew anyway where you stayed when you were in town, and I knew for some time where you worked, and where your offices are.'

I was surprised, and it obviously showed.

'Don't worry, I wasn't stalking you or anything, but about two years ago there was a picture of you in the Times with some business group, you were announcing some deal or other. It was easy enough to find out where you stayed, but last night was pure chance. Well, maybe serendipitous, as I had decided a few months ago to try and make contact with you.'

'So, my question still stands, why now?'

'Well, a few reasons. I'd been living with this secret for the first twenty years of my marriage, no one knew, I mean no one. Like I said, a day wouldn't go by that I wouldn't think of it, stress over it, and some times were harder than others. Like on Freddie's birthdays. In fact, what should have been the happiest times were sometimes the saddest and the hardest. And it was breaking my heart that I was lying to him, that I was living this lie, that the whole thing was false, my life was false. I hated myself. By the way, for what it's worth, I hated you too. And I started drinking a lot.' She took a deep breath and sipped some water.

'As Freddie grew up it was becoming obvious, to me anyway, that he and Rob were very different, and I was becoming anxious that Rob was seeing it too. Although that was probably all in my head. I think just the knowledge alone was poisonous. Even though he really was a good father to him, they just didn't seem to get on. They fought constantly, especially when Freddie was in his teens, and I know fathers and sons do that, but it really upset Rob. He'd ask me what I thought, what was it that he was doing wrong as a father, what could he do to fix it, and would I talk to Freddie and so on. But they were very different people, and not just physically, their mannerisms, their personalities, their temperaments. Things were becoming strained too between me and Rob. It's ridiculous but I started to resent him for my situation. Everything he did annoyed me, we were arguing more and more, and we were less and less intimate. I actually didn't want him to come near me. The family was becoming fucked up, dysfunctional; everyone was suffering - including Ellen. Then one day it blew up completely, they started arguing over something stupid, but it actually turned physical and Freddie left the house. He was twenty, but he left for almost a week, moved in with one of his friends. In the meantime, Rob was blowing a gasket, it actually felt like he was coming close to a breakdown, and I knew then that this was tearing the family apart and I made a decision there and then that I had to deal with it. A friend of mine recommended a counsellor whom she was attending and so I booked my first session, my first of many sessions, and it was the smartest thing I had done in my life. I explained everything, poured everything out to someone else, to another human being. She was good, non-judgemental, and calming. I went to her for about a year before I was ready, and then one day I felt that it was time, I felt that I had the courage and confidence to take the first step.'

'And?'

A long pause.

'And so, I told Rob.'

4

Boston, Friday 12th May *(22 days to Nadir)*

Anthony relaxed in seat 4A as the Airbus went through its take-off routine and climbed to ten kilometres above the earth's surface. He sipped his double gin and tonic and nibbled on a fruit and nut mix. He loved this part of his work life - going home. He had phoned Jessie from Heathrow, letting on that he was still in Dublin and that she'd see him Friday night, but because of the opportunity to reschedule his flights he would now touch down in Logan International at 5.30am, and be home by 7.00am Friday morning. What a surprise she was going to get. Anthony didn't do surprises, but he was giddy in himself that he had thought this one up, all on his own. He sang to himself the Simon and Garfunkel anthem '*America*' as he always did on westward transatlantic flights. His mood was ebullient. He thought of his last few weeks with Jack and glowed at how successful their working relationship had been over the years, hoping that when he no longer worked for the firm then he and Jack and their wives would remain close. They had been through so much together, as professionals and as friends.

His mind drifted back to their first assignment in the crazy days of 2007 and the initial murmurings of the impending financial meltdown. Their organisation had been approached by the Spanish government to help rescue a family-owned banking business headquartered in Barcelona which was on the verge of failing. Hundreds of European and US jobs depended on the survival of the company. But it was a Spanish-Catalonia political football and they were thrown a hospital pass. They were only a few days into the assignment when their lives had been threatened by nefarious phone callers in the middle of the night. At one point even a small explosive was detonated outside their hotel. They had a choice to make; to continue their work or get the hell out of it and give in to the terrorists' threats. The Madrid government promised them around-the-clock protection, which would have been very comforting in Madrid, but less so in Barcelona. But they saw something in each other that they liked and so they took a punt on one another and, in spite of the risks, they both agreed to continue through to the completion of the assignment. The company was successfully turned around, made leaner, rebranded, and, unlike other financial institutions, actually survived the global financial crisis of the following years.

And they had done it together. As a team. Like brothers in arms, he and Jack.

His thoughts drifted to Jessie. *I really need to get Jessie back to Connemara to the Sommers' place the soonest* he thought, *and they must stay with us. I'll mention it to Jack when we talk next week.* As he hummed his tune and sipped his drink, he had the same thought he always had on this particular journey, and it was of his grandfather and grandmother when they first crossed the Atlantic almost one hundred years earlier. Crammed into a little ship and working their passage, they had given up their meagre savings to get to an unknown new world. He marvelled at their endeavour and their courage and ambition. They had only been teenagers for God's sake, and they had succeeded against all the odds. They'd eloped from a little village called Valloni which was in a very poor region at the base of the mountains in Northern Italy, a few kilometres west of the town of Castelletto. They had given their names as Tony and Renee Castelletto when they arrived at the Immigrant Station on Ellis Island, where they were officially processed and given their papers which allowed them to embark on American soil and find honest labour. And they did just that, working hard to assimilate into American life. They settled in Boston where Tony set up his own shoemaking enterprise in a little chaotic workshop on the south side of the city. Within two years of their arrival in their new world, Renee gave birth to Tony Jr. and eighteen months later, baby Sylvester came along.

They worked tirelessly to build a successful shoe-making business. They hunkered down and somehow weathered the Great Depression following the stock market crash of '29. And in the mid '30s they moved from the little workshop in south Boston to a large old renovated warehouse on the waterfront, which gave them direct access to the interstate transport network and was also close to businesses in the city centre. They supported and gave patronage to the city municipal bodies, particularly the Boston police and fire departments, and of course greased the palms of the Irish and mafia-controlled unions. The '*Castelletto*' brand became synonymous with affordable, high quality, durable footwear for the working men and women of New England. Nothing fancy, they were the Levis of shoes. But in spite of their success, or maybe because of it, the Castelletto dynasty also experienced personal tragedy. In 1974, when Anthony was just fifteen years old, his parents, Tony Jr and Isabelle died in a freak accident during a January storm when a falling tree crushed their car. The following year, his uncle Sylvester lost his only child at the age of six in a tragic drowning accident. Soon after his parent's untimely deaths, his uncle Syl took Anthony under his care.

Anthony loved his grandparents. He remembered when he was a child and he used to stay over at the beach house, his grandfather would put him on his knees and bounce him up and down, singing nursery rhymes. Then, without warning, he'd suddenly open his legs so that Anthony would fall through, only for his grandad to catch him just before he hit the ground. He'd screech with fright and delight and his stomach would lurch to his mouth and his grandad would let out a great roar of laughter. Even though it nearly made him sick he'd plead *again, Grandad, again, again.* His granny, Renee would scold her husband, saying, 'For God's sake, what are you doing, you old fool? One of these days you'll drop that child and then what will we do?' When she was out of sight his grandad would give an exaggerated conspiratorial wink and do it all over again.

As Anthony grew older, his grandfather would tell him stories about how, in 1919 he and Renee eloped and left their little mountain village in northern Italy, making their way through France. He'd thrill and regale him about all the strange people they met, the robbers and the highwaymen and the wild beasts and the deserted German soldiers hiding in fields and ditches. His grandad would always ask: 'But child, have I ever told you about the time I saved your granny from an evil dangerous bandit?' And Anthony would answer, 'No, Grandad, you never told me that story,' even though he'd heard it a thousand times. But it didn't matter what the lad replied because his grandad carried on telling him the bandit story anyway.

'You see, Anthony, me and Renee were making our way through France, and every night we'd be exhausted from travelling all day. This one night we found a barn and we crept into it and found some straw to sleep on and we cuddled together for warmth and comfort. But while we slept, a bandit, who must have been hiding at the back of the barn, bided his time and then jumped out and grabbed your granny and threatened to kill her with his butcher's knife unless I handed over what precious little savings we had. He was a big man and he had his arm around your granny's waist and the knife to her throat. Well, I looked into her eyes and she looked into mine and then, as if both our minds were one mind and we were - how do you say it, telepathic, yes, we were telepathic, your granny opened her hand and gripped the bandit's crotch, vice-like, just as I jumped into action and grabbed his knife-hand.'

'And were you and Granny scared, Grandad?'

'Well, I'd be telling you a lie, child, if I said I wasn't scared, but your granny gave me courage and strength. She was so brave. Anyway, I grabbed his hand and we were both fighting for the knife, but he was a strong bastard and the next thing I knew I felt the blade glance off the side of my head and then this fierce pain in my ear. And with that,

I gave him an almighty punch into his face and knocked him on the ground and the knife fell from his grasp.'

'And what happened, Grandad, did he cut your ear off?' As Anthony had heard the story many times he was well ahead of his grandfather.

'Shush lad, take your time, wait till I get to that part. Anyway, he fell to the ground and your granny got loose and crawled away and I jumped on top of him and we were both scratching on the ground for the knife, but then he found it. As he tried to stab me, I grabbed his wrist and I turned his hand around and the knife -' Anthony always covered his ears with his hands at this point '- sunk deep into his throat.'

'And was he totally dead, Grandad, and was there lots and lots of blood?'

'Yes child. You see, it was either me or him.'

'Then what happened, Grandad, is that when you met the farmer?'

'No, no lad, will you wait for me to tell the story? Then I grabbed our belongings and I pulled your granny by her arm, and without looking back we ran from the barn as quickly and quietly as we could and we held each other's hands tightly as we walked all through that night until the dawn came. Then we found a ditch a bit away from the road and we lay down together and fell asleep. And after a few hours, we woke up and Renee looked at me and said, "Holy mother of God, Tony, half your ear is gone." So, we started out again and eventually came to a farmhouse where a kind farmer and his wife cleaned and bandaged my ear and gave us a little bread and cheese and warm milk, and when the farmer asked us our names I quickly said: Tony and Renee Castelletto.'

'You didn't give him your real name 'cause you killed a man, isn't that right, Grandad?'

'Shush, child, I'm nearly finished with my story. Anyway, later when we left those kind people and we were on the road again and on our own Renee asked me; "But why didn't you give him our real names, Tony?" And I said to her, and I remember it to this day, I told her:

"Renee, we can never use our old names again for we have killed a man, and as we have taken his life, he in return has taken our identity.'"

While Anthony was in wonder at his grandfather's stories, Renee would often shout from another room, 'Never mind those old stories, child, most of them are made up. Don't believe half of what comes out of that old man's mouth.'

Anthony would think about this and he'd always wonder which half of the stories he should believe, the first half or the second half. But he believed the entire bandit story because his grandad was the only person he had ever known who was missing half his ear. And when he used to play in his room on his own or when he'd dream superhero dreams, he re-lived these stories, he became his grandad, fighting the ever-evil bandits and always saving his granny.

The Airbus touched down on Runway 2 in Logan International exactly on schedule at 5.35am. Anthony had already shaved and refreshed before landing and, once he had collected his luggage, he stopped off at the flower stall in Arrivals and bought an extravagant bouquet of red roses, and by 6.00am he was switching on the ignition of his Mercedes. He took the tunnel to the Mass Pike and on to route 90, and because there was hardly any commuter traffic this time of the morning, he estimated that he'd be home in forty minutes. He turned on the car radio to catch up with any local US news; some presenter was interviewing one of the wounded survivors of the Orlando nightclub massacre. The first anniversary was coming up in a few weeks' time. The guy was saying that the scene had been horrific; the shooter was just killing indiscriminately, bodies everywhere, and all in the name of religion. Then the presenter cut to a Trump commentary that seemed to imply that maybe if they weren't gay, they wouldn't have been at the nightclub and Anthony thought, *what kind of a screwed-up world are we living in? Forty-nine innocents killed in a gay nightclub and we've just elected this homophobic moron as president, what are we doing to ourselves?* He couldn't listen anymore, so he silenced the radio.

As he drove west on the highway, he shook himself out of the moment of gloom and forced himself to think more positively and so he thought about Jessie and the prospect of them spending more time together once he left the firm. *But first I must tell her about my decision, no, I'll involve her in the decision. Maybe we'll go for dinner to Hernández this evening and I'll tell her then, I mean involve her then, she loves the desserts and the atmosphere and the fuss they make at Hernández. And we could tell the kids if we see them over the weekend.* He was so proud of the kids; they were doing really well for themselves. Beautiful Maria, who was completing a PhD in applied physics in his old alma mater at Harvard and recently dating Paul, a lovely guy from Medford. And Julian, who was studying art at MassArt and was already recognised as a special talent, working in oils and metal and even exhibiting at the South Boston Art Show. Jessie thought Julian might be gay as he had yet to show an interest in a female partner even though most of his friends were females. She had finally had the courage to broach the subject the last weekend that Anthony was home, in as casual a way as possible:

'Met any nice girls lately, darling?'

'Girls? Course, lots, but you've met most of them.'

'Ah yes, I've met most of them, not all of them of course. But tell me, is there any one of them particularly special to you, you know, like in a special kind of way?'

'What do you mean by special, Mom?'

'Well, you know, special, maybe one of them that you particularly fancy?'

'Hm, no, not particularly, I kinda like them all, but any reason why you're asking?'

Jessie turned to her husband for inspiration: 'Anthony dear, you know what I mean by special don't you?'

'Best to keep me out of it, Jess.'

'Oh, come on Anthony, you know what special means.'

'Son, your mother is trying to find out if you're gay.'

Jessie gave a little scream and her body jerked, spilling hot coffee on her lap which caused her to jump and yelp some more while at the same time protesting:

'No no no, that's not what I was implying, and that's a terrible thing to say Anthony, don't listen to him, Julian. You know I didn't mean that, you're so crass Anthony, where do you get these things from?'

'Hm, methinks the lady doth protest too much,' Anthony mocked. But to both their surprise Julian offered:

'I don't know actually.'

'You don't know what, darling?' Jessie asked, trying to recover her composure.

'Well, if I'm gay or straight of course. I don't know yet, but I'm probably bi. Is that a problem for you guys?'

Except for another little yelp, Jessie was speechless and so Anthony offered: 'Course not Son, you follow whichever star makes you happy, and the most important thing to know is that we're always here for you, if ever or whenever you need us, that right Jessie?'

Jessie, still in shock, said, 'Yes, yes of course Julian, your father is right of course, we're always here for you, just like we're always here for Maria.'

'Great,' said Julian and he jumped to his feet, gave his mother a kiss on her cheek, winked at his father, and said: 'Well I'm off then, meeting some friends for lunch, see you guys later.'

End of conversation.

Jessie took to her bed for the afternoon.

Their house was a large log house off a tree lined avenue in a woodland area just two miles west of Framingham. He loved this house, a Norwegian chalet design, which they had built fifteen years earlier, even getting the logs imported from Norway. He especially loved soaking up the smells of the woods and that tactile feeling of the bare exposed log walls. As he drove down Eucalyptus Avenue at 6.40am, just as he had calculated, most of his neighbours' cars were still in their driveways and their curtains closed, he caught the familiar sight of the gable end and the half-roof of his own house through the trees. Turning into his own drive, he was surprised to see, sitting alongside Jessie's VW Tiguan, a blue BMW, parked in front of the double garage. *Maria must be staying over,* he thought, *I'm sure Paul drives a Beemer.* He subconsciously registered the number plate and parked his car behind the VW before carrying his luggage into the hall, dropping it by the hall table as quietly as he could so as not to disturb anyone. Just as quietly he started to climb the stairs, carrying the beautiful bouquet of flowers. But as he reached the top and as he was about to put one foot on the landing, he heard noises coming from his bedroom. Grunts, squeals, obscenities. He stopped in his tracks, every muscle in his body seized, frozen. His brain stopped computing, his mind went blank, a terror blank. His eyes stopped taking in his familiar surroundings; every sense failed, except unfortunately his hearing. A man was grunting and swearing, and Jessie sounded demented, possessed, her voice guttural, pleading. 'Fuck me, fuck me, oh Jesus baby, yes, yes …' was this his wife? He had never heard the woman sound like this before in his life.

Deep, deep in the molecular soul of every human being lies the complex strands of instructions which decide who we are and what we do, and when triggered they produce breath-taking clarity of decision and consequent action. And in this specific and unique moment the question asked of Anthony's cellular soul was one of fight or flight. His consciousness told him to turn around and walk down the stairs and quietly slip away into the safety of oblivion. But his molecular instructions told him to walk to the bedroom door, open it and confront his future, and there wasn't a single muscle in his body that could prevent him from following that instruction.

He didn't remember opening the door. He just remembered standing there, in the doorway, watching - no, not watching, observing, like an observer to a surreal drama of which he was playing a not too unimportant role. He saw a man with a hairy back and a hairy ass and hairy legs - *how often had she said that she never liked hairy men* - between his wife's thighs, her knees bent, one of her arms around his neck, the other gripping his ass, her face buried in the crook of his neck and his head arched back. But if the sounds were visceral, the urgent gyrations and thrusting of their bodies was animalistic, and he was acutely aware of the sweaty suction noises as their bellies slapped against one another. He was fucking her relentlessly and she was loving every thrust of it.

The man moaned, 'fuck, I'm coming, I'm fucking coming.'

The woman grunted, 'come in me, fuck me, oh yes, I love you baby, come in me.'

Anthony was fixated momentarily by a stain on the bed sheet, a stain that resembled the face of a clown, animated by the movement of the sheet, sneering at him. The stain of adultery, of betrayal. And then he heard a cough, and quickly realised that it was his own. (And he noticed, rather bizarrely considering the circumstances, that he showed surprisingly good manners to cough behind his hand).

The man quickly arched his head around in the direction of the new sound, but he couldn't stop the involuntary jerking and twitching of his ass cheeks as he emptied his load into the woman. He tried to tear himself off of her, and out of her, but she held on, determined to finish her own orgasm, unaware of the drama unfolding, unaware of the threatening abyss.

Anthony was transfixed, fascinated by his wife's reaction as she belatedly became alerted to the instant paralysis of her lover, and slowly she turned her head and saw him. From ecstasy to agony in the refocusing of her pupil.

Something flipped in his brain, a metamorphosis. He knew this scene; it had been described to him many, many times over by his grandfather. Suddenly, it wasn't his wife on the bed, it was Renee, his grandmother, and he knew that he must act quickly now to save her from the evil bandit. With the weapon of flowers tightly gripped in his right hand, he leapt toward the bed and in a second bound, he was kneeling on it and pushing his grandmother away from her attacker, screaming, 'Get away Renee, I'll save you. Run, run, get away.'

As he pushed and shoved her off the bed, he jumped on the stunned naked man, straddled him around his waist and pinned him by his throat. And now that Renee was safe, all his attention was directed at the attacker, and Tony (the metamorphosis being complete) screamed, 'you fucking bandit, I'll fucking kill you, trying to steal our savings.'

As he had one hand on the throat of his enemy, and with the weapon in his other hand, he stabbed and slashed him across his face and chest and arms. 'You fucking bandit!' He screamed over and over as short thin lines of blood began to appear all over the man's upper body and face, as the thorns scraped and snagged flesh, and blood-red rose petals flew randomly in the air and onto the bed, and broken rose stalks turned and spun and fell harmlessly to the ground. He became aware of Renee, screaming hysterically for him to stop. Now he felt her beating his back with her fists and trying to drag him off her assailant. *She's confused* he thought, *she doesn't understand what's happening*, and still pinning the man by his throat, he turned to explain to his hysterical wife their imminent danger from this bandit when, from nowhere, he was hit by a terrible blow to the side of his head which left him senseless for a few seconds. This was followed by a second and a third blow from the attacker's fist which knocked him sideways and, partly concussed, he was easily thrown off and he slid off the bed and fell to the floor.

'Jesus Christ, you've killed him, you've killed him,' his wife screamed at her lover.

'He nearly fucking choked me,' her bloodied lover croaked, 'it was self-defence.'

Anthony lay crumpled and semi-conscious on the floor as Jessie rushed to help him move so that he was in a sitting position with his back against the bed.

'Quick, Bill, get me some water, hurry for God's sake.'

Handing her the water, he said, 'He's fine for fucks sake, look at me, I'm ripped apart from those fucking thorns. Look at my face, how the fuck am I going to go home after this?'

'Get out, get out of my house,' she screamed; 'Sweet Jesus, what was I thinking, what was I doing?' She was mumbling, crying.

Her lover swore as he dressed and then, at the door, he turned and said, 'He's a crazy bastard Jessie, what was all that bandit shit about and calling you Renee? Don't worry babe, I'll call you when all this quietens down.'

'Please, please get out now,' she cried.

Although groggy and dazed, Anthony was no longer confused. His brain hurt like it had been hammered, but the blows had also readjusted and straightened his consciousness; he was back in the present. Through double vision he saw his wife putting on a dressing gown, it hurt to concentrate but slowly his focus returned. But her voice seemed disembodied, distant, he could hear her talking but he didn't understand the words and they seemed to be coming from a different part of the room. She knelt in front of him, crying and saying how sorry she was and it was not what it seemed and she loved him, and now the words began to synchronise with her mouth and the repetition of them sank in and made sense. Made sense, but not the truth. He started to get up from the floor with the support of the bed. She tried to help him, but he pushed her away.

'Leave me alone.'

'Darling, I'm so, so sorry, please let me help you.'

'I said leave me alone,' he said more determinedly as he got to a sitting position on the edge of the bed.

'You're concussed, darling, let me call Mark, he'll come over straight away.'

'Listen, please leave me alone, and I don't need your bloody doctor, or anyone else for that matter.'

She kneeled in front of him, crying, sobbing, her hands on his knees, pleading. He stood up, pushed her away. She begged him to sit back down, to talk to her, it's not what it seemed, she loved only him. But he fought to regain his balance as he stood for a minute. Then, unsteadily, he walked past her, out of their bedroom, down the stairs, picked up his keys from the hall table and his bags, and pulled the front door closed after him. He sat in his car for a minute, looking at his watch, 7.08am. He calculated. Twenty-eight minutes. Jesus! It didn't take hours or days or weeks or months, just twenty-eight bloody minutes.

He started the Mercedes and drove back towards Framingham and checked into a Best Western motel in a most insalubrious part of town.

5

Martha was told of her husband's death at 9.00pm on a wet November evening. She remembered it was at that precise time because she had just sat down to watch the national news at nine o' clock, as was her evening routine. It came from nowhere. He was due home from work for seven-thirty and he hardly ever got his timing wrong, but on rare occasions events dictated otherwise. Martha wasn't concerned, the twins were up in their beds sleeping, and she had his dinner on a slow cook in the old range. And although she wasn't conscious of a worry, she afterwards remembered that there was something there in her subconscious, an itch that wanted scratching, which she wasn't awake to at the time. And so, when the knock came to the front door and she could see the fragmented blue of the police uniforms through the frosted glass, she knew even before she opened it that he was dead. The driver of the other car survived without a scratch. The randomness of life. Or was it the randomness of death? She could never figure it out. Either way she thought it didn't matter in the end.

Her husband Tommy was an engineer with the Irish electricity company and had a very good, permanent job and decent wage and benefits. Two of those benefits were a generous widow's pension and a very generous death-in-service insurance payment, four times his annual wage, tax-free. Tommy also had personal life insurance and mortgage protection insurance, tax-free. Not that money was in any way compensation for losing a treasured spouse, but the car insurance company also paid out a handsome sum in compensation, tax-free. Even the loan that they had in his name with the local credit union was cleared upon his death, tax-free. But Martha had loved Tommy, and everyone agreed that Tommy loved Martha, and together with their two beautiful, clever children, Lizzie and Jack, they were by all accounts the perfect family. Lizzie and Jack were twins, the baby girl born six minutes before her brother.

Soon after her husband's passing, Martha's health took a turn for the worse. Like vertigo of the mind, she lost her mental balance, her cerebral equilibrium. Sometimes her thinking became muddled and sometimes it slipped into a void, a blackness, a hell. Although she appeared initially to have come to terms with the arbitrariness of Tommy's death, she now obsessed about the reasoning for the car crash. She wasn't questioning the physical stuff, like the torrential rain, or the greasy surface, or the road cambering the wrong way. No, nothing physical, nothing you could touch, more the intangible stuff, as if the crash itself had been a living organism with a mind of its own, and therefore with choices to make. Some Greater Force must have been pulling the strings and that Force must have had options. For instance, it could have decided that one car could have gone a little slower approaching the bend, or one car go a little faster, or it could have contrived that either driver had left their place of work five minutes earlier, and so on and so forth. There were many variables that the Force could have applied to avoid the crash. Or, and this was the ultimate choice, if the Force wanted a crash, why not let Tommy walk away without a scratch and the other driver instead made into a corpse, driven to an unrecognisable pulp of flesh and bones and skin and blood. She never met the other driver, a voiceless, nameless, featureless cunt (All her life she had hated this word, the despicable 'C' word. But now she found a home for it, a meaning for it, and now it slipped off her tongue easily, and repeatedly, albeit under her breath). The cunt had reached out to her at the funeral but she had ignored him, best to keep him featureless, voiceless, it made his unrecognisable bloody pulp of a corpse easier to manufacture in her mind. Of course, Martha was a Christian, a Catholic, and therefore this Greater Force could only be one thing, her God. Her charitable God. Who knew only mercy and love. Maybe the featureless cunt had been a better Christian, a holier person, closer to God … or else she and Tommy were bad. But she knew that Tommy wasn't bad, she knew his soul was pure, unstained, so it must have been she who owned the sin. And she knew what it was. It was the sin of love, of possessiveness and greed and pride and desire for Tommy, to the exclusion of everything and everybody else. The sin of selfishness. She knew deep down in her soul that this was not a random accident, no; this was retribution from an angry god.

A cunt of a god!

The twins were ten years old when their father died. Martha had been a kind, loving, and caring mother, but was naturally distraught and beyond grief when she lost her husband. Now that the responsibility for the twins rested solely and uneasily on her shoulders, she worried and stressed constantly about their upbringing and their future and, above all, their safety. Her personality began to change, cracks began to appear. She fussed and chided them often if they put themselves in the slightest perceived danger. The outside world became nightmarish, full of demons and potential risks, and certainly the twins couldn't be trusted to navigate all the hazards without her presence. But even with her supervision, the simple act of crossing busy roads became a particular knot of stress in her temporal lobes. She'd walk them a kilometre up the road to find a Zebra Crossing and then walk back the same kilometre on the other side just to arrive across the road from the point from whence they had left. Her anxieties soon led to a condition of severe procrastination. In preparing the kids for school, for instance, she'd calm herself with a cigarette, then she'd rush them through their breakfast in case they were late, then she'd worry about forgetting her house keys, then she'd get them to empty their school bags to check that they had all their correct books and exercises completed for their classes even though she had completed the same procedure the previous evening after their homework, then she'd have another cigarette, which generally triggered the worry again about forgetting her house keys, then she would do a tour of the house, making sure that all the electrical switches were off, and plugs were unplugged, and windows were closed, and then she would ask them to check if they had their correct assigned lunches (the lunches being almost identical except Lizzie liked her cheese cut a little thinner. But years later when she and Jack would reminisce, she'd good humouredly recount that she had only mentioned it to her mother once in passing, but it had become gospel in her mother's head), and then they would eventually get to the front door and go through the locking-the-door procedure. Of course, by this time they were hopelessly late for school and occasionally, depending on her level of anxiety on any given day, their mother would theatrically look at her watch and complain; 'What's the point in bringing you to school now, it's obviously too late at this stage. And it's not my fault, you two take too long over your breakfast' and, despairingly, they would open the front door again, go back home, and she would ring the school and tell the teacher that her children were sick today and wouldn't be attending classes. And then Martha would sit down and have a cigarette, but now at least she wouldn't have to worry about forgetting the house keys.

Of course, the kids suffered too. Whereas they were initially disoriented by the emotional shock of the abruptness of their father's death and the vacuum of silence and loss of intimacy in its wake, it was further compounded shortly afterwards by their mother's mental disintegration. The moorings that had once held them firm became loose and insecure. Taut chains suddenly rattled. The solid ground that they had once carelessly trampled on, once unmoveable, unwavering, had turned to mud overnight, their footing slipping here, sinking there, causing insecurities and exposing vulnerabilities. Kids who were once glowing and confident became cautious and dulled, and even appeared to physically shrink.

But sometimes, against all the odds, children dig deep and mine their survival instincts and develop a resilience that belies their age. They learn to duck and dive, to negotiate unfirm ground, and to recognise emotional and physical hazards in the distance and would develop little strategies to avoid them, to survive them. And Lizzie and Jack had a further advantage; they had in each other a twin who was hardwired to their own wavelength, and instinctively they had each other's back. They stood up for each other in the schoolyard when the bullies scented blood. They stood up for each other when adults 'who knew best' encouraged them to compromise their relationship with their mother. And they stood up for each other when either one was feeling especially sad or low-spirited, when they hankered for their dad.

Everyone apart from Martha and her children saw what was unfolding. If the initial cause of their trauma was an unwitnessed car crash on a dark and wet lonely road, then this was a car crash in slow motion and in broad daylight and on display for all to see - their families and friends, their neighbours and teachers. However, just the fact of knowing that a problem exists doesn't always guarantee that interventions are made, or indeed, even when they are made that they are helpful, or that they add the intended value. Sometimes, good people do nothing. Sometimes good people do terrible damage. The wisdom of 'we don't want to interfere', or 'someone else will do it', or 'we shouldn't stick our nose in other people's business' becomes a pervasive cowardice.

It was to everyone's great relief then that Tommy's older brother, Martin appeared to step in and take charge. Notwithstanding the urgency for an intervention, there was added legitimacy in Martin being the right man for the job. You see, Martin had been the couple's best man at their wedding, and, because of that, he was also godfather to the twins, as was the custom back then. Now, he was a little older than Martha, ten years in fact, and although he was still single, enjoying his bachelorhood and especially enjoying his nightly few pints in Mulligans, he was seen by all as the best man to steady the ship. The wise and the clever however (who themselves, of course, had done nothing to help) observed wryly, "But who's going to steady Martin?"

But life has a funny old way of managing its checks and balances. Once Martin entered the scene, Martha became a different woman. Not that her new man knew anything about being a husband, or caring for children, or helping them with their homework, or getting them to school, or even crossing busy roads (he himself was once knocked down by an early morning milk float on a very quiet road as he weaved his way home from an all-night lock-in at Mulligans). No, none of these missing attributes bothered Martha, because all that mattered to her was that Martin *was* there and that he shared the responsibility, or to put it another way, the total responsibility didn't solely rest on her shoulders. In fact, by the very aspect of his arrival and his commendable offer to support her and the kids, Martha's ship was steadied and slowly but surely, she recovered her confidence and sensibilities and her mental equilibrium, and she enthusiastically took to the task of steadying Martin. (It was actually Martha who contrived the proposition, but they were only too happy to let the opposite be known).

The twins, too, slowly emerged from their nightmare. The only imaginative leap they had to make was reconciling the previously much-maligned and indeed slandered Marty (by their parents), to their supposedly new (well, if not quite new then certainly reconditioned), daddy. But with their now fine-tuned resilience and newfound ability to operate in a world of smoke and mirrors, they enthusiastically saluted the flag. At least outwardly; inwardly, they never really bought into the project. But they were very happy to play along, and indeed they developed their own rules and language as they competed with each other in this new and interesting game of playing happy family. Of course, they were happy to play along because they were free! Free to take their lives into their own hands crossing busy roads without having to walk a marathon to get to the other side, free to hang out with their friends without supervision, free to climb trees and jump off walls, free to ride their bikes with dodgy brakes (dodgy even after their new daddy, who had assured them that he was 'good with his hands', attempted unsuccessfully to fix them, but instead nearly killed them).

Then, when the twins were twelve, a new danger came out of the blue. They were asked to join their mother and Uncle Marty in the parlour, and because they were invited to sit on the good couch, they knew something serious was afoot. They were never allowed to sit on the good couch, or indeed use the parlour at all, as that was the preserve of special visitors; doctors and parish priests, and - once at the time of their father's death - a bishop. Their mother led the discussion with Uncle Marty nodding appropriately for emphasis.

'Well, children, now that you're finishing in St. Patricks in a few months you'll need to select a new school for your secondary education.'

They both nodded, and thought, *phew, just school, thank God they weren't talking about having babies or anything disgusting like that. No threat yet.*

'And I, I mean Martin and I, have given this some considerable thought.'

They both thought simultaneously, *crap, Uncle Marty's involved, trouble coming.*

'And it's important that you both get the best education possible, in fact the best education that money can buy. And because of the, ehm, interruption to your studies, which of course wasn't my fault - and neither of course was it your late dear father's fault - we both feel that you may need to play catch-up now, and what better environment than in schools which produce the highest results in the country?'

The twins heard 'schools' in the plural. Up to the point of being marched into the parlour they had assumed that they would be attending the Community School just a mile or so from their neighbourhood. It was co-education and most of their school friends were going to attend there.

'And so, darlings ...'

Darlings? Holy shit, this is really bad, thought the like-minded twins.

'... we have decided to give you both the golden opportunity of the finest education that your dear father would have wanted. So, we have selected two of the best boarding schools in the country.'

The kids were completely blindsided, jaw-droppingly speechless.

There was a long silence until Uncle Marty jumped in. 'You know, an awful lot of kids would eat your hand off for an opportunity like this, I wish I had been given this opportunity when I was your age.'

Yeah, and you'd have drunk it, thought the twins. They looked at each other for some kind of secret signal that would get them out of this crisis - and a crisis it certainly was - but their antennas couldn't either handle the shock or weren't designed to work in a parlour that had once hosted a bishop, and had simply shut down.

'Well, I've never known the two of you to have nothing to say before, and Martin is right, this is a great opportunity.'

Then Lizzie, being the eldest - if only by six minutes - spoke up, 'We don't want to go to boarding school, we want to go to the Community School.'

'All our friends are going to go there,' followed Jack.

'Our dad wouldn't want us to go to boarding schools,' offered Lizzie.

'Yeah, he wouldn't have let you send us there,' charged Jack.

'Well, he and I spoke about it before he died,' lied Martha.

'The problem with you two is that you don't know how lucky you are,' fumbled their new daddy.

Now, maybe Uncle Marty was right, maybe the ungrateful brats didn't really know how lucky they were to have lost their dad, but the chances were that he was probably wrong.

Led by Lizzie, the twins decided to mutiny:

'We're not going to go there, wherever it is.'

'And you can't make us.'

'We'll go on hunger strike.'

'And you can't make us eat.'

'We'll run away.'

'And we'll die.'

'We'll burn down the schools.'

'And we'll burn to death.'

'We hate you.'

'Me too.'

'And I hate this feckin room.'

'Me too.'

Then they both jumped up and stomped out of the parlour.

Martha put her face in her hands and cried and cried, and Martin sat alongside her and awkwardly put his arm around her shoulders and said hush hush hush repeatedly as he patted her arm continuously until Martha said, 'That's really not helping, Martin. It's actually quite annoying, please stop it!'

So, whichever side of the fence your sympathies lie in the battleground of adults versus children, kids are never going to win. It's not that they're too short, or too weak, or lack courage, or cleverness, or financial resources. No, it's none of these things. They always lose because they're just always hungry. And adults own the keys to the kitchen.

And so, the twins were separated for the first time in the September of their twelfth year. Lizzie had to leave two days before Jack as her school opened their semester earlier. Her school was in county Clare, about seventy kilometres south of Galway, and Jack's was in county Donegal, about two hundred kilometres north of Galway. Before they separated, they swore to each other that they'd write and telephone every week. They didn't give each other any little mementos and they didn't prick their fingertips and spill blood together as they weren't in love that way (they rationalised anyway that as they shared the same blood and, as their hearts were already broken, there was no point in causing each other more pain). But they did promise each other that they wouldn't cry in front of their mother and Uncle Marty as they left home and each other.

But they did.

6

I don't remember much about that time. I have little vignettes of memories, nearly all of them bad. I remember not talking to my mam and Uncle Marty for the two days after Lizzie went, and when I was alone in my bedroom I cried and cried from the pain of missing her so much. I actually thought that my heart would break. I remember sitting in the back of the car, my suitcase on the seat beside me, and hating the two people in front. And I remember arriving at the school for the first time, being driven up the winding tree-lined driveway and seeing the enormous gothic style, three-hundred-year-old monstrosity of a building. There were lots of families dropping off their sons and you could easily tell who the freshmen were, with their mothers trying unsuccessfully to hold back the tears and the boys giddy with the excitement of their new adventure. But whatever stories their parents had told their unsuspecting children - and indeed themselves - to lure them thus far, it didn't take long for their enthusiasm to be replaced by a previously unknown sensation developing in the pit of their stomachs. And it wasn't the monstrous gothic edifice ripping apart the skyline, or indeed the shock and dread of the barked orders by the Christian Brothers staff. No, the nausea came from the dawning realisation that they would shortly be separated from their parents and would soon feel the dread of; 'But who's going to mind me now?'

And unfortunately, the answer was: Nobody!

I survived the first year, just. Although there were only ninety or so students in the college there were strict hierarchies in place. Like all such structures, the ruling order was naturally from the top down. And the fifth years ruled the roost, with their lackey fourth years doing their bidding and chumming up for favours and special considerations. The fifth years had the luxury of having their own individual bedrooms, which were used for sleeping, studying, hanging out with their cronies, and other activities, mostly heinous, which included time-honoured rituals - and of course sexual liaisons - with their chosen boys, or victims. This cohort, the fifth and fourth years, kept themselves to themselves and never mixed with the three junior years, except of course for fun and humiliation, beatings and sequestering their personal goods (food parcels from home, alcohol, cigarettes, or anything that could be traded, there was nothing sacred). The third and second years were the middle level and were made up of little groups and cliques, and they had established servile relationships with the higher years. These were the enforcers, who themselves would be severely punished if they crossed lines. The first-year students, the lowest of the social classes, were fodder, the whipping boys, the shoe polishers, the gofers, the targets for humiliations, for beatings, the butt of jokes and horrible tricks. They were assumed to be stupid and were despised for their weaknesses and innocence.

Lizzie and I kept our promise to write to each other every week and telephone, when possible, which was always difficult as there was only one public phone in each of our schools with limited use for students. That first year we didn't see one another for four months until we came home for the Christmas holidays, but even before that point I knew that in the game of chance I had pulled the short straw, as I guessed that we were on very different trajectories. I hated every minute of life in my school, whereas Lizzie took to hers like a duck to water. After trading our first few letters I could see that our experiences were vastly different. In her pages it was obvious that she deliberately played down her newfound excitement so that the difference between our situations wouldn't be so obvious and hence would be less painful for me. Although we would continue over the school years to trade letters and experiences, and we were still unnaturally close as siblings, the trauma I felt from the physical and emotional separation from Lizzie in those first four months was all-consuming.

But I fared better than most first year kids. I suspect the coping skills which I had acquired after my father's death helped me in negotiating the pitfalls of those early days. Yes, I was targeted like all new boys;

in fact, I was once beaten into an unconscious state in a random and unprovoked attack by a group of second year students, which required me to spend the best part of a week in the infirmary. But in the main I was left alone. I never understood why, but I can only assume that I must have exhibited some survival behaviours which protected me. The inescapable routine, the drudgery, the militarisation, were anathema to my core being. We slept in dormitories with long lines of beds; washed in washrooms with long lines of sinks (smelling of disinfectant); ate in the cafeteria with its long rows of tables and its stale smell of yesterday's meals. And we studied in a study hall with its long lines of desks. There was no privacy. It was de-individualising and dehumanising. It was an environment which seemed designed to break spirits and stunt growth. And, sadly for boys experiencing their teen years, there was no guidance in relation to their developmental needs, their curiosity, their sexuality; the formative years became the de-formative years. Boys were bullied by boys who themselves were bullied by adults, the very ones who were charged with their care, development and education. Looking back now, even as I try to mitigate their appallingly self-serving behaviour in the context of the Neanderthal norms in the Ireland of the day, they stand charged for failing the test - the test of basic human decency and kindness. Upon every boy who was given to their care they left their mark, their stain. I find them guilty as charged!

And then one day, a miracle occurred. When we returned to school in September of our third year, we were introduced to Madame Rouault who had joined the heretofore all-male teaching fraternity. Up until this point, Greek and Latin classics were mandatory but now French was introduced as an optional subject. The college dean, Brother Bartholomew (known to all as The Bull because of his grunting noises and his charging gait) told us at assembly that because we were expanding our curriculum, no one should ever again question the progressiveness of St. Declan's. This caused most students who, up to that point, thought they understood the meaning of progressive, to recheck their dictionaries. The Bull stood in the centre of the stage and grunted and beckoned Madame Rouault to join him, and I swear to this day, the woman didn't walk but floated across the stage. She introduced herself in French and then English, but I understood no words, all I heard was the sweet sounds of a nightingale. But the *piece de resistance* came when the Bull rudely interrupted her to stress that the classes would only be offered to the junior grades, as the senior students were already locked into their Leaving Certificate cycle. There could be no better ending to the drama unfolding in front of me on this stage. I truly was witnessing the performance of a lifetime of Beauty and the Beast, and I had to stop myself from jumping to my feet, clapping furiously and shouting *bravo bravo bravo!* Then the Beast grunted something completely unintelligible and the Beauty sang *au revoir* - and I think I shed a tear!

I signed up immediately for French classes, held on Tuesdays and Thursdays, and I studied like a boy possessed so that I would impress the beautiful Madame Emilie Rouault. She told us that she hailed from Brittany in Northern France, she was engaged to an Irishman and that she had fallen in love with the Irish countryside. Although I had never really noticed the Irish countryside up to that point (in truth I found it dreadfully stupid and boring), I too suddenly fell in love with it. And when she said that she loved taking long walks on her own while contemplating life and beauty, I enthused that I too loved that simple pleasure (even though I actually hated walking aimlessly, up to that point). Everything considered, I couldn't believe how alike we were.

I wrote to Lizzie telling her what a wonderful teacher Madame Rouault was and my sister replied, 'Ah, you *love* your French teacher, I know the feeling, I'm in *love* with my English teacher.' I thought, *that's disgusting, of course I don't love her, it's just that she's such a wonderful mentor and such an insightful human being.* After trading many more letters with Lizzie on the subject of teachers and love, I discovered that she was indeed in love with her English teacher, and that her English teacher was Miss Courtney. And the following year she fell in love with her gym teacher, Miss Barnes, and then her maths teacher, Miss O'Neill. Lizzie's sexual bias continued into adult life, with her never having any interest or curiosity in the male species but having wonderful happy relationships with the female sex

Towards the end of our third year, Madame Rouault offered to take any interested third year French students to Brittany for two weeks of language immersion once the junior exams were completed. It seemed that my mother and Uncle Marty were only too happy to have me away for a further two weeks and vouched for my fare and expenses. Five other boys also successfully convinced their parents to support the trip. But Emilie needed a second teacher to accompany us and it was agreed that Mr. O'Mahony, or 'Shavers' as he was known to his students, would join in the adventure. (He earned his nickname because he invariably arrived to school for his morning classes with pieces of bloodied tissue covering self-inflicted shaving cuts to his chin, his upper or lower lips, his cheek, or his neck. He once arrived with a bloodied piece of tissue stuck to a razor cut on his temple, what *was* he doing?). He taught history and art up to junior level and had a good understanding of French, and anyway he was the only other lay teacher in St. Declan's. It all seemed like the perfect fit.

And so, at the tender age of fifteen, I took off on my first big adventure accompanying the woman I loved, with Shavers driving the rented minibus and the five other boys who had thoughtfully come along to make up the numbers. Little did I know that the other boys and the sly Shavers (who never once cut himself shaving during the two weeks we were there) were as infatuated with Madame Rouault as I was, and we all fought like dogs in heat for the two weeks to get her attention.

We stayed in a little town called Loudeac in the middle of the beautiful Brittany countryside. This was Emilie's parish and she had organised for us to stay in local family homes for a nominal rent for the two weeks. We spoke no English while we were there and my love for the French language blossomed during that initial brief visit. However, I never did get any closer to Emilie over the two weeks. How could I with her other six admirers forming a continuous human wall around her. But I continued in her classes for the next two years in St. Declan's and I came back each year to Loudeac, spending two full summers there.

During my years in boarding school, I adopted a relatively low profile, deliberately not attracting the attention of the staff or the other boys. I was neither an obvious overachiever nor underachiever in academic or sports life. I was neither the bully nor the bullied, in fact I went relatively unnoticed, due mainly to my survival strategy. Relatively unnoticed, that is, until my fifth and final year.

This was when Alex joined our class. Alex Connelly had attended a secondary school in Galway town and had sat his leaving certificate exams but had failed them miserably. The youngest of a large family of boys, his parents decided that he should re-sit his exams including his final year but that he needed a quieter and more secluded academic environment. And so, they enrolled him in St. Declan's, far removed from any of his local distractions. Now, nearly all of the students in our school were from a scattering of the four provinces of Ireland, and even one or two unfortunates from England, sent by their Donegal expatriate parents. But very few were from Galway town except, as it turned out, Alex and me. And more surprisingly, he lived in a neighbourhood quite close to where I lived. The first day we met we both recognised each other's faces but that was all. Alex could actually have been living in the bedroom next to mine at home and I wouldn't have known him as I had spent the previous four years locked away in an institution, or in Loudeac for the summers.

As we were from the same parish, I was asked by the Bull to show Alex the ropes and he was given a room close to mine. Alex was a paradox: a natural conservative but also taken to complete recklessness at times. Although I wouldn't have been able to articulate my own values back then, I was developing into quite the little liberal, diametrically opposed to Alex's views. I was the yin to his yang. And so, we got on like a house on fire. He was tall, at least four inches taller than me, and he had one overwhelming attribute: he was fearless. He didn't understand or care much about the hierarchical pecking order within our structure. He had arrived without baggage and he had no intention of paying homage to anyone else in the school, bar the staff, and even then, only if they played fairly. He never looked for trouble, and when it came, he did his best to circumvent it with his '*do nothing*' philosophy but, sometimes when it became unavoidable (as it did in his first few weeks when some of the senior fifth years didn't think that they were getting his full attention or respect), he dealt with it with a frightening efficiency, not just with his strength but with his fearlessness. Alex ignored or in some cases dismantled, hundreds of years-old rituals and traditions with the minimum of effort and fuss. Sometimes it just took a 'no' and sometimes it took a little more investment, but Alex never took a step back. Customs that we all thought were made of bedrock were actually without foundation and were as brittle as eggshells. Once you accepted the demise of one, then the domino effect helped to dismantle others. He was violently opposed to the singular but ubiquitous behaviour which underpinned most of the antisocial and aggressive traditions of the school: bullying. And whenever he came across it, no matter the age or circumstances of the victim, he intervened. It was the one area where he broke his own rule of 'do nothing'.

There was an early example of his intent which I understand has since been adopted into the school myths and folklore. One of the freshmen, a small guy for his age, was found buttoned into his own overcoat and, with the aid of a couple of wooden clothes hangers, was left hanging on a hook on the back of the dormitory door. He wasn't discovered until that night, by which point he had cried himself into a delirious state and had passed out. By the time he was discovered, he was dangerously dehydrated, and his arms and neck were very severely bruised but worst of all, to his shame, he had messed himself. The following morning three boys went missing from roll call, the fifth-year prefect and two fourth year students. After an extensive search they were discovered in the woods nearby. They were each naked with their backs against trees and their wrists tied behind them. They had pillowcases over their heads so that they could not identify the perpetrator(s), and written in red marker on the prefect's chest was simply 'Quia oculo ad oculum' (an eye for an eye). Because of the code of silence even though everyone, including the Bull and his staff, suspected who the perpetrators were in both incidents, no one was ever disciplined. Although I didn't condone vigilantism or revenge beatings, I did get a certain thrill in writing the biblical words on the prefect's chest.

But of course, Alex's interventions (*rebalancing the scales,* he termed it) had a major disruptive effect on the status quo, upsetting not just the student hierarchies but also the staff norms and sensibilities. It made their lives far more difficult when the old order was broken and they now had to get involved, or at least be seen to get involved, in student misbehaviour and actually do some work. But Alex was never designed for a school like St. Declan's, and in a way, I guess neither was I. If in the previous four years I had taken the path of least resistance and unquestionably turned blind eyes here and there (and in the process, something I regret even to this day, compromised my values even if I wasn't fully awake to them), I was now about to make up for lost time. So, I went a little wild in my final year. Except for French and the ever-elegant Madame Rouault, who had grown more beautiful in the intervening years, my studies took a back seat. Having my own room was a game-changer. I could close my door to the outside world and drown in my own pool of privacy. I discovered music and Playboy magazine at the start of the eighties, and was blown away on hearing the first play of Bowie and Queen's *Under Pressure* on pirate Radio Luxembourg. This I thought is my kind of scene as I drooled and pleasured myself over Vicki Lasseter's body in the Playboy centrefold (with my mental image of Emilie's face superimposed on Vicki's). Alex and I also became nighthawks, experts at night-time manoeuvres which always involved the risk and excitement of getting caught. There was an old, dilapidated, and barely functioning pub called Murphy's some distance from the college and we'd often make our way down the dark, narrow unlit road with overcoats over our pyjamas to break into its storeroom and help ourselves to as many bottles of Harp beer as we could securely carry back up the road to our rooms. Or we would easily open the locks in the Sacristy and borrow its dreadful altar wine. (We justified the verb 'borrowing' as we were just getting it sooner than everyone else at the daily masses). We once executed a daring raid into the Bull's own den while he slept, relieving him of his precious bottle of Paddy whiskey and his Cuban cigars.

But, of course, we were eventually caught. It was never really a question of if, but rather when. There were too many forces working against us, too many eyes watching and waiting for us to screw up. It happened quite easily and when we least expected it. We were returning one night from a routine escapade to Murphy's and decided that we'd have a bottle or two of Harp in Alex's room before we hit the beds. We made it back to the college without any difficulty but when we entered his room and switched on the light, we were blinded by the explosion of a flashbulb. And when we could eventually see again, we were confronted by the Bull and accompanied by, surprise surprise, the grinning fifth year prefect holding a whirring Kodak Instamatic as it spewed out the evidence. We were summarily charged and found guilty, then the evidence was heard and the next morning our parents were telephoned. They arrived a few hours later to be advised that we were forthwith suspended for four weeks. As we had only a few months remaining before our final exams, this had the effect of an expulsion, but it saved our parents the embarrassment and shame of the label.

We studied in our homes for the rest of the school term and weren't allowed to hang out with each other, but in spite of the disruption we both did reasonably well and achieved the results we needed for university. Lizzie, on the other hand, excelled and thrilled our mother and Uncle Marty by getting A's or B's in every subject, which of course they shoved in my face at every possible opportunity. But their enjoyment was short-lived when, while introducing them to her new girlfriend, Lizzie announced that her friend was lesbian - which of course was her way of coming out. Compared to Lizzie's news, my little fuck-up disappeared into the annals of history and was never mentioned again.

Merci encore Lizzie!

7

Dublin, Thursday 11th May *(23 days to Nadir)*

I watched her closely as she told her story. Listened to her voice. *Is there sincerity there? Am I hearing the truth?*

Marianne must have read my scepticism. 'Listen, Jack, I'm not here to ask you for anything, at least not for myself. I know you find this hard to believe, but it's the truth. I swear to you on my mother's soul, I swear to you.'

I stared at her, looking and listening for the truth but hoping to snare the lie.

'And I know I'm now fucking with your life, everybody's life, but you have to hear me out.'

'Ok, so you told your husband, what happened then?'

Marianne laughed a little, but humourlessly. 'Well, he went berserk, didn't he? Screaming and shouting at me. Calling me names, horrible names, you whore, cunt, liar, coward. He picked up his coffee mug and smashed it against the wall of our kitchen, and then he followed it with mine. I thought he was going to hit me at one point, and I knew he really wanted to, to hurt me, but he didn't. Then he sat at the kitchen table and cried.'

I continued to look, continued listening for the lie.

'I was just apologising over and over again, sorry sorry sorry. Then he stopped and lifted his head and looked at me. I could see him processing the information, and then it seemed like a penny dropped with him, and he said stuff like our marriage was all a lie, a lie from the start. I'd never loved him, I married him because I was pregnant, I'd used him, manipulated him, cheated him. Was Ellen his? How could he be sure that Ellen was his, everything was a lie, every-fucking-thing … and of course, in a way Jack, it was.'

Remembering what Alex had advised, I said nothing. *But where do I go from here, fuck, she sounds genuine, it sounds like the truth, it could have happened like she said.* Ignoring Alex's advice (anyway, I reasoned, that bollix has been more wrong than right, for Christ's sake) I asked her:

'For the moment, let's say you're telling the truth, Marianne, and you say you're not looking for anything, so what are we doing here?'

'You're his father, Jack, you're Freddie's father. I'm here for him of course.'

'So, and let's say that this is true, does he know that I exist? He knows your husband isn't his father?'

'Yes of course he knows, after I told Rob, I told Freddie - which was the hardest thing I ever had to do.'

'So, he knows it's me, he knows who I am?'

'No no, he doesn't know who you are, he has no idea who his father is. He just knows it isn't Rob. But he wants to know, he wants to meet his father.'

'And how do I know it's not someone else altogether, like you didn't *fuck* someone else after me.'

Marianne went silent for a little while. 'That's horrible, Jack, I know you hate me right now, but that's horrible. Anyway, you've seen the photograph; he's the head of you.'

I put my head in my hands and exclaimed exasperatedly, 'Fuuuck!'

Marianne ignored my reaction and carried on. 'He was obviously shocked when I told him, shocked and surprised, but not overwhelmed by it. He blew up of course, but eventually calmed down. He said it explained some stuff between him and Rob, and later he said he understood why I did it, especially with all the other shit that was going on in Ireland back then. So yeah, he said he understood why I did it but that it was a bad decision, a really bad decision that has changed lives and I should've been more honest, it would've saved all this fucking pain.'

I looked at my watch: eleven o'clock.

'I'm sorry, Jack. I truly am sorry for all of this; if I could turn back the clock, I'd do it in a heartbeat.'

'Yeah, whatever … Tell me, does your ex-husband know who I am?'

'Not from me he doesn't, but he did ask me a few times and I know for a while he was making enquiries around Galway because I got a call from my cousin in Salthill. But I don't think he ever discovered who you were, he would have said it if he knew.'

'And your son, where is he at?'

'Over the last year since he's become a dad himself, he's been obsessing about meeting his real father. I think Saahira, his partner, is pushing him, too.'

'And what have you told him?'

'Nothing, I swear, I haven't promised him anything. I needed to talk to you first … listen, Jack, even if Freddie wasn't interested in meeting you, I had planned to tell you anyway.'

I was tired and losing patience. 'Why, for fucks sake? Why couldn't you have just left it all alone? Why drag me and my family into the fucking thing, you made your own bed thirty years ago, Marianne, you want me to be your conscience now?'

'Jack, he's your son for God's sake, he's got your blood, your genes, and so has his child, so has Fabeena, she's got your genes too. I know it's the last thing you might want to hear now but there were two of us there that night. I didn't dream him up all on my own, there were two of us involved. He's your son, Jack, and Fabeena is your granddaughter whether you like it or not! … And yes, I should have told you back then. You don't think I've regretted that every day since? I've hated myself for what I did, and I'm sorry I've hurt everyone, but it's got to be fixed now, you needed to know.'

Christ, I thought to myself, *I came into this day with three kids and I leave with four and a grandchild, how the fuck did that happen?*

'Ok, Marianne, it's getting late. So, tell me, where do we go from here? You've obviously thought this out; you've certainly had plenty of time to do it.'

'I've nothing planned out, Jack. My only plan was to tell you. But you'll need time to think about it, to think through it, to decide if you're going to do anything about it.' Marianne hesitated. Then she searched in her bag for something and produced a little ornate box, smaller than a matchbox, and placed it on the table. 'I know that this is a little weird, Jack, but I probably always knew that this day would come, so I kept this. You can use it, you know, to check, to check that you're his father. It's his DNA.'

I walked Marianne to a taxi a short distance from the hotel and opened the rear door for her, and we stood there for a few seconds. Saying goodbyes in normal circumstances can be awkward, but when one party has offloaded a small family and the other hasn't quite grabbed the bundle then it can be downright hazardous. 'Ok,' I said, 'see you then.'

She quickly leaned over and kissed me on my cheek, saying, 'you have my number, Jack, please call me.' She climbed into the taxi and I closed the door. As the car began to pull away, I watched her as tears rolled down her cheeks. Real tears, or tears for my benefit? Tears of relief from a problem shared, or of a well-executed production?

Once the taxi was gone, I made my way to the hotel bar and ordered a double Jameson on ice. The barman asked as he poured it if I'd had a nice evening, *a nice evening*? Who the fuck was he kidding? I think I grunted something and sought out a quiet dark corner and collapsed in an armchair. I took a long sip of the whiskey and reflected on the evening's events. Ok, where the hell do I go with this. Then I remembered the little casket in my pocket, and on opening it I found a small see-through jewellery bag wrapped in cotton wool, and I could make out what looked like a child's tooth in the bag. His DNA, she said, she kept it all these years, just in case. Fuck!

Ok, I thought, what are my options? It's unlikely she'd give me something that would disprove his parentage if she wasn't one hundred percent sure of her facts, that wouldn't make any sense. So, let's assume that she's telling the truth and he is my son, so where does that leave me. I could just pretend this never happened; just innocently walk into tomorrow as I walked into today. After all, she kept the secret for over twenty years, no reason why I can't do the same. The husband doesn't know who I am, the young fella doesn't know who I am, and she said her only plan was just to tell me, she didn't want anything else, the rest was up to me. But I didn't believe that for a second. She's a mother, his mother, she won't rest until son meets father, and anyway, maybe he already knows who I am, maybe she's told him.

I thought of what Alex would say if he was here with me right now. He'd say, 'For fuck's sake do nothing, this isn't your doing, just keep your head down and it'll go away.' And if Lizzie was here, she'd say, 'Embrace the truth, bro. It wasn't your fault, you're as innocent a party as everyone else, put it out there and let it play out.'

And then I imagined telling Bea. Bea with her conspiracy theories, her insecurities, and her jealousies. Bea who twice walked out on our marriage because she overreacted to perceived wrongs against her, wrongs by me, secrets I was supposedly keeping from her, collusions stacked against her by me and the kids, her friends, her business partner. And each time they were followed by bouts of depression - or was it vice versa? Maybe the depression drove her paranoia. Fuck, I was always behind the curve with her depression, I never saw the tell-tale signs, I was too busy, or too preoccupied with my own shit. Her friends would call me and ask if I'd noticed a change in her.

As I downed the last of the whisky, I thought, *maybe she doesn't ever need to know, and maybe the kids need never know*! But I was delusional that evening. I was trying to solve a problem. No, worse, I was trying to get rid of a problem and not embrace the truth, as Lizzie did indeed say the next morning when I called her:

'Jesus, bro, they're your flesh and blood, they're my flesh and blood, embrace the truth.'

'I knew you'd say that, Lizzie, and for the record, they may be my flesh and blood but they're not yours.'

'Well, if they've got *our* mother's and *our* father's genes in them, I'm claiming a piece of them.'

'Stop joking, sis, this is fucking serious.'

'I know Jack, but you can't deny your son and grandchild, that'd be like denying Ben or Sean or beautiful Sadie. My advice: get the test done soonest and, whichever way it goes, embrace it.'

'I'll say one thing about you, Lizzie, you're consistent. Predictable maybe, but consistent.'

'What's she like?'

'Who?'

'The mother, Marianne, what's she like? You know I'm sure I remember your first girlfriend way back then.'

'Well, I'll tell you one thing; she doesn't look like a grandmother. I think you'd like her though, she's kinda like you.'

'Really? How like?'

'Like a pain in the ass.'

'Bye Jack, love you. By the way, that baby toothy thing is so cute.'

I got through Friday's work schedule on autopilot. I met my own solicitor and gave him the casket with the tooth and a swab from myself. I told him that I was helping out a client. He said he'd quietly organise the DNA match which should only take a couple of days.

I was in my car, as I'd hoped, at three o'clock and heading for the M50 and out of Dublin. As a distraction I switched on the radio and a discussion was taking place about Brexit, two political talking heads, a pro-man and an anti-woman. The phrase 'perfidious Albion' caught my attention and then the woman went on a rant; '... kings and politicians declare war, but citizens die for their vanity. British politics has reached an all-time low when we're playing on people's insecurities and stirring their nationalistic prejudices, creating anti-emigration sentiment. Brexit and Trump, no difference, the same rhetoric. Protect the borders, build walls, kick out immigrants, keep America for Americans, keep England for the English. And in doing so we're playing into the hands of right-wing boogies and loonies; the world is going crazy and crazy things are happening....' I thought about what she was saying, about recent crazy stuff, like the five people killed in March in the Isis attack in Westminster. Was that symptomatic of the problem? Or, earlier this month, another so-called Isis-inspired suicide lunatic bombed 22 people at the Ariana Grande concert in Manchester.

The bloody world is going crazy.

I wasn't even listening to the talking heads; I'd got myself into a frenzy all on my own. I switched stations - music, thank Christ. The Isley Brothers were saving my sanity with *Summer Breeze*. I let Brexit fade into the distance and sang along.

Once I got on the motorway to Galway, I began thinking about something Lizzie had said, 'Flesh and blood, they're your flesh and blood, bro'. Jesus, imagine if I actually do have a thirty-four-year-old son and a granddaughter. When I first met Bea, this child would have been what, maybe eight? And when we had Ben, he would have been ten. And I never even knew that he existed. And when we had Sean, he was a teenager, the same age that I was when I was sent to boarding school. I wondered what he was like, and what his baby was like. And then the thought hit me, jaysas I could be a grandfather, a pappy, at fifty-four!

I negotiated Galway's Friday traffic and headed out the Spiddal road, stopping for a bunch of flowers on the way. I loved that last stretch of road from the city to home, on my left, twenty kilometres of beautiful wild Atlantic coastline, and on my right, rugged sheep in rugged little fields and both protected by Connemara walls. First through Barna, then through Carraig, and eventually on home to Spiddal.

I parked the car in the drive exactly at six o'clock. I called out to Bea from the hallway and Sadie shouted from the kitchen that she was out in the back garden. Sadie hurried out and gave me a kiss and a warm hug, and I found myself holding on to her longer than normal, at which point she said, 'Everything ok, Dad? How was your week?'

'Good, good,' I said.

But before I could take another breath, she launched into a 'life is so unfair' drama between herself and her best friend Joanne; 'like, Dad, I couldn't believe how Joanne has virtually not even thanked me after I'd given her the present of that beautiful bracelet for her birthday, remember I showed it to you, and all she was saying was how lovely Claire's present was, who by the way, as you know, Dad, Joanne hates and always calls her a bitch behind her back. And do you think I should ring Joanne and tell her that I think she's a bad friend? … oh, those flowers are lovely, are they for Mum? By the way I don't think her mood is great, we just had a few words, and you know how dramatic she can get?'

Pot calling the kettle black came to mind.

Out in the garden, Bea was on the phone to one of her friends and she waved to me, saying hi. She was apologising for not being able to meet her friend for coffee earlier but that the shop was super busy and she was working it on her own because Helen, her partner, wasn't well enough to come to work again today.

'Yes yes, I know I need to mind myself. Listen, Jack is here. Yes yes, you're right, you're right, I promise I'll take care of myself, but the show must go on, and it's not easy when you're running your own business. Ok, bye-bye, see you in the morning for coffee.'

I kissed her on the cheek and gave her the flowers and she admired them but then said, 'Oh they're lovely Jack, but I hope they're not a guilt gift.'

Even though I knew that she wasn't really serious, I really hated when she said that, it took the good completely from the thought (and it also made me think, *well maybe they are a guilt gift*, and then I actually do feel guilty for something even though I don't even know why … well, except for this evening, of course, because I really did know why).

I flopped into a chair next to her and looked out beyond the fields to the blue-green ocean which was bathed in beautiful evening sunshine. The sun was still high above the mountain range to the west, and I guessed that there was probably another two hours before it sank behind the ridge.

'God this is beautiful, isn't it, darling?'

'Yes of course, but I've only just sat down myself, so I haven't had a chance to enjoy it.'

'Tough day again by the sounds of it?'

'Well, Helen is still out so I had to manage the shop on my own and we were super busy. I didn't get a break all day.'

'Yes, I heard you saying it to Margaret - it was Margaret, was it? How is she?'

'Oh, she's fine, why wouldn't she be fine, a well-paid secure job working for the city council, no responsibilities, no worries, of course she's fine.'

'I think you're understating it a little there, darling. I'd say she has loads of crap going on, as CFO she's virtually running the council. And her kid is a twenty-four-hour worry. I know she gets help from the health services, but I can't imagine that Tom takes any of the load. How long are they separated now? Three, four years?' I said all of this quite casually, conversationally, agreeably - but at what age must I be, or after how many years of marriage does it take, for me to learn to engage my brain before engaging my mouth?

'Well Jack, if you're so worried about Margaret, why don't you go over there right now and mind her and her kid? In fact, why don't you marry her altogether? After all, she *is* single.'

'Hey, hey, Bea, I was only saying that it can't be easy for her either. But you're right.' *(Serious backpedalling, which is difficult to do while you're still on forward momentum).*

'I know you've got the responsibility of the shop and your investment to worry about and I know there are no guarantees. And I know that

Helen's situation is awful for you, but maybe that's a nettle that we need to grasp. Maybe we could give it some thought over the weekend.'

'Yes, sorry Jack, it's just I'm really tired right now. I shouldn't have said that about Margaret, that was mean. And yeah, maybe we can chat about Helen over the weekend.'

(Phew, back from the edge)

'Good, good, well, will I make us a nice cool drink? A wine maybe?'

'Yes, that'd be lovely darling, and the flowers are lovely too, and it's good to have you home for the weekend.'

I got up, kissed her on her lips, and went inside, leaned against the fridge and let out a long relieved sigh. I poured two glasses of a cool chardonnay, drank half of one glass in one gulp, then refilled it and thought *for fuck's sake, I might as well go straight over and marry Margaret right now cause the day I ever tell this woman about discovering a whole new family fully formed, I'll be found impaled on Margaret's front door!*

And with that Sadie walked past me and, a little too triumphantly, quipped, 'well I did warn you, Dad.'

8

Boston, Friday 12th May *(22 days to Nadir)*

Having checked into the Best Western motel, Anthony left the reception and found his cabin, threw his bag on the bed, checked his watch - which told him it was 8.00am - and went outside and walked a little distance until he found an all-night liquor store at the rear of a shopping area. The back lot was shabby, littered, some parked cars looking abandoned, a couple of boarded-up storefronts, a bar called The Black Cat Club, advertising: *'Budweiser, King of Beers'*; *'Five-star bar food'*; *'Live music nightly'* and *'Company Girls'* (he wondered what was meant by the '*Company Girls*'). Alongside the bar was a massage parlour with the neon sign in the window flashing: 'The Delta of Venus' and proclaiming; '*Professional, Asian-trained massage therapist $50/30mins, satisfaction guaranteed*'. Leaving the liquor store with a bottle of Jack Daniels in a brown paper bag and two packets of Marlboro's, he headed back to his room. He closed the curtains and sat on the bed and lit his first cigarette in twenty-eight years, his last one being on the eve of his wedding, with his promise to Jessie that he'd quit before they were married the next day. But he thought that it was ok to break his promise now as bigger promises had been broken. He coughed on inhaling the acrid smoke and, although his brain went into a spin, he quickly took another drag, a deeper drag, and then another until his coughing eased and his head stopped spinning. He was surprised at how much he'd missed the taste of cigarette smoke in his mouth and the powerful hit to his lungs after taking a deep drag. Cracking the seal of the whiskey bottle and pouring himself a generous helping, he drank half in one gulp, letting the burning liquid flow down his throat, and almost immediately he felt its effect on his brain. His cell phone buzzed, but without answering it he saw lots of missed calls, mostly from Jessie, but also from his kids, Maria and Julian. There were texts too which he didn't open; instead, he switched it off and threw it in the general direction of the writing desk, or the floor, which is where it landed. *Good shot,* he thought.

Over the next hour he steadily smoked and drank, making a big dent in the Jack Daniels, lying on the bed, his head propped up on pillows, which allowed him to smoke and drink without drowning or setting himself on fire. Laughing out loud, he pictured the headlines: '*Man ignites himself in motel cabin while wife takes it up the ass in log cabin.*'

Anthony's mind drifted further from reality as the alcohol warped his cognitive pathways; *I wonder did she do it,* he thought. *Did she do what*, he answered himself. *Take it up the ass of course, that's what we were talking about, did she take it up the ass, or suck his cock, the fucking cock sucker*. He shook his head and said out loud, 'Don't know, don't frickin know, and stop frickin asking me, Jesus I'm pissed.' His eyelids were beginning to feel heavy, so heavy. They were closing on their own and as he struggled to keep them open, he thought; '*I'll just let them close for a second, it's so frickin hard to keep them open, that's better, just for a second.*'

He screamed and jumped as the cigarette burned his fingers. 'Jesus Christ, my frickin fingers.' Dumping the still-lit cigarette in the ashtray and sticking his fingers into the glass of whiskey, he laid back on the bed and fell into a very drunken stupor.

Anthony awoke with a start. A car horn blared from outside his window, voices were raised, and men were shouting abuse at one another. Too much noise. He felt like he was about to die (like the nightmares that had terrified him since his 9/11 flight), his head was pounding, and his mouth felt desert-dry and tasted like an ashtray. His neck hurt from the position his head had been in while he'd slept. In vain he tried to open his eyes. The left side of his face, his cheek bone and his eye socket, felt sore and swollen. With great difficulty he slowly tempted his right upper eyelid up a fraction. Through the slit he saw that the room was dark. Tempting the other one to open a little, he tried to locate his left hand (which he didn't immediately), and eventually found it under his back, completely numb. He moved his body slowly to free his hand and eventually felt it coming back to life as pins and needles shot through his arm and electrified his fingers. *What's the time?* Forcing his hand to move in the direction of his face, he tried to read his watch through his slits, but they refused to focus so he closed one eye and tried again. His watch said that it was four-thirty, but was it in the middle of the day or night? Searching for his mobile on the bedside table, he remembered that it was on the floor somewhere. Christ, *I need to pee, badly.* Anthony moved his body and rolled onto his side and rested for a few seconds. Then he threw his legs off the bed and forced himself to sit up. Resting his head in his hands for a while, he heard noises like someone groaning, until he realised it was himself. He attempted to stand, lost his balance and staggered, but he found the safety of the bed and sat down again. This time he stayed there for a while, opening his eyes slowly, and eventually he got used to the semi-darkened room, and he began to make out shapes. *I really need to get to the bathroom, or I'll piss myself* he thought. Fumbling around in the dark, he eventually found the bathroom, but also found the toilet bowl with his shin; bone against unmovable ceramic. '*Holy Christ*' he shouted. He'd found it.

Once he had relieved himself, he came back to the bedroom and slowly got to the ground on his hands and knees and searched for his cell phone by feel and touch. Crawling under the writing desk he eventually located it, switched it on, and covered the screen so it didn't blind him. It read 16.45. He crawled to the bed and pulled himself up until he was again lying on it. There was a bottle of water on the night table and he opened it and drank half before seeing that the whisky bottle was three-quarters empty. He groaned as he fumbled for a cigarette from the pack and the matches and, once lit, he dragged deeply on the poison, like a hardened smoker. When the cigarette was finished, he closed his eyes and drifted back into a deep sleep.

Anthony's eyes flickered open; he felt less pain, less torture, his hands worked. He lit a cigarette; it didn't feel like twenty-eight years!

He opened his phone, 20.50. 'No wonder I'm bloody starving,' he said out loud. Slowly getting off the bed and finding the window, he opened the curtains and unlatched a window and bristled at the gust of fresh air. It was sundown and thankfully the evening light matched his optic nerve's ability to absorb it. He got undressed and poured himself a whisky and figured out the shower controls. Letting the strong hot water-pressure pound him for fifteen minutes, he sometimes sobbed and sometimes his body shook uncontrollably. But in the end, it made him feel almost human again. Sitting naked on the chair at the bedroom dresser and staring in the mirror, he barely recognised the wreck looking back. His left temple and cheekbone were bruised and they felt tender to the touch, and his left eye looked like it was a little closed. Anthony hoped that in return he had maimed the asshole for life.

He made his way back down the street in search of the bar that promised everything. He found it, but it looked different by night. Darkness had done its magic and had cast a welcoming veil over the tackiness of the place. He saw and heard on entering that there was a band on a little stage in one corner playing country music with a Dolly Parton look-alike singing '*Trouble in the Fields*'. The bar was lit for some kind of atmosphere, and the atmosphere felt like death warmed up, no, no, on second thoughts, not death, just indifference. He found a table which allowed him a good view of Dolly and the happenings. There were maybe twenty customers scattered around the bar and a couple of men and three women were sitting on high stools at the counter. He studied the large A3 laminated menu and shortly a waitress appeared in a cowgirl outfit complete with hat and polka dot kerchief.

'Hello honey, my name is Candy, welcome to the Black Cat, I'll be your waitress for the night. Eating on our own, are we?'

'Yeah,' he drawled. He wondered why he suddenly felt the need to talk like a cowboy.

'And do you like what you see?' She said this leaning towards him, her cleavage almost in his face, and it took up eighty percent of his line of vision. 'I mean on the menu, baby.' She gave a well-rehearsed laugh and threw her head back, which allowed her breasts to protrude even further, now occupying ninety percent of his vision.

'I'll have a bottle of America's king of beers and a platter of your five-star bar food please.'

'Coming right up honey, and would you like a bit of company with that?'

'Company?'

'One of the lovely ladies at the bar, they'd be only too happy to join you, that's a lotta food you've ordered there.'

'No, no, I'm good, thanks.'

'No problem honey, but make sure you just shout now if you need anything.' and she winked theatrically as she left, swinging her ass for extra effect.

His Bud arrived, quickly followed by his food - disturbingly too quickly. Candy was right about one thing, the platter was enormous, but he dived into it, eating and drinking beer (*like a real cowboy,* he thought, although he had to admit he really didn't know how a real cowboy eats as he's never had the pleasure of having a meal with one). He called for another Bud and watched Dolly-look-a-like launch into '*Jolene*'. Candy must have missed her cue on the beer because it was brought over by one of the ladies sitting at the bar.

'Hi handsome, is there room for two on that seat?' She didn't wait for an answer but sat beside him on the couch.

'I noticed you all alone there and thought you might like a little company.'

'Well …' He didn't even have his refusal formed when she called out across the bar for Candy to bring her a fresh beer, too.

'My name's Maxine, what's yours? I haven't seen you here before, new in town?' She held out her hand and somehow found his, and the joining was complete when she rested her other hand on their handshake and kept it there, gently patting and squeezing.

'Anthony, my name's Anthony. I live out towards Worcester.'

With introductions over and a new beer for Maxine, she took up a more intimate position closer to him, and to Anthony's surprise, they started talking.

They talked about everything and nothing. Their kids, their jobs, their towns, their lives, the dire state of the Democrats, the repugnant Republicans, they told some truths and told some lies. The story of their current relationships was nearly right in both cases, and nearly wrong. In the game of age guessing, she rightly guessed that he was in his mid-fifties; he lied that she looked to be in her late thirties - he knew he was gifting her at least ten years - but to her credit she claimed that she was forty-eight. She looked younger. She looked good. She smelled good.

The evening flew by. Dolly was finishing the night with '*Nine to Five*' and customers were beginning to drift away. Anthony took care of the bill and Maxine went to the bathroom and returned with her coat, suggesting that she walk him to his car.

'Well, I don't have a car, I'm actually staying in a local motel, and I really appreciated your company tonight, Maxine, I promise you it did me the world of good but I need to be getting back, I've a big day tomorrow.' As he reached for his wallet in his jacket to tip her, she suggested:

'Listen Anthony, I really enjoyed myself too tonight, you seem to me like one of the good guys and we can close out the tip now but I'd really like to spend a few more hours with you, I mean just as friends, just some company for both of us. In case you're wondering, it's not my job to sleep with customers, I don't do that, I promise you no pressure, no scams, I like you.'

Was this the ultimate scam, he thought, or is life itself the scam? He took her at her word. He wanted to. He needed to. They walked back to the motel, she linking his arm, still talking about everything and nothing.

Along the way, she ventured, 'I hope you don't mind me saying but that's some ugly bruise you've got there, cowboy, are you in trouble or something or did you just fall off your hoss?' He unconsciously put his hand to his cheek.

'No, no trouble at all, you should see the hoss!'

He opened the cabin door and apologised in advance for the state of the room. They both automatically started tidying stuff and then as naturally as if they knew each other as lovers for years, she undressed to her bra and panties as she walked casually between the bathroom and the dressing table, still chatting, cleaning off her makeup and brushing her teeth using his toothbrush. And then she climbed under the bedclothes and told him to hurry and get undressed and come to bed. He undressed to his shorts and joined her under the covers. He put his arm around her, and she cradled into his chest. It felt good to hold her close, the feel of her, the smell of her, her bed voice telling him about some childhood memories. He kissed her head, deeply inhaling the scent of her hair. She turned her face up and found his mouth with her lips and kissed him; he welcomed the intimacy, but then gently pulled his mouth away. 'Don't be cross, Maxine, but I'd love to just enjoy this pleasure, holding you in my arms.'

She laughed and slapped his chest with her palm; 'Don't worry darling, I won't be cross. And don't be afraid, I won't eat you alive.'

He laughed lightly. 'Good, then stop talking and go to sleep.'

And they did sleep, she in his arms, her head resting on his chest. Then after a while they tossed and turned in their own ways and their bodies separated, and they slept back-to-back and side to side, a hand resting here or there. And at some point in the night, he ended up wrapped around her, her back against his chest, her ass against his crotch. And around dawn she pressed her ass against him, rubbing against it, feeling him get hard, and he responded and pushed his hardness against her and felt her breasts and pulled at her thighs and kissed her neck. And she made involuntary little sounds of pleasure and they took the last of their clothes off and she turned to him and kissed him, whispering, 'You're lovely, you're a lovely man.' She climbed on him, straddling him, guiding him into her and they made love like that, like only new lovers can do, hungry to explore each other's bodies and wishes and needs.

He woke to the sound of the shower and then she came out of the bathroom wrapped in a towel, and she was smiling at him and drying her body and fixing herself and getting dressed, and his watch said that it was eight-fifty.

'I've gotta go honey, I'm meeting my friend at the mall at ten and I need to get home and get changed.'

'Man friend?'

'Well, if his name is Rebekah, yes.' She laughed. 'What are your plans for the day? Are you going out to Worcester?'

'Dunno, I've a few calls to make and I'll see how the day goes.' After a pause he said, 'It was really great being with you last night.'

'No guilt then?'

'Well, some maybe, but no regrets, you've helped me find my self-worth a little.'

She sat on the edge of the bed and put her fingers through his hair. 'My poor baby, with your bruised cheek and your sad eyes. Lose your self-worth, how could that be? You're a good man, Anthony. If you stay over tonight, will you be in the bar later?'

'Will you be there?'

'From about eight.'

'Hm, don't know if I fancy meeting you in the bar, you know.'

'Blast, look at the time, I really gotta go babe, tell you what, here's my number. If you're staying over, give me a call in the afternoon, but it has to be before two and I'll see if I can get a swap for tonight and we can go somewhere else. I'll let you buy me dinner in a posh restaurant.' She bent down and kissed his mouth and grabbed her bag and at the open door she turned and blew him a kiss.

Anthony had breakfast at a diner a couple of blocks away and then came back to his cabin and sat at the writing desk and prepared himself for some important calls. But first he shot off an email to his boss, the managing partner, blind copying his PA to say that he'd picked up some viral infection in Europe, and his doctor had told him to stay out of the office for the week as he was likely to be contagious. His boss immediately replied, *'stay the f**k away from the office and especially from me :) get well, see you soon'*

The first call he made was to the Boston Chief of Police, Jimmy McCarthy, who was an old friend. He trusted him completely and he didn't have time to fabricate stories, so he told him briefly about what he'd found when he arrived home the previous morning, and that he needed the most trusted private investigator that he could recommend. Jimmy didn't take too long to come up with the right guy and gave him a name and an address. Anthony wrote out the instructions for the investigator, put them in an envelope along with his house key, the house alarm code, and the registration of the blue BMW - or at least the bit he remembered - and dropped them off at reception for currier delivery.

Next, he called Julian and Maria and explained that he and their mother had had a bust up, and that he was staying away from the house for a few days, but that he was fine and he just needed a little space; he'd meet them for lunch during the following week. If they knew anything about what had actually happened they didn't let on, and he suspected that Jessie hadn't told them. Then he called his lawyer and set up a meeting for the following week, by which point he figured he'd have the information.

Leaving the hardest call until last, he rang Jessie and told her that he didn't want to discuss anything over the phone but that he'd be staying away for the week and he'd meet her on Wednesday next week. She begged him to talk more, she couldn't wait that long to see him, she loved him, she was sorry. Hanging up, he figured to himself that he needed that much time to be able to meet her face-to-face and have a rational discussion with her.

Once the call was closed he poured himself a whiskey, lit a cigarette and lay on the bed propped up on the pillows. He thought, how in the name of Christ did we get here? Was it destiny? Was this *his* destiny? And if so, from what point was it destined? From when he was five years old? Ten years old? Or maybe from the day he married Jessie? Or did the clock of fate start ticking from the moment of his own infidelity?

He sucked on his cigarette and, smiling to himself, he thought of what Maxine had said after he had taken a few drags from her half-smoked cigarette, 'Funny, I never had you as the smoker type.' What type was he then? Was he a different type now than a few days ago? Can your world be turned upside down so dramatically, so fast? He thought, *'course it can. A heart attack or a stroke will stop you dead in your tracks - or half-dead if you're really unlucky - with no warning. Have I changed from last week? 'Course I have. I'm drinking whiskey at noon for Christ's sake and smoking my fifth cigarette of the day already, and I spent the night with a woman I picked up in a bar. Do I still love Jessie? Dunno, right now I hate her. Do I want to love her? Dunno. She's slept with a guy - no, screwed a guy. Maybe there were reasons for it, and maybe I own some of those reasons. Away for weeks on end, maybe not as thoughtful as I should have been, or as attentive, or as loving? And I'm not exactly whiter than white, I've been unfaithful, and she never knew. Not that that matters. Would she forgive me if she knew? Hm, she probably would, she's pragmatic that way, she understands human weaknesses, the human condition. But would she ever get over it, probably not. But it's one thing to hear that your wife has been unfaithful, it's a completely different thing to see her actually getting screwed by a stranger.*

He found the piece of paper with Maxine's phone number and without hesitation texted her.

'Hi, staying over tonight, would love to buy you that posh dinner if you can get out of work duties, A x'

Within a minute his cell phone buzzed with a received text.

'I'm on it, looking forward to it … really :)   meet u at 7 at your hotel xxx Max'

9

I don't remember much about my father. He died in 1972 when I was ten years old. The bond between Lizzie and me grew stronger then. I remember him as a big man but quietly spoken, and I suspect that he was in possession of a bohemian spirit. I also remember that he had big strong hands; everything that he held appeared miniaturised in their minding. As I study my own hands in recent years, I think that they have morphed into my dad's. And his face and arms were bronzed from working outdoors in all kinds of Irish weather. He worked for the electricity company maintaining the regional network, fixing broken cables and climbing poles with harnesses and tools strapped around his waist and a hard hat. We'd sometimes tease him and ask him what he did at work and in response he'd sing *Wichita Lineman* and then he'd grab my mam and dance her around the kitchen table, singing Kristofferson's '*The silver-tongued devil and I*'.

Each year we'd spend the two weeks of his summer holidays camping over in Dogs Bay on the Atlantic coast beyond Roundstone. It would take us over two hours in our Ford Anglia to drive there, stopping on the way in Maam Cross for ice-creams. My dad would sing American country songs or Elvis's songs, or sometimes Bob Dylan, the whole of the journey, and my mam would sing along and Lizzie and I would be giggling in the back seat at how awful they sang, but how wonderful it was too. The car would be packed to the roof with sleeping bags and towels and food and camping gas and pots and pans and beach stuff, everything my mam would think that we'd need for two weeks of holidays. Then, finally, the tenting gear would go up onto the roof; a big pile of it balancing precariously and tied to the roof rack with ropes and straps. Lizzie and I would worry that we'd lose the whole lot going around tight bends on country roads, because our dad would say that if it fell off, then the holiday would be over and we'd have to go home again. But it never fell off. The car was so weighed down that every now and then the exhaust pipe would clank and scrape off the road when we went over bumps or when we couldn't avoid the ubiquitous potholes. Then when we'd eventually get to Dogs Bay, we'd empty everything from the car onto the grass by the sand dunes and spend ages setting up our tent. And our mam would go to the nearby farmhouse, to farmer Daly, and he'd give her a billycan of fresh warm milk, and a pot full of big brown speckled eggs with feathers still stuck to them, and a bag of new potatoes just dug from the ground.

Hail, rain or sunshine we'd go the short distance to the beach every day. When the tide was out it seemed we'd have to walk for miles to the water's edge, but even when it was fully in there would still be a little exposed sandbank where we'd stake our claim. Dad would hammer windbreaker poles deep into the sand and then he'd lay out a blanket which would be our sand-free base camp for the day. I remember he'd chase me and Lizzie along the beach and grab us and hold us under each arm like trapped piglets, running as fast as he could into the breaking surf as we screeched with excitement and terror, and then he'd fling us like ragdolls into the Atlantic Sea. But I know from recent efforts at corroboration that my memory is suspect, even damaged, and so I wonder if he did that just once or if he did it fifty times. But I do remember the vinegary smell of egg, onion, and tomato sandwiches my mam used to make, and that special taste of milked and sugared hot tea in the open air and the smell and taste of sea salt spraying off the crashing waves on the shore. I have an old black and white photograph of the four of us on the beach when Lizzie and I were just two naked babies lying on a bath towel. The last photograph I have of my dad, in glorious technicolour, is of the four of us again lying on the same spot, but we were ten years old then, so it must have been taken just four months before he died.

Lizzie tells me that the night he died we were woken from our beds and brought in to our next-door neighbours, the Muldoon's, where we spent the night and she says that that was the first time that we heard the song. I don't remember that, and I don't even remember the point at which I was told about his death. I do remember worrying about who was going to tie down the tent to the roof rack if my dad wasn't there because me and Lizzie were too small, and our mam couldn't even keep clothes on the washing line. But of course, it didn't dawn on me then that, as our mother couldn't drive, we wouldn't be going anywhere anytime soon. The song, our song, was *American Pie,* released that year and played on the radio every day. We were ten and we thought that Don McLean was singing about our dad; *the day the music died*. Because we thought everyone knew our dad. Of course, we didn't actually think that, but we really wanted to believe it. That was the last year we went to Dogs Bay. Uncle Marty wasn't exactly the camping sort. In fact, we were never quite sure what sort he actually was. I find it hard to understand, though, why I haven't been back there since. It's not because I don't want to, in fact I keep meaning to visit some time, but I guess I've just never got around to it.

But now, every time I hear our song on the radio I can only think of my dad, and even though it was linked to him in death I never remember it in a sad way, but in a happy celebratory way. Camping in Dogs Bay and *American Pie,* is that the summation of my memories of him?

My memories of my mother are different however, to this day I can't figure out the boarding school decision. What was her motivation? After all, there were only two of us kids to manage (and not five or six like other families of that time), and although Uncle Marty was of little actual support as a parent, he did give her the confidence to regain her balance after our dad's death. On each of my own kids' twelfth birthdays, I held them close and I couldn't even conceive the prospect of sending them away at that age. I can only conclude therefore that it must have been as hard on my mother to be separated from us as it was on Lizzie and me. Lizzie has a more generous reflection of that time, but I wonder if that is because her school experience was a very positive one. She told me once that the night before she was due to leave for that first semester, she was wandering into my mother's bedroom to get something or other and she heard Mam crying. She stopped outside the door and eavesdropped on her and Uncle Marty. My mother was sobbing really hard and questioning if they were doing the right thing in sending us away. I always assumed that it was Uncle Marty who forced my mother's hand, but Lizzie swears that it was definitely all my mother's doing. She said that when she herself was in her twenties she'd had many a chat with Angela, our mam's sister, who gave her that insight. Angela said that our mother became a completely different woman after dad died and that she didn't trust herself to manage us into our teens.

Lizzie and I took a gap-year before university when we finished secondary school as we were only seventeen. I didn't get up to much during that year, but I was living at home for an extended period for the first time since I was twelve. Lizzie spent most of the year staying with friends down in Limerick, so I didn't see much of her, and Alex was in the States with his brother. And so, as an adult, I got to meet my mother. It was awkward at first, staying out of each other's way, almost avoiding each other. Not so Marty; there was no awkwardness, we just didn't communicate. Not in a bad way, just in an indifferent-to-each-other way. But gradually as the house got smaller and my mother and I found ourselves in the same rooms more often, it became less awkward and we started to have conversations. During that year I got the impression of a woman who seemed to have prematurely aged because of her laboured loss. There was clearly a void in her life, a resignation. But to my shame, I never broached the subject and hence we never spoke about it. She hid her brittleness behind a stern front. Mostly, though, she was kind and generous to me, but I never experienced softness or demonstrations of love. She never gave me a hug or put her arms around me or told me she loved me. She seemed almost afraid to show affection. I said this once to my sister and she scolded me and said, 'Why are you waiting for her, why don't you grow a pair of balls and give her a hug, that's what I do, and after all, you are bigger than her.' And she laughed.

* * * * *

One evening Lizzie and I were staying over at Angela's place and with a bit of encouragement from us, and a glass or two of wine, she told us the story of how our mam first met our dad. Apparently, as sisters, Angela and Martha were inseparable when they were growing up and shared everything; their bed, their clothes, their accessories, but most of all and best of all, their secrets. She said that Martha and Tommy fell in love almost instantly. Angela and our mam were with a group of friends in Shanahan's pub in Galway and they were having a mighty session. There were two guitars playing and Angela had her fiddle, and the Child of Prague (Billy Pragg was his name and he suffered from a nervous disposition of constantly blessing himself), had his tin whistle and bodhran. It was a Thursday night in early December and outside it was raining cats and dogs, and as always during the winter, there was a roaring turf fire in the hearth. They were playing for their own amusement and the few locals that were gathered there. Then two lads came into the pub, definitely strangers in town. They took off their soaking hats and coats and ordered their pints, and a few of the locals moved their chairs to give them room to warm themselves by the fire. He was sitting across from her and immediately they caught each other's eye, and he nodded his head and smiled, and she could feel the heat rising up her neck and into her cheeks. She thought he was so handsome.

There was a bit of a break in the music and his friend encouraged him to sing, so he asked for one of the guitars and he stood up, pulled up the collar of his shirt, put one leg on a chair *a la* Elvis and sang *Jailhouse Rock.* The pub went wild and shouted encore, encore, and then he broke into *Johnny B Goode* and he had the whole pub singing along to the chorus. His name was Tommy and his friend's name was Paddy. At one point in the night, Tommy came across and sat down next to Martha. They were sitting very close, their arms sometimes touched, or their legs, and when they did she could feel the electric energy jumping between them. It was raw and exciting and scary. She knew at that precise moment that this was it. She knew this was *him.*

Although his job had him based at the Limerick depot, he was with a gang who were helping restore power to areas around Galway following a recent storm. Paddy was his boss, but they were also very good friends. Eventually the session ended, and the barman cleared the pub and, as the rain had stopped, Tommy offered to walk her home. Angela said that she walked behind them and out of sight; 'Just to keep an eye on him you see, after all, we didn't know him from Adam.' When they got to the start of her road, he pulled her over against a wall and held her close and without any please-or-thank-you he kissed her hungrily. Later, in the small hours of the morning, as the sisters whispered and giggled in bed Martha said that she didn't want the kiss to end, and she didn't want him to go, and she didn't want the spell to be broken.

After that night they'd meet whenever and wherever they could. Although it was the start of the sixties for the rest of the western world, it might as well have been the forties in Ireland. He drove a motor bike and he'd come up to Galway as often as he could at weekends. Her parents forbade her to travel on his bike, so she'd meet him in town and then climb on the back and wrap her arms tightly around him and put her face against his leather jacket covering his broad back, and they'd head off out the Connemara coast road. After a few miles they'd stop in a quiet place and, with the freedom of the wilderness, they'd embrace and kiss passionately and cuddle and tell each other how much they missed and loved one another and how lucky they were, and they'd laugh and cry and make plans. Angela sounded a little sad when she recounted that their plans always only involved

Tommy and her sister, no one else. There was no room for anyone else in their relationship, in their dreams.

Tommy soon got a transfer to the Galway depot and he took up lodgings in a family home out by the dog track. At the time, Martha was working in a shoe shop in town and now they were able to see each other three or four times a week. A year later, when Tommy was twenty-four and she was twenty-one and an independent lady, they were married, and they moved into a one-bedroom flat down by the docks. And they were ridiculously happy. They lived for each other. Lived to see each other after work every day and lived to wake up to each other every morning. They'd make love whenever they could, at night, in the morning, and as Martha once confided to Angela; scandalously during the daytime at weekends. They had no shame!

Unsurprisingly then, Martha became pregnant within six months. Unsurprising because family planning in Ireland was, at that time, more science fiction than science, and to avoid being damned for all eternity the only allowable forms of birth control was either the Rhythm Method (which involved charts and baby stickers and abstention, when you least wanted to be bridled), or the Withdrawal Method (which involved bringing frustration to a cerebral injury level). Needless to say, they practiced both methods, but very badly. And so, true to the science of the day, Martha didn't know that it was twins she was carrying until we were delivered in the bedroom of their little flat. But there was a problem with the birth, and old doctor Daly realised too late that her home birth really wasn't a good idea. Although we were born healthily our mother began to haemorrhage and was rushed to the Galway General hospital. She underwent immediate surgery, but the cure included the removal of her womb. She spent three weeks in hospital during which she was only occasionally allowed to see or hold her new babies.

Notwithstanding Martha's near-death experience, Tommy was ecstatic at the birth of their twins. Martha was ambivalent. She saw us as a threat to their union. She told Angela after we were born; 'I now have to share him; my total is reduced to a third.' She figured out much later in life that she had probably suffered from postnatal depression, which naturally went undiagnosed back then. The treatment was stern advice, "Pull yourself together, girl. Women have babies every day of the week so stop thinking only about yourself; be strong for your husband and your children." And this coming from nuns who themselves would never bear children … Well, at least not officially anyway.

But in time, as her health slowly recovered, she grew to accept a union of four and she came to love her babies. As we listened to Angela tell the story, and although she was quite modest about her own involvement, we understood that she was hugely supportive, minding and caring for us babies during the times when our dad was at work and when our mam didn't feel able, and minding her too.

By our first birthday Martha felt that she had emerged from the dark side and that Tommy and she were as before. He was doing well in his job and had a good steady wage, so they moved out of the tiny flat to a brand-new house just fifteen minutes from town. Their lives were idyllic. She knew that Tommy would have loved more kids, but the fact that she couldn't conceive suited her just fine. She was perfectly content with Tommy, Lizzie and me.

The years flew by. In the blink of an eye, we were attending our first day at school in our new grown-up school uniforms. Soon we were making our First Holy Communion; Martha had us dressed to dazzle the sun and, according to Angela, everyone said how cute and gorgeous 'the twins' were, and all the women remarked that Tommy looked so handsome in his new tweed suit. Martha was so proud of him. She loved him so much. She confided in Angela that sometimes the intensity even surprised her, when it actually caused an ache in her chest.

And then he left her. Without warning. And all that intense love turned to immense pain. And anger. Her beautiful man, her lover, her soul mate, her rock. The father of her children stolen from her. Gone. One evening Angela saw her sister hold a photograph of Tommy to her lips and cry; '*How could you leave me, Tommy Sommers? Why didn't you take me with you? You promised we'd never be apart.*'

As her love turned to indescribable anguish she felt that she had lost a great part of herself, but not a physical part, more like her soul had died. Her world had simply fallen apart. She couldn't think straight. If she couldn't comfort herself, she thought, what was the point in trying to comfort the kids? She was so caught up in her own loss and self-pity that she was absent for us and our grieving. Some days she couldn't get out of bed and other days she worried about our welfare so much that it paralysed her and all she could do was cry for us. She didn't see the point in doing house chores and even meals became irregular. She smoked more, sometimes lighting a cigarette but forgetting that there was one already burning in a different room. She lost weight. Angela demanded that she attend her doctor, but either he had nothing to offer or she didn't take his help.

The months went by and things continued to deteriorate and so one day Angela took her sister aside and said that they needed a woman-to-woman chat. She told her that if she didn't care about herself, then she needed to care about the kids, they were suffering so much. She said that Tommy was alive in the kids and if loving Tommy meant anything, then it meant loving them even more. She said lots. And Martha didn't seem to feel hurt or angry by what her sister said, or feel insulted or threatened by her attitude, but most of all, and worst of all; she didn't seem to feel anything. Of course, she nodded in agreement with Angela, but agreeing about something and doing anything about it are two very different states. But her sister persisted. She wouldn't give up. She had promised herself that she wouldn't let Martha continue to wallow in her grief, and doing nothing was not an option. So, she challenged her again the next week, and then the week after that and every week following until eventually her sister finally heard her.

Although she was only thirty-five, Martha confided that she would never love another man. But she also said that she couldn't bring up her twins on her own. There were obviously lots of single mothers and fathers who were doing an excellent job rearing their kids, but she knew that she didn't have that capacity, that capability. A dilemma for sure. But one to which she had found a solution. And so, she hatched a plan. An audacious plan. And she conscripted Angela in its execution.

One day soon after the hatching, Angela happened to 'bump' into Tommy's older brother, Martin, and suggested to him that he should pay Martha a visit; 'You know, just to show family support, Martin' He gratefully thanked Angela for the suggestion and he said in fact that he knew just the right time and occasion to visit her over the next few weeks.

And so, on the evening of May 02nd Martin knocked on Martha's door, his arms loaded down with presents. One was a large doll in beautiful hand-made clothes and the other was a full train set with passengers and a station master with a little red flag and a perfectly detailed train station. Martha brought him into the sitting room and as she poured him a cup of tea remarked; 'These are lovely presents Martin; you really shouldn't have gone to so much trouble and expense.'

'No, no trouble at all Martha, sure I'm their godfather.'

'Yes, of course, but are they for any special occasion?'

'They're for their birthdays of course, Martha.'

'Ah, their birthdays, but you know when their birthdays are?'

'Sure, they're tomorrow, that's why I brought them over this evening, so they'd have them first thing in the morning.'

'Well, no Martin, their birthdays aren't actually tomorrow.'

'What? But I wrote it down, from last year.' He fumbled in his pocket and pulled out a piece of paper. 'Look, the second of the fifth, which is tomorrow.'

'No Martin, it's the other way round, it's the fifth of the second. Their birthdays were in February, three months ago.'

'What? Oh Martha, I'm so feckin' stupid, and I really wanted to do something nice, surprise the kids. They've been through so much recently.'

'Don't worry yourself,' she offered, 'the twins will love their presents, better now than their actual birthday, a bigger surprise.' She also didn't tell him that the kids were eleven and had outgrown dolls and train sets years ago.

'Thanks Martha, that's kind of you.'

Without asking, she refilled his teacup again and pushed the little plate of biscuits towards him. After a few minutes of silence while Martin worked his way through the biscuits, Martha thought to herself; *well, I suppose this is as good a time as any.*

'Martin, can I ask you a personal question?'

'Of course, Martha, don't worry, you can ask me anything.'

'Well, can I ask if there's anyone special in your life at the moment?'

Martin looked a bit stumped but then, having given it some thought, the penny dropped and he said, 'Ah, you mean Jimmy Mac and Joe and the lads?'

'Eh, no no, Martin, I don't mean any special male friends. I mean a special female friend, like a girlfriend?'

Martin blushed. 'Ah, I see what you mean, no no, sure who'd have me at this stage, ha-ha?'

'Don't be silly, there are lots of women in town that'd love to have you.'

'Ah, that's kind of you Martha, but sure I'm too set in me ways for any of them.'

'Well, I have a proposition for you Martin, something I'd like you to think about.'

'A proposition? Go on, go on.'

'Well, since Tommy died, I'm sure you've noticed that I've struggled big time on my own with the kids. I've tried to do the best I can but I'm finding it very difficult without the support of a man.'

'Don't be silly Martha, you're doing a fine job with them.'

'No no, Martin, I'm not, and they miss their dad so much. They miss a man around the house, they need a father figure.'

'Ah yes, a father figure.'

'Yes, a man about the house, someone to look up to, especially for Jack, you see what I mean?'

'Yes, I see what you mean,' Martin said soberly.

'Really?'

'Yes of course, I know exactly what you mean.'

'Oh Martin, really?

'Yes, yes Martha, you don't need to say any more, I know what you mean, and I know what you're asking me.'

'Really? Oh, Martin, you're so clever and thoughtful, I knew you'd understand.'

'Good, well that's settled then, now that wasn't so bad, was it?'

'Oh, not at all, and you're sure you don't need to think about it overnight or for a few days?'

'Course not, as me friends say, "once Martin Sommers makes his mind up then that's the end of it, there's no movin' him."'

'So, your answer is yes, then?'

'My answer is a resounding *yes,*' Martin said enthusiastically and with a little flourish slapped the table with the palm of his hands.

'Oh Martin, how can I ever thank you enough, you don't know how much this means to me, you being Tommy's brother and everything.' She reached out and put her hands on his hands.

'Sure, how could I say no Martha, I'm so honoured that you'd want to ask for my consent.'

'Ask your consent, for what?'

'Well, consent to marry again, of course.'

'Jesus, Martin, tis you I'm asking, for God's sake!'

'And once Martha had peeled Martin off the floor' Angela continued humorously, 'and dusted him down, she offered him a generous glass of Jameson and, over the course of the rest of the bottle, they hammered out a pact.'

As Angela told her story I had a picture of Lizzie and me upstairs in our bedrooms sleeping the sleep of angels, blissfully unaware that the rocky road of our young lives was about to again careen sharply around the next bend to God-knows-where, while, in the heavens above, our dad was frantically trying to steer our tender lives safely between the ditches.

* * * * *

And their pact lasted for the next thirty-seven years, up to the point when Martha died. She hadn't been sick or anything, except for the usual old age complaints. Arthritis prematurely twisted her joints, and as her mobility reduced, she gained weight which further exacerbated her tortured bones. It was early in October and Bea and I were in Lyon doing some maintenance on our apartment on Rue Foch. Lizzie rang me to say that our mam had taken a turn and her doctor was admitting her to hospital for tests, just to be on the safe side. I didn't worry too much about it but later that night Lizzie rang me again to say that she had suffered a major setback and to get home as quickly as possible. The only scheduled flight to Dublin the following day was in the afternoon, and by the time we got back to Galway and to the hospital it was close to nine o'clock.

And it was too late. She was gone. She had died just thirty minutes before we arrived. But Lizzie had been with her the whole time even though our mother hadn't been conscious for a few hours. Bea drove our car home to Spiddal and Lizzie and I stayed with our mother for the night. We reminisced, recalling the big events and also remembering the silly little details. We talked and cried about her, but mostly we laughed about her. And we remembered our dad too, and we even agreed that Uncle Marty was after all 'an ok lad'.

And when the doctor came to chat to us about the cause of her death, he said that it was most likely a myocardial infarction, or in everyday language, a heart attack. Lizzie turned to me and said, 'In the end she did die of a broken heart, Jack.'

10

Boston, Tue 16th May (18 days to Nadir)

The grey-haired man in a grey suit and in a non-descript car drove up Eucalyptus Avenue at 2.00pm keenly looking for the image which was described in the notes contained in the envelope. 'You'll be able to see the gable end and the half-roof of the house through the trees.' Once he had his target in sight, he pulled over to the kerb just across the road and about twenty metres from the driveway. As he passed, he saw the VW Tiguan in the drive. He turned his car so that he had a clear and uninterrupted view of the entrance. Then he slipped his favourite CD into the machine and listened to Hall and Oates sing *'You've Lost That Lovin' Feeling'*. From a brown paper bag, he took out a homemade tuna and sweetcorn sandwich and poured a cup of steaming coffee from a flask and settled back in his car seat in the shadows for an afternoon of observation. Over-endowed with the patience gene but sold-short on imagination, he thought; *life really doesn't get any better than this.*

At 5.15pm the VW pulled out of the driveway and drove down the avenue. Once it was out of sight the man got out of his car, and from the rear seat took out a backpack and threw it over his shoulder and walked casually and unhurriedly down the road and up the driveway. He let himself into the log house and went directly to the alarm system to check if it had been activated. Having completed a reconnaissance of each room, he logged on to the house Wi-Fi and proceeded to attach a miniature electronic device discreetly above the door frames of the bedroom, the kitchen, and the living room. Opening his cell phone, he activated an app, checked that each camera was operational, and captured the images of the three rooms. He then made his way to the cellar and found a comfortable chair and settled down for his wait.

An hour later he heard her car returning and listened as she closed the front door. He settled back in his chair, reckoning that he still had four to five hours to relax before he needed to re-energise. But this was what he did best; he was a master of the waiting game. He had spent ten years in both the army intelligence and the intelligence wing of the Boston Police Force. He opened the app on his phone and watched her as she moved around the kitchen preparing food, and after an hour or so she disappeared for a while and reappeared in her bedroom, getting undressed and changing into her nightdress and dressing gown for the evening.

A minute later she appeared in the living room, switching on the TV, and settling down on a couch. The noise of the TV irritated him, so he muted his device. She received two phone calls, but neither was of any consequence. At one point she left and returned with a drink and settled back into the couch. At 10.45 she switched off the TV, which was his cue to be ready to move. His screen virtually blacked out when she switched off the living room light and then he saw her enter the kitchen. She made herself a drink, as his notes correctly suggested, and his screen again blacked out when she switched off the kitchen light. A minute later she appeared in her bedroom and placed her drink on the bedside table nearest the door. *Sometimes you just get lucky*, he thought. He made his way from the cellar across the hallway and crept up the stairs to the landing and waited outside her bedroom door. He checked his app and saw that she had taken her dressing robe off and that she was sitting at her dressing table fussing and moving things. After a short while she got up and went into the en suite bathroom and he could hear her electric toothbrush activate. He opened the door just enough that he could slip into her bedroom and empty a sachet of powder into her glass. The powder clouded the liquid for only five seconds before completely disappearing. He slipped back to the landing, quietly closing the bedroom door and retraced his steps to the cellar.

He checked his app and saw that she had switched off the light in the bathroom and was climbing into bed. The reading light above her head was on, and she propped herself up in bed and opened a book and was sipping her drink as she read. Within fifteen minutes she had finished her drink and she threw the book on the other side of the bed, switched off the reading light, and was sleeping within a few minutes.

The intruder waited a further thirty minutes, during which time he was busy setting up his laptop and other accessories, and he then repeated his journey back to her bedroom. He knew that she would be in a deep drug-induced sleep at this stage and that she would remain like that for at least four hours, although he only needed two or three hours max to complete his work. Inside her bedroom, he went directly to her cell phone on her bedside locker where it was charging, unplugged it, and slipped it into his pocket. As he made his way back out of the bedroom, he noticed that the bedcover was only partially covering her body, so he pulled it over her to cover her exposed flesh.

Back in the cellar he quickly got to work on her phone. He checked his notes for her code, which allowed him access, and once opened he hooked it up to his computer and began the download. He copied everything from the phone and her sim card; emails, notes, pictures, videos, music, phone contacts, everything, and then he got to work on her history, her emails, internet, phone calls and texts. Within two hours he was done. He had mirrored her phone to his computer, and he had captured every piece of data that had moved in and out of it since it was updated three years earlier. Finally, he opened the back of the phone and attached a microchip to the inside of the back cover, closed it and checked on his computer that it was activated. Once finished he returned her phone back to her bedroom and plugged it in. 'And now for the old-fashioned physical search' he said out loud and he turned to her wardrobe and dressing table and forensically went through everything that was kept there, coat pockets, drawers, folders, envelopes, files, handbags. He lay down on the ground on his belly and looked under the bed for any tell-tale hidden signs of secrets. He even swept his hand underneath her pillows in case he had missed anything. Once he was satisfied that he had captured everything of importance, he surveyed the room to make sure that nothing was out of place. He washed her glass in the bathroom and replaced it on her bedside locker and finally he removed the camera from above the doorway and pulled the door closed behind him.

Back in his car he checked his watch. 3.50am. Good, he thought, she'll sleep until six or seven and she'll wake up a little drowsier than usual and maybe with a mild headache but nothing that will bother her. He slipped the car into drive, pulled away from the kerb and headed for home and sleep, satisfied with his very productive night's work.

Anthony's phone buzzed with a text late on Tuesday afternoon. 'I have the info and can pass it to you later.' Anthony texted back, 'My cabin at 7.'

At precisely 7.00pm there was a knock on the door and Anthony invited the private investigator into his room. As they shook hands the man said, 'You can call me John.'

'Em, well ok, good to meet you, John.'

'Right, I've got everything you need in digital format and I've also got a hard copy of some selected documents like pictures, emails, addresses etc. Everything is catalogued and indexed on this front page.' He had taken a dossier from his backpack and placed it on the dressing table.

'Thanks, I'll go through them later, but you might just fill me in on the two specific things I asked for.'

'Yes of course; who is he and how long have they been seeing each other.'

'Yes, and obviously if there's anything else that's relevant.'

John leaned back in his chair, folded his arms and began his story.

'The man that she is currently seeing is William Johnson, but he goes by Bill. He lives in Hopkinton, just twenty minutes from here. He's married with three teenage kids. He works as a sales and marketing manager for a gym equipment company and he covers quite a large territory west of Boston city. They met on an adult dating app three years ago and the affair proper started six months after that, so they have been seeing each other for the past two and a half years. They meet mostly in your home, but they have also met in restaurants and hotels and last May when you were in the Far East they went to Florida for a few days. This of course is all detailed in the dossier, with texts and emails and images to support it.'

'You say images, what kind of images?'

'Pictures of them together of course. By the way, I should warn you, there's a health warning with the images, some are very explicit.'

'But how did you get the images, surely she didn't have them on her phone?'

'Yes, of course on her phone, and in her emails. Listen, Anthony, people hold on to compromising stuff all the time, particularly digital images on phones or computers. Fifty years ago, lovers kept letters, or a risqué photograph hidden under the floorboards or somewhere safe, but these days they're hidden in digital-broad-daylight. I'm never surprised at how stupid people can be.'

'One thing you said earlier, John, and I suspect you chose your words carefully, you said "the man she is currently seeing" When you say currently you mean up until last Friday morning, yeah?'

'I say currently because she has been in contact with him since Friday morning. They met for two hours in the Hopkinton State Park on Sunday afternoon at which time they were intimate in his car and there have been a number of calls since. For instance, they've discussed the fact that you're meeting her tomorrow.'

'Jesus Christ, John, what the Christ have I unleashed in you.'

'I'm sorry, sir, but once you engaged me you were always going to get everything, every detail. But I can just as easily take all the evidence and destroy it so it never sees the light of day. You've already paid me for my services and after all you now verbally have the information you need.'

'No, no, of course not, I'll need the evidence. Trust me, I appreciate the work you've done. Anything else?'

'Not about your wife, but I can tell you more about him if you'd like to know.'

'No thanks; I think I know enough about him for my own good.'

'Well, it may be useful information for you, depending how you might want to use it.'

'How do you mean?'

'In the conversation with your wife.'

'Go on then, what more do you know?'

'The guy is cheating on your wife too.'

'Yeah, he's married, is that what you mean?'

'No, come on Anthony, wise up, he's seeing someone else as well.'

'You mean there's a third woman?'

'Yep, you don't need to know any details but yes, he's been having an affair with another woman for years, and it predates your wife.'

'Holy Christ, poor Jessie.'

'Well ok, that's it. I'll leave you with the dossier and the memory stick. The key and the instructions you gave me are in this envelope. Your wife's phone is currently active, which means it's giving me information in real time, but it deactivates automatically in two weeks' time unless you instruct me otherwise. I can deactivate it remotely at any time between now and then. If there's nothing else then I'll leave you to it, but please don't hesitate to give me a call if you need anything.'

They shook hands and Anthony saw him out of the cabin. On the front steps the private detective turned and said, 'Have a good life, Anthony,' and he walked to his car.

'Have a good life.' What the hell does that mean? Anthony thought as he poured himself a whiskey, lit a cigarette, and threw himself on the bed. He picked up the dossier and flicked through its pages until he came to a group of images. There were maybe six pages in all and each one contained four pictures. Each image was dated and laid out in chronological order. The first few images were of both of them together, having a drink at a bar or in a restaurant or sightseeing

somewhere, taken by a third party. The next batch was of Anthony's wife seductively posing naked on their bed, his bed, licking her lips and using her index finger to entice the photographer to come to her, and a few pictures of her lover naked and posing like a bodybuilder. Then he came to the images which carried the health warning, selfies of them screwing, or each of them alternatively controlling the camera while being screwed. His wife in various positions.

He flung the dossier on the bed. He tried to get a handle on his feelings, to really understand how he felt; was it disgust; or anger; or sadness; or bitterness? Or worse still, indifference? Why didn't the images distress him or incite him to a violent response, or at the very least, revulsion? *Possibly because you can't beat watching the real thing,* he thought. No image, no matter how explicit or grotesque, could match the memory of actually seeing her being screwed - no, no, not just seeing her, hearing her. And anyway, it didn't look like her in the images, posing seductively like he'd never seen her before, and happy in a way that he'd never seen her. Yeah, that was it, she looked different, younger, fresher, with more vitality, more energy.

Then the penny dropped, and with the clang of an anvil it hit the ground, and the moment of comprehension was exquisite. In total surprise and shock at his own revelation he sat bolt-upright on the bed and said, 'Christ, I'm married to a different woman.'

But as fast as it came, the moment was slipping away from him. 'Say it again', he told himself. 'I'm married to a different woman than the one screwing in these pictures.' *Ok, hold that thought, what do I mean? Yes, that's Jessie, my wife, but she's not the woman I'm married to or the woman I've spent the last thirty years with. She's a different woman.* 'Christ!' he exclaimed. He slowly lit another cigarette.

'What in God's name have we been doing?' he said out loud. 'Have we been only living half-lives, and half lies? Do we actually know who the hell we are, or know each other at all? What have we been doing, playing bloody games, playing hide and seek, just showing bits of ourselves to each other? Have we ever been honest with one another?

Or even honest with ourselves?' He picked up the dossier again and flicked through the pages, with facsimiles of emails and texts, and stopped at one random page and read some lines.

Her: 'my darling I want to suck your thick cock this second.'

Him: 'oh me too Jess I want you on your knees looking up into my face.'

Her: 'oh baby I'm so hot my fingers are in my cunt now.'

Him: 'fuck me too babe I need you soooo badly.'

Anthony looked at the dates of the texts, June 24th. That's familiar, he thought. He checked the calendar on his phone for June of last year. Yes, as he thought, June 22nd to 25th Galway, when he and Jessie were staying with the Sommers all that weekend.

'Jesus,' he shouted, 'even when she was with me, for Christ's sake.' He took the dossier and fired it as hard as he could across the room; it hit the window blind but then fell harmlessly to the floor. He looked at it and thought with a wry smile, '*I can't even break something.*' He laughed but with a little edge of hysteria.

He texted Maxine to see if she could meet him for a drink, and although she said that she was working, she encouraged him to come over anyway as the bar was very quiet. He grabbed his pack of cigarettes and his jacket and with unnecessary force slammed the door after him. As he walked the couple of blocks to the bar, his thoughts were on that weekend in Galway. The Sommers' and the Castelletto's, two loving couples on a mini-break, while unbeknownst to him his wife was surreptitiously texting her lover. And the moment of exquisite clarity, which he had experienced earlier, faded further and further from his consciousness with every step and every dark thought.

11

Galway, Saturday 20th May (14 days to Nadir)

I was determined to dedicate every minute of my weekend to my family, no work calls, no emails, no strategizing work meetings even in my head, and especially no 'other' family ruminations. The only exception to that was a prior commitment to go to watch Connacht play Munster with Alex in an early kick-off at the Showgrounds on Saturday. The local derby match was hugely anticipated in the rugby calendar and Alex had managed to get very good stand tickets. I even thought about cancelling, and suggested it to Bea, but she insisted that I get some 'boys' time with Al. Anyway, I'd booked La Porte restaurant in Spiddal for Bea and myself for dinner that evening. We were also treating Sadie to breakfast in Galway on Sunday morning. Al lived in Poreen, which is a little village a few kilometres west of Spiddal, and he'd agreed to collect me on the way and promised Bea that he'd have me back to her by 5.00pm. And so, we set off towards Galway, two old friends who hadn't met in a few months and with the added excitement of a mouth-watering bruising game of war ahead of us.

'I can't fucking wait to watch Munster weep after 80 minutes, Jack, I've a real good feeling about our gang today.'

'Hm, I think you say that before every game, Al, and we haven't beaten them in over two years. I wouldn't be betting my house on them any time soon.'

'You see, that's your problem lad, you've no confidence in the team, and you know they can pick that up from you and all the other depressives during the match. The team isn't the problem, it's the fucking supporters.'

'Ha, ok, ok, I'll will them to win, I'll beam laser-like positive karma in the direction of their changing room the minute we get to the park, but right now I'm looking forward to a pint in O'Connell's.'

'So, tell me, what's all this nonsense about babies being sprung out of the blue on ya, I hope you did like I told you to do and invoke the do-nothing principle?'

'Well, it's not a baby anymore Al, it's a fully grown 34-year-old man with a daughter to boot, and the do-nothing law may not quite work here.'

'But you haven't done anything yet, right?'

'No, no. Well, other than doing a DNA test for paternity.'

Al braked hard and nearly steered the car into a ditch. 'You did what? Why the fuck did you do that? Are you mad?'

'Jesus Al, mind the road, and calm down for God's sake, no one knows it's my test and I'm the only one who'll get the result. I need to know bud; I have to know.'

'Well, I'll tell you something for nothing, I wouldn't need to know, I wouldn't want to know - like why draw all this on you?'

'I didn't draw it on me, it's come out of the fucking heavens and landed on me, and anyway if you're so clever, what would you have done, walked away?'

'I keep telling you, you gotta revert to first principles lad, you do nothing! Me, walk away? I wouldn't have walked away, I'd have legged it out of that hotel and be tearing down the M6 to Galway so fast, that the hotel doors would still be fucking swinging by the time I had me arse on a barstool in O'Connell's.'

It wasn't long before we were sipping pints in said O'Connell's amid the hustle and bustle of Munster and Connaught fans mingling and good-naturedly jibing each other, with both sets of supporters telling their opposites, 'Jaysas, I think ye'll do it today lads, I've got a feeling ye'll be too strong for us, that's a great team ye're putting out there today.' That way, when the fans met again after the match, if your side did lose, at least you were clever enough to predict it. But if, on the other hand, your side won, it made the winning all the sweeter. 'Jaysas, I really thought ye'd do it today, ah well, sure there's always next year.'

All this to the utter misery of the poor losing supporter. It's an inverse-bragging, passive-aggressive soup. Lethal.

Alex glanced at his watch. 'Jaysas look at the time, drink up lad, we don't want to be late for your laser-like karma.' We finished our pints, Al shouted to the barmen that we'd see him later, we grabbed our coats and headed out through the crowded bar.

Just a little over two hours later we were back in O'Connell's nursing our pints.

'Jaysas Jack, I really didn't see that coming, I really thought we had the measure of 'em today, but how can ye win when you're playing the ref too.'

'Al, we got fucking hammered, and I didn't see the ref touch the ball once. And, come to think of it, I didn't see our backline touch the ball once either in the whole game.'

Some Munster supporters arrived at the bar and shouted over to Alex, who they knew from old. 'Jaysas, I thought ye'd do it today Al, still, sure there's always next year.'

Alex lifted his pint in recognition and forced a grim smile. 'Yeah yeah, well done lads.' Then he turned to me, and half under his breath mumbled, 'Fucking assholes, I hate them Jack, I hate 'em worse than Leinster, I nearly fucking hate them worse than England.'

'Tell me something I don't know, Al.'

'Well, ok, I hate them for Kinsale.'

'Kinsale? What about Kinsale?'

'Sure, we'd have won the battle of Kinsale if the Munster clowns weren't a bunch of chickens, and then we wouldn't have had the Flight of the Earls, and we wouldn't have had Cromwell's plantations, or the Ulster plantations, and the great famine wouldn't have happened and we'd be a thirty-two county Republic now, a united Ireland.'

I looked at Al in bewilderment. 'But the Battle of Kinsale was Hugh O'Neill and Red Hugh O'Donnell, they were from Tyrone and Donegal, it only took place in Kinsale, for crying out loud.'

'Yeah, but what about their chieftain, what was his name - yeah, O'Sullivan Beare from West Cork, what help did he give? Fuck all. It's because of him and his cronies that the battle was lost.'

I threw my eyes up to heaven and finished my pint. 'I'll say one thing for you, Al, you never cease to amaze me.'

'But we'll get it fairly shortly anyway.'

'Get what?'

'A united Ireland, we'll get the six counties back, you know, because of Brexit.'

'How do you make that out?'

'Well, the Brits have fucked themselves up, haven't they? How can the North be in the UK and the EU at the same time when the UK leaves? Mark my words, it'll only be a matter of time when their artificial Union splits asunder. And anyway, they don't give a flying fuck about the North, they'll play the Unionists like the muppets that they are.'

'Well, for once I agree with you Al, God only knows what's gonna be released from this Brexit Pandora's box.'

Driving back in the car Alex offered from nowhere, 'I remember her, you know.'

'Who?'

'The so-called mother of your so-called son, I remember her, Marianne.'

'Really? You sure? What do you remember?'

'I remember that she was blonde, tall, beautiful, what's she like now?'

'Still very beautiful, she hasn't changed much. But tell me, what do you remember?'

'I remember the first time you met her.'

'In Neachtain's, you remember us meeting her in Neachtain's?'

'That wasn't the first time we met her.'

'Yes, it was, when she came over and asked me for a light.'

'Christ you've a lousy memory Jack, we first met her on the Aran Islands, on Inis Mór, that's when she came over and asked you for a light.'

'No way lad, I distinctly remember being in Neachtain's, I even remember where we were sitting when she came over to us.'

'Nah, I bet ya a fifty that you're wrong. And I can prove it. Yes, we bumped into her the following night in Neachtain's, but the cigarette ruse happened outside Watty's pub on Inis Mór.'

'Al, do you actually make stuff up in your head, this is worse than your Kinsale farce.'

'You, me, and Lizzie had gone over for the craic for the day because Lizzie had got us a free trip on the ferry over and back. Remember the sun was splitting the stones and we were sitting outside Watty's with pints and garlic mussels and their gorgeous soda bread, debating whether to go for a dive off the pier? Then she came along and specifically targeted you for a light and you started fumbling and blabbering incoherently, and then, like you were suddenly struck dumb, you just shook your head. Remember, Lizzie offered her a light and the four of us started chatting - well, three and a dummy at least.'

I couldn't believe that my recollection of my first-time meeting Marianne could actually be so wrong, but somewhere in the fog of memory the scene outside Watty's started to emerge and take shape.

'I'll never forget that afternoon, Jack. Remember that I had the hots for Lizzie, and Lizzie had the hots for Marianne, and Marianne had the hots for you, and you just had the hots. You couldn't make this shit up.'

'Yeah, I do remember you were always trying to get off with my sis in spite of the fact that we all knew she preferred girls.'

'No Jack, you're hopeless, not in spite of, but because of the fact that she preferred girls.'

'You're incorrigible Al, you're fucking incorrigible.'

'No rush with the fifty by the way, and no need to admit "you're right, Al."'

'Ok, ok, you could be right, it might've been outside Watty's, but it was definitely in Neachtain's the next night that she bumped into us again, so I'm half right.'

'You can't be half right Jack, that's like being half pregnant. And you should know more than anyone that you can't be half pregnant - unfortunately in your case.'

'Low ball, Al.'

'She seriously wanted your bones Jack, she was all over you like a rash and it was no coincidence that she was in Neachtain's the next night, but you were so naïve you couldn't see it.'

'But how did she know where we were going to be the next night?'

'Em, well I might have said something to her about where we hung out.'

'Ah, so it's your fault that I'm up shit creek, I should have known that you were stuck in the middle of it somewhere.'

Alex laughed. 'Not my fault that you couldn't tell the difference between a bed of feathers and a bed of thorns lad.'

I thought back to that time and remembered it as the hottest summer for years and remembered Marianne being the hottest thing I'd ever met. My only previous comparator was the lovely Madame Emilie Rouault who obviously wasn't available (being married, having a child, being much older, but probably most significantly, not even noticing that I existed). And so, replacing her in my heart with the very exotic and available Marianne caused me feelings of great guilt. Mind you, I soon discovered that my degree of guilt decreased proportionally with her degree of increasing availability. In other words, the more I got, the more I forgot, so to speak. But that feeling of inferiority and punching above my weight was pervasive, and in hindsight I now believe that it contributed to my inability to engage in a normal intimate relationship with her. Not only was I the country boy and she the city girl, but I had also only just emerged the previous summer from my five-year chrysalis of horror and was struggling big time to comprehend life in the fast lane. I was faced, for the first time up close and personal, with the female form and biology, and, even more impenetrable to me, the female mind, with its alien characteristics and vanities. Their complexities and unfamiliarity were both a mystery and a wonder to me.

And I was confronted by my own sexuality, and in my confusion and awkwardness I lacked any appropriate responses. I remember that Al had gone to stay with a brother of his in the States that summer, so I was left on my own to navigate this new and intimidating world. Without my mentor, I knew nothing of its rules or customs. I felt like a navigator without a compass. I'd decided not to go to France so that I might assimilate back into my own community, but I soon discovered that I was a stranger in my own village. Teenagers who lived locally and should have been my friends had gone to local schools and were already in well-developed groups and cliques. So, I stumbled around that summer and autumn desperately attempting to understand the rituals and manners but instead finding myself in an emotional cul-de-sac. And my confidence and self-belief took a hammering. I saw myself as ugly, unattractive, stupid, and worst of all irrelevant. It was only in the spring of my nineteenth year and in the company of Al and Lizzie that I gradually began to understand the impact that the previous five years had had on my arrested development. I understood then that if I was to grow and be successful in this new reality then there were habituations and behaviours that I needed to shed. I was very conscious of the fact that I was on a journey of deconstruction and rebuilding. And although it would take me years to fully grow into the independent, confident, and developed individual who became the identifiable Jack Sommers, I'm convinced that it was that first year at the deep end, sometimes waving and sometimes drowning, that formed the foundation of my rebirth.

'Anyway, sorry to interrupt your daydreaming, Jack, but what about Marianne, what're you gonna do if the test is positive?'

'Hm, dunno, have a breakdown or something. Don't really know bud, it changes everything.'

'What does Lizzie say?'

'Embrace it, you know that's what she says, you know her as well as I do.'

'And what about Bea? You could be walking into a shit-storm there, lad, I know Bea only too well too, and you don't wanna mess with Bea.'

'Who the fuck are you telling Al, don't I know it, and she's not exactly in the best shape at the moment.'

'Yeah, Sylvie dropped into her in the gallery during the week just to say hello and she said that she was as high as dough, stressed. She says that she needs to dump Helen, that she's a liability and that she's just using her.'

'Yeah, I agree with Sylvie, she's got a good sense of things. Although I can never figure out how the she's put up with you for so long.'

'Charm Jack, pure fucking charm, and animal attraction, that girl can't fucking wait till I come home from work every day.'

'Aha, brill, Al.'

'Listen bud, be very careful with this thing. Sometimes we can get sucked into stuff in the belief that we can step out of it at any point. You know, get off at the next station, but then we realise that we've missed our stop, we've gone too far. Call me when you get the DNA result, I don't want anything to happen between you and Bea.'

'Yeah, I promise I will Al, in spite of what everyone else says about you, I think you're the best.'

We pulled into my driveway and Alex beeped the horn and Bea stuck her head out the front door and shouted down to Al, "Well? Did you win?"

'Lost by a hair's breadth, Bea, and your husband didn't help much, no belief.'

As I walked up the driveway, Bea was laughing and waving him goodbye. 'There's always next year Al, love you.' She blew him a kiss.

* * * * *

Over dinner at La Porte that evening we chatted comfortably about the intertwined stuff of our lives, the important and the not-so-important. Centre stage always was Ben and Sean and Sadie, each with their individual worries and challenges and ambitions. As the discussion wandered here and there, I told Bea about Anthony's plans to leave the firm.

'Really? Jeez, that's big news, darling. What's his problem?'

'Ah, I think he's just had enough, says he wants to spend more time with Jessie and the kids.'

'Hm, I hope he realises that they may not want to spend more time with him.'

'Yeah, probably not, but he'll find out soon enough, I suppose, when he tells them.'

'You're going to miss him hugely, Jack.'

'I know, the job won't be the same without him to be honest. It gets you thinking about stuff.'

'About yourself, you mean? You're not thinking about leaving, are you?'

'No, no, not at all, but I will miss him.'

And then the conversation flowed to Bea and her Art Gallery and the problem of Helen. Bea seemed relaxed in the comfortable and familiar environment of the restaurant, with its blazing turf fire at the gable end of the room which always gave the place that smoky, earthy aroma and country kitchen atmosphere. Careful not to overplay my hand, I suggested an approach for her which should result in a soft landing for Helen and would allow Bea to bring someone else into the partnership. To my surprise, she warmed to the plan and promised to sleep on it overnight and we'd discuss it further in the morning.

We walked the short distance from the restaurant through the village and out the coast road to our home. It was one of those beautiful mild, cloudless nights and the stars sparkled like diamonds in the sky. The full moon seemed to shimmer and just hang there, casting a glow on the bog and hills to the west and illuminating our way home. I loved this walk at this time of the evening. Bea linked my arm and leaned in against me as we strolled lazily along the twisting coastal road. Once home, we threw our coats on the hall stand and I guided her into the sitting room as she giggled and, without turning on the lights, I pulled her close to me and kissed her, tentatively at first, but then more persuasively as our passion rose. We kicked off our shoes and I sat on the couch and with my hands around her waist, pulled her close to me. 'Oh, la la, mon cheri, tu es tellement audacieux,' she whispered as she slowly unbuttoned her blouse, revealing her satin bra and full breasts. She undid her bra clip in one elegant seamless movement and threw it away. I buried my face between the warmth and smoothness of her breasts and she, in turn, pressed my head against them more firmly. She opened a button on the back of her skirt, unzipped it, and let it fall to the ground. I cupped her ass and stroked her thighs and she automatically opened her legs and sighed deeply. I sat back and admired my woman. 'Oh, tu es belle mon amour, tu es très belle.'

Unlike me, Bea had always been comfortable with her nakedness, unencumbered by sexual inhibitions, by taboos. She had a natural sensuality and playful eroticism and she loved the stimulation of foreplay, of kissing and touching. She teased open the buttons of my shirt and pulled it off my shoulders, then unzipped my jeans and I eased them off and threw them into the darkness. Bea pushed me back against the couch and falling to her knees she kissed my nipples which she knew drove me wild while she massaged my prick. She eased my shorts over my erection and slipped her own panties off. It had been a while since we enjoyed this level of intimacy, and right now we hungered for one another, getting lost in each other's sexual arousal, breathing hard, our passions rising. She climbed on me, straddling me, her legs bent at the knees, her thighs hugging my waist, and I clasped her ass as she manoeuvred herself over me and I likewise into her. She gasped as she eased herself down on me and she moaned as I entered her. She started working her bottom, grinding onto my prick as she bent over so that our mouths could make love. We were two familiar lovers surrendering to each other's desires and as we hungrily kissed we ground our bodies against one another, making those animalistic sounds, involuntary, unrestrained noises and cries. And as always, because we understood each other's bodies so intimately, and measuring each other's movements, we quickly came in overwhelming tremors, whispering and evoking our love for each other, 'Je t'aime cheri, je t'aime beaucoup.' We stayed locked in each other's embraces until our spasms subsided, and when we were calmer, she kissed my hair and gently eased herself off me and fell, exhausted but sated, on the couch alongside me.

The rest of the weekend couldn't have gone better. Sadie even remarked to us over breakfast in Galway that we looked like a couple of lovebirds and that we must have been up to some mischief last night, to which I responded, and to Bea's embarrassment; 'hm, maybe, and maybe this morning as well.' Sadie covered her ears with her hands and pleaded, 'stop it, Dad, keep your voice down for God's sake, that's revolting.'

After breakfast, and having dropped Sadie off at her friend's house, we took advantage of the spell of warm May weather and went for a long walk over the hills behind our house as we fine-tuned the plan to remove Helen from the gallery. It was important to ensure that her friend wouldn't lose face and that both women could remain good friends after the separation.

That evening, as the weather continued dry and unusually wind-free, I fired up the barbecue and cooked steaks and onions and peppers and of course hand-cut deep-fried chips, and we sipped a chilled Sauvignon.

'I hope you know that I love you, Mr. Jack Sommers.'

'And I hope you know that I love you, Madame Beatrice Dufort.'

'We are lucky to have one another, aren't we,' she said rhetorically.

'Well, you're definitely lucky to have me.'

She punched my shoulder. 'Why can't it always be this peaceful, Jack, peaceful and happy?'

'But of course it can be. I agree that this was a beautiful weekend but there's no reason why we can't enjoy the next one just as much.'

'Do you think you'll get home from London Friday evening? It would be great if you could, by the time you get home on a Saturday the day is half gone and there's nothing left of our weekend.'

'I promise I'll do my best to get home Friday night, darling, I should be able to … but now, Madame Dufort, as I did all the cooking and fed your belly you need to earn your keep, so get off your sexy ass and start the cleaning up, anyway I need to get my case ready for the morning.'

12

Dublin, Sun 21st May *(13 days to Nadir)*

Marianne climbed under her bed covers, exhausted. She was alone in her house in south Dublin, but over the last few years she was used to the house being empty, with Freddie and his little family in London and Ellen in her apartment in town. Empty, of course, except for Romeo the tomcat who had adopted Marianne two winters ago and came and went as he pleased, but generally roamed within a circle of four or five neighbouring houses. But tonight, for some reason which only tomcats know, he decided that he'd keep her company at the end of her bed. Marianne lay there in her comfortable foetal position, her knees tucked into her tummy, listening to her CD of classical music which promised *The Only Classical Album You'll Ever Need*, and true to its title, it *was* the only music that Marianne needed to fall asleep to every night. She suffered chronically from that condition called tinnitus which presented as a constant noise whistling through her head. She had wrestled with it for as long as she could remember. Paradoxically, quietness was her enemy. Night-time was when silence and stillness allowed the incessant noise to amplify and permeate through her consciousness. But that particular music seemed to distract, or at least drown out, the high-pitched, wind-like noise. A well-respected neurologist once advised her, as they fucked in her bed (her friend Andrea said to her the next day that, on balance, she did well to get his advice as normally his fees were exorbitant), that the noise was probably psychosomatic, most likely driven by anxiety or stress. At the time this sounded plausible, especially as she harboured a profound secret, but now that she had finally told it to the last and probably most significant person, she knew that the specialist was a fraud ... the noise was still there, and anyway, he had been lousy in the sack.

But lying now in bed, she couldn't think of anything else except the conversation she'd had with Jack the previous week. Every night since, she'd replayed it over and over again, sometimes almost saying some of the words out loud. Did it go ok? Should she have been stronger? Maybe she should have forced him to agree to meet her again next week, but that was silly because she couldn't force Jack to do anything. But it was open-ended now and she'd have to wait and see if he came back to her - crap, she should really have tied it down better before she left. 'Stop, stop' she said out loud, 'you're driving yourself mad.' *Be more positive*, she thought, *it went ok, be proud of yourself, maybe it could've gone better but it could've gone an awful lot worse.* But the question she kept returning to was: did he believe her? She had felt toward the end of the night that he seemed to accept her story, a little anyway. But even if he did believe her, what would he do in any case? Would he reach out to Freddie? *God, that's all I'm asking,* she thought, although not much point asking God as she had little confidence that he was actually up there. *But*, and she addressed this directly to her undetermined God, *I could be convinced you know, if I got a little sign, like Jack reaching out to Freddie. See what I mean, God? Big deal for Freddie, tiny trick for You.* Then she thought about Jack and remembered what she had liked about him all those years ago and what she continued to see in Freddie. Jack certainly had a mind of his own, more assured now, confident, clever. *His own man,* she thought, *and very handsome.*

Each time she took a significant step in making good the problem she created many years ago, she thought of the day she had walked into Janet's office. Her name had been recommended by a friend who had become pregnant at nineteen and who had travelled to London on her own to have her baby. Her friend had no idea what she was walking into, and once her baby was born, he was taken from her and given for adoption to an English couple. The girl never saw her baby again and, although she later married and had other kids, she was forever tormented by losing her firstborn. When Marianne heard her friend's story it seemed only to compound her own guilt and emphasise her own shame and her own weakness. At least her friend had the courage to go to London, whereas she herself hadn't even the moral mettle to tell the truth.

Janet went through the preliminaries quickly and then asked her:

'So, Marianne, tell me, how can I help you?'

'I've got a secret.'

'Ok, does anyone besides you know this secret?'

'No, I've told no one.'

'And how long have you kept this secret?'

'Nearly twenty-two years.'

'Ok, that's a long time. So then, how can I help you?'

'I need to talk to someone, tell them what I've done and figure out how to fix it if it's possible, and I know that it may not be possible but I have to try.'

'Ok, and how has keeping the secret to yourself this long made you feel?'

'Well, I've been living a lie for as long as I remember and I've hurt loved ones terribly badly, and they don't even know how much I've hurt them. I feel so guilty, so ashamed, I hate myself and there hasn't been a day go by in the last twenty-two years that I haven't regretted what I've done. I so want the hurt to stop, I can't live with it anymore. But I know I need to deal with it properly and that's why I'm hoping you'll help me.'

'Ok, well I'm here to listen, Marianne.'

Marianne started her story and talked and talked nonstop, with Janet all the time nodding encouragement.

'When I missed my period, it began to dawn on me that I might be pregnant but I couldn't figure out how it happened because I hadn't had penetrative sex with Jack. I couldn't understand how I could conceive. Even though I was twenty-one, we were all so naïve back then. I found this book in a bookshop in town about pregnancy and I couldn't take the chance of buying it, so I tore out the pages I needed. And then one of my friend's sisters was a nurse and I asked her some questions 'on behalf of a friend', and although I know she suspected that I was talking about myself, she didn't let on.'

She took a long drink of water. This was the first time she'd ever spoken the truth out loud and it poured out as if a dam of words had been breached.

'My parents were ok parents, but very old-school and I just didn't think that I could tell them. Then I met up with Rob who I knew was crazy about me, and I liked him too and after only a few dates we made out - I mean, we had intercourse. And I knew that even though I hadn't made any decision about the pregnancy, I knew that I was being manipulative and deliberately putting him in the frame. I even pretended a few weeks after we met that we couldn't have sex one night because I had my period. In all of this I really did try to contact Jack a few times but to be honest I suppose they weren't really very serious attempts. And I don't know why that is, I've asked myself that question lots of times, but I don't have the answer. Then I told the first big lie, the lie that I'm still living with. I told Rob that I'd missed my period and I was worried that I might be pregnant. I was in tears, distraught, like really very upset and I even brought up the prospect of an abortion or that I could go to England to have the child and give it up for adoption. But Rob was having none of it. He would stand by me and we would have this baby and love this baby and be proud to have it, and we would tell both our parents when the time was right. He had a good job and he said we could get married and he'd get a mortgage and we'd get a little house. He was so supportive and caring and fearless. In the first few days I told myself that I'd tell him the truth, but not today, tomorrow. But of course, as each day went by the lie became more and more the reality and the truth became harder to confront. Then we told our parents and friends and the lie was embedded, sealed; I couldn't go back.'

She stopped talking for a few moments, drank some water, not looking at Janet, and cried.

'You have no idea what it's like to live with a secret all these years, to live your whole life a lie. Every day you face it, every day you want to come clean. You know that there's only a half dozen words separating the truth from your conscience. There's the real world that everybody else lives in and then there's your world, but you don't *live* in it, you just exist in it. It's the world of your lie, and you're trying to live in both, but they're not always in sync and they're never, ever compatible. Some days are easier, some harder, but it doesn't matter because it eats away at you like a cancer, eats away at your mind - or maybe it's your soul I guess - either way you hate yourself, your self-worth goes down the toilet.'

She remembered Janet bringing that first session to a close even though she wanted to keep talking until her story was told. She remembered going home exhausted and lying down on her bed to rest, Rob coming home from work that evening and that she was still there. She told him that she had one of her migraines and he made her a cup of tea and a hot water bottle and they chatted for a while. But she picked up her story the following week and all the other weeks after that, and each week she couldn't wait for her Thursday session to come around.

She pulled her knees up tighter to her tummy and wrapped her arms around them and made herself into the tightest human ball she could manage. Human balls offered better protection from the world, she thought, I'm like a human porcupine. And as Rachmaninov's *Rhapsody on a theme of Paganini* faded into the night she closed her eyes, and, untroubled by secrets in her soul or noises in her head, she relaxed her body, letting it uncoil and unfold as she slipped into a deep welcoming sleep.

* * * * *

About a year after her first session with Janet, Marianne made the decision to tell her family the truth, knowing that nothing would ever be the same again and she could very easily lose everything: her husband and her children, her home and her family and friends. But she had come to the view that she never really had them anyway. The narrative of her family up to this point was virtual, not real. She turned to her poetry and her music for resilience and inspiration and indeed courage. She loved Yeats and repeated his lines over and over again, which she believed had been presciently written for her:

He, too, has been changed in his turn,
Transformed utterly:
A terrible beauty is born.

Her terrible beauty would soon be born. Nothing would ever be the same again. The family photograph would spontaneously combust, and it could never again be made right, and even knowing that, she was still determined to press on, and tell the truth to her husband first.

She knew that Freddie would be staying with one of his friends for the weekend and she had therefore arranged for Ellen to ostensibly mind her grandmother for the Friday and Saturday nights. She lit the fuse after breakfast on the Saturday morning while they were sitting at the kitchen table with cups of coffee. She had prepared her announcement well in advance and now this was the moment of truth.

She took a deep breath. She could actually hear her own heart pounding in her chest. Her mouth had gone dry but she steeled herself to get the first sentence out:

'Rob, I've something to tell you, and please hear me out. I've an admission, something I've kept hidden from you since before our marriage. I know that this will be one of the hardest things you'll ever have to hear and I'm deeply, deeply sorry that I've kept it from you all these years. I know that this will hurt you beyond what I can imagine.' She spoke slowly and evenly, doing her best to manage the tremor in her voice. She took another deep breath. 'Before I met you, I had been with a guy in Galway during the summer and although I didn't know it at the time I had become pregnant by him. We didn't even have full intercourse and I didn't realise it until I was back in Dublin and I'd met you. He never knew that I was pregnant and doesn't to this day, and I've never seen him since.' She stopped talking. Her voice box seemed paralysed. She swallowed and inhaled deeply and forced the next sentence. 'That pregnancy … that baby … is Freddie.'

At first Rob had a vacant look in his eyes as he stared at her, which then turned to a look of bewilderment. It seemed to take ages for his thought process to register the weight of her words. His forehead wrinkled and his eyes became smaller, his mouth tightened, and as if he had completely misheard what his wife had just pronounced, he said:

'Sorry, what did you say? What are you talking about, Marianne?'

She repeated in a little frightened voice, 'I'm so sorry, Rob … before I met you, I had met a guy in …'

'I fucking heard that part of it, girl … What did you say about Freddie?'

Her voice faltered and cracked, her throat tightened, her breathing became difficult, she felt faint.

'Well, the guy I met … before you … is his father.'

Rob laughed nervously; 'Are you trying to tell me that I'm not Freddie's father?'

And in the tiniest of voices, hardly audible: 'Yes … I'm sorry.'

He just stared at her for a long time in disbelief. Registering the impossible, the unbelievable. And then he exploded. She sat there rigidly, her eyes tightly closed, amidst the anarchy, amidst the crashing splintering delft.

And then, as quickly as he had erupted, the energy seemed to leave him and he slowly retrieved his upended chair from the other side of the room and slowly and deliberately sat down again.

'Tell me you're fucking winding me up Marianne, you are, aren't you?'

Marianne said nothing, she didn't need to say anything. Her face said everything.

The die was cast.

The next few days in the house were like hell on earth. Rob's mood oscillated between bouts of menacing silence and near-violence, slamming doors and screaming obscenities at no one and everyone. Eventually he told her to move out of the house. He couldn't stand to be around her, to even look at her. He was not going to give up their home when it was she who was the home-breaker and it was she who had fucked everything up. But she had expected as much, and in anticipation, she had done some apartment searches in the weeks before she told him. She found a two-bed flat close by and she moved in without much fuss. When she had broken it to him, she had apologised genuinely and profusely and although she knew that she had mortally wounded him, she hadn't pleaded with him to forgive her or to keep their marriage together. Too much water had flowed under that bridge and she knew that he couldn't ever forgive her. She was prepared to take whichever road was left open to her.

However, in breaking her silence she had caused immense collateral damage and created a huge dilemma for her husband and her children. Once the decision was made that she would move out of their home, Freddie couldn't live under the same roof as Rob because of their years of antipathy towards each other. This was now especially the case when they discovered that they weren't even sharing genes (even though at that point Freddie's greater sympathies lay with Rob, and his loyalty to his mother was stretched to the point of breaking). So, Freddie too moved out. He was in his second year studying law in Trinity and he found student accommodation on the campus. Ellen was eighteen at the time and her reaction to the whole thing was that this was the most exciting news ever to come into her life. Her family up to this point had been a fairly boring affair, other than the odd bust-up between her dad and her brother and her dad and her mum, but nothing like the intrigues in some of her friend's homes. She also saw the advantage of now being able to move between two homes, which offered up all sorts of opportunities.

And so, Marianne's secret was out. Once over the shock of it, her parents bemoaned the fact that she hadn't felt that she could tell them when she'd become pregnant, and that saddened them the most. But other than that, their relationship was neither damaged nor improved. Rob's parents had a very different reaction, and within a week of moving out, she received an eight-page handwritten letter delivered to her new address from his mother (who, incidentally, had been very close to Marianne and had given her immense support during both her pregnancies and subsequent child-minding whenever asked). The letter captured brilliantly and eloquently their summation of the deceit as they saw it:

" *… your weaknesses, not just the weakness and cowardice of your original sin which pales into insignificance compared to the cowardice of this new sin, the sin of confession … by relieving your own guilt you have wilfully destroyed the lives of those who loved you … you have left an indelible stain on our lives … you should have had the courage to go to the grave with your secret of shame … you are so single-mindedly selfish and stupid that you don't even understand the impact on our son and our grandchildren, and we stress* our *grandchildren because Freddie will always be our grandchild and Rob will always be his father, no matter what you say, you cannot take him away from us …*"

Her girlfriends had mixed reactions which in general reflected the state of their own lives and marriages and their individual values, but unanimously they sympathised with Rob. One or two drifted away from her but her two closest girlfriends took the *c'est la vie* attitude and even seemed to be excited to be helping her decorate her new apartment.

Within a year of the breakup, Rob reached out to her and suggested that they should make an attempt at reconciliation, see a marriage counsellor, and that she could move back into their home. She agreed to go to joint counselling but not to move back, at least not for the time being. So, they dated again and, with the exception of his parents and Ellen (Freddie was agnostic about their relationship), everyone was happy for them. They even stayed over in each other's beds a number of times. But then it just seemed to run out of steam, lose momentum, and even began to get a little staid and tetchy, and so they both agreed to separate formally and bring to an end their relationship and marriage before it became acrimonious (to everyone's disappointment, except for his parents, and of course Ellen who celebrated with a bottle of Bollinger with her friends when she heard the news). They sold their large family home in South Dublin for a considerable sum which they shared equally, and which allowed them each to downsize to smaller houses in the same general area.

And their kids too moved on. Ellen graduated from UCD with a business and marketing degree and joined Guinness in St. James' Gate, and Freddie moved to London to a new life after cutting his 'law teeth' in Cox's in Dublin.

And then, one afternoon, a few years later, when the divorce had come through and the dust was well-settled and Rob had found a new partner, Marianne was chatting with one of her friends over a coffee, and the conversation, as always, turned to relationships. Her friend asked her if she was happy.

'Hm, yes, I think so, Jill, although happiness can be elusive. But I'm certainly happier than I was three years ago, you know, before I came clean.'

'You're happy even though you're not in a relationship now?'

'Ha, or maybe *because* I'm not in a relationship now.'

'So, no regrets then, no looking back?'

'Christ no, no regrets and no looking back … but you know, there's still some work to be done.'

'Ah, so you're *not* fully happy then. So, what's left to be done?'

'Find Freddie's father, silly, find Jack.'

'Really? And what happens when you find him?'

'Well, unite him with his firstborn, of course.'

'Hm, be careful, Marianne, you don't want to be playing God with other people's lives.'

'Au contraire, darling, If I thought I could play God, Freddie, Jack and I would be the perfect little family by now.'

Part 2

* * * * *

The art of living is more like wrestling than dancing, in so far as it stands ready against the accidental and the unforeseen …

Marcus Aurelius

13

It was the autumn of 1998 and Saif Butt sat in the front passenger seat of his brother-in-law's station wagon as they drove to Islamabad International Airport. His wife and their three children were packed tightly in the rear seat, and their luggage was even more tightly packed in the boot and on the roof. Other luggage would follow at a later time. They were coming from the southeast and in order to get to the airport they were nervously navigating roads to avoid getting sucked into the gravitational pull of the city. Saif thought about what he was leaving behind; his old life, his friends, his extended family, his furniture business, his house. But although he was nervous, and hence irritable, he was also optimistic and upbeat about his decision to start a new life, a new beginning. It didn't dawn on him to consider what the rest of the family were leaving behind, nor did it bother him that his wife didn't share his optimism.

Islamabad, the capital of Pakistan, lies in the northeast of the country and sits restlessly and noisily - but proudly - in the foothills of the Himalayas. About sixty miles southeast of the city, in the Mirpur District of Azad Jammu and Kashmir, sits the little town of Mangla. The town is singularly famous for its eponymously named hydroelectric dam which was constructed across the Jhelum River in 1965. The Mangla Dam is a godsend for the entire region as it harnesses and tames the mighty force of the river Jhelum and stores the seasonal monsoon excesses which help to mitigate the otherwise devastating droughts. The Pakistani Government selected a British engineering firm of designers and engineers as the lead contractors in the building of the superstructure, and this was to be a significant factor in the future migration of peoples between both countries. In the damming of the Jhelum, an immense area of land was flooded and hundreds of towns and villages were submerged, and over one hundred thousand people were displaced. The discommoded families were rehoused in newly-built towns close to their original villages or were moved to the nearby city of Mirpur. Others, about five thousand souls, were given work permits for Britain, and many moved to East London, Birmingham, or the textile towns of northern England, like Bradford. This then forged the great cultural bond between the Mirpur region and the Pakistani communities in Britain.

A few miles from Mirpur lies the city of Jhelum where Saif Butt and his family once lived in relative comfort and happiness. Saif traded in local furniture but also bought and sold some British-style pieces in his well-presented shop. His wife kept their house and reared their three children, Saad, Haleema and Khuram. They lived in a little village community and were surrounded by family and friends. Some of their extended family and neighbours had already emigrated to Britain and the reports back were of opportunity, prosperity and, significantly, religious tolerance. This was in stark contrast to Pakistan in the nineties, where the economy was in freefall - unhelped by a corrupt polity - and a worrying religious shift towards Islamic fundamentalism.

But if Saif's life had been prosperous in the past, things certainly weren't good now. Nobody was buying furniture, 'how can they', he'd say, 'when they need to buy food and clothes with the little money they have.' He spent his days dusting the pieces in his shop, dropping his prices every month, but to no benefit, and gradually eating into the savings he'd accumulated. It was June, 1998, and Saif's mood had not been good for months now. He blamed everyone and anyone for the economic collapse and turmoil of his country, and consequently, his business. But he especially blamed the Americans for their interference in his country over the previous decade, as they waged a proxy war with the Soviet Union, played out in Afghanistan.

'They've dumped us now that they've no more business over here. They've used us and interfered in the delicate balance of our country and now it's broken … and I can't sell any of my furniture.'

'Things will settle down,' his wife would soothe, 'things always settle down in the end.'

'That's foolish talk, woman, when my business is gone and you've no money left to buy food for the family, tell me then how settled you are, that's if there's anything left of us to settle.' And then, wistfully, he mumbled; 'if we could only move to Britain.'

Saif's sister was already living in London and he was also in correspondence with a cousin of his who had emigrated many years before, and had a well-established restaurant there, which purportedly was doing a thriving business.

'Jalal tells me that he's making a fortune in his restaurant and that he could open two or three more if only he had the help from someone he could trust.'

'But you know nothing about the food business, Saif, you know the furniture business, stick with what you know, trust me, things will settle down in the end.'

'What do you know about *any* business, woman, I *know* about business and the business of selling food and selling furniture is the same thing.' His wife struggled to see the logic in his argument - *you can't cook a chair and you can't sit on a curry* - but she understood her place in the marriage and knew that it was time to hold her tongue.

In addition to the economic meltdown there was also real and justifiable fear in the air. Just the previous month, India had carried out a second nuclear test and in doing so had ratcheted up tensions with its Muslim neighbour. As he read about the fusion test in the newspapers, Saif had had enough; 'They're going to blow us to pieces and we're going to blow them to pieces and there'll be nothing left, just a huge hole for the Indian Ocean to fall into.' His wife was about to say something but he cut her off; 'and if you say it'll settle down in the end, woman, you'll be the first one down that huge hole.' And then, he mumbled to no one in particular, as had been his habit recently; 'yes, if only we had British citizenship.'

But everyone in the family knew that Saif had already made up his mind to leave Pakistan, and his irascibility and venting over the previous few months was his way of justifying to himself, and his family and friends, the validity and righteousness of his decision. So, when he officiously called his wife one evening to sit at their prized antique dining table to tell her that he had an important announcement to make, she said, even before he had a chance to say anything; 'you're taking us away from our home, aren't you.' And although she knew that in stealing his thunder she was inviting a worse thunder on herself, she didn't care; she needed to show him that she knew him better than he knew her, and by doing so, demonstrate some small degree of control.

And so, they packed their bags, upped sticks, sold out … in a word; Emigrated.

They travelled to Britain on a visitors' visa and arrived on the cusp of a new millennium, with high hopes and shiny new dreams, and enough sterling to give them a little seed money to start a business. They initially moved in with his sister and since they then had an address and sponsors, Saif quickly set about applying for asylum. Though they were practising Muslims, they weren't especially religious, which reflected the general local environment, and so they fell in easily with the large Pakistani community in Barking, east London. Having weathered the initial culture shock - including the vagaries of the London weather - the family settled into their new world, their new English life. Saif's wife had been right of course (but wrong to be right), the restaurant experiment didn't quite work out and so he picked up where he had left off and opened a furniture business. They moved to a rented flat and his wife did the best she could to transform it into a home. The children made new friends in the neighbourhood and at their school in Forest Gate, and they didn't disappoint academically. But what was disappointing was the news that their asylum application had been refused and so, like other immigrants in the same predicament, they kept their heads down and their noses clean, and started the process of appealing the decision, and in the meantime, carried on regardless. After all, there was a Labour government in place and the new millennium was within sight and the feeling of hope, optimism and prosperity was seductively in the air.

But the butterfly effect that had first disturbed the air back in 1979, when the Soviet Union invaded Afghanistan, was still rippling its way throughout the Middle East twenty years later, and then, fatally, the turbulence crossed the Atlantic in 2001. On 11th September at 8.46am, the first plane, under the control of an al-Qaeda pilot, and by the order of Osama bin Laden, crashed into the North Tower in Manhattan, and suddenly, and without warning, the optimism and hopes of the new millennium came to a shuddering halt.

Terrorism had arrived in the West.

The al-Qaeda attacks on America sent the world into a spin. By that October, the US had invaded Afghanistan, supported by Britain, and Saif Butt was inconsolable. Just when they were succeeding in their new world, events had again conspired against them; 'This is all the Americans' fault. It's they who gave arms and ammunition to the Taliban and al-Qaeda, they only have themselves to blame.' One of the consequences of the war was a backlash against Muslims and the rise of anti-Islamic sentiment in the West. Saif worried constantly about their wellbeing, their future. As their asylum appeal still hadn't been granted, he feared that they could be deported back to their old world in Jhelum. And it was all too much for him. The tightly-wound ball of anxiety that pressed against the inside of his skull, and the weight of disappointment that hunched his shoulders seemed too much for him to bear. One very ordinary night in their flat in Barking, he went through his usual rituals for bed, locking doors, undressing, attending to his personal hygiene, and finally his prayers to Allah; *keep the family healthy and bring the business back to prosperity.* Then he climbed into his bed and was soon asleep. But he was never to wake again. During the night he suffered a fatal heart attack and, very quietly, he died with his dreams.

* * * * *

Khuram Butt, Saif's youngest child, was thirteen when his father died. Like his siblings, he had settled easily into his new life in east London, doing well in school, making friends, assimilating the urban accent. He was soon talking with a distinctive east London inflection. Then, early in the new millennium, although their father didn't live to see it, the family were granted indefinite leave to remain in Britain; finally, they had what their father always craved: British citizenship.

The younger Butt's teenage years were unremarkable, playing football with his friends, hanging out in the parks, meeting girls, smoking, occasionally cannabis, growing his hair in dreadlocks, listening to reggae music and keenly supporting Arsenal football club. He graduated from secondary school at nineteen with good results, particularly in business studies, and readily found employment in office environments. Although easily influenced, and obsessive in his interests, he was developing well in his early adulthood, and successfully making his way in the world. Then, in 2012, at the age of twenty-two, a change occurred. It happened at the wedding of his sister, Haleema. After the ceremony, as Khuram was chatting to family and friends, he was introduced to a guest who he was soon to discover had strong Muslim beliefs. His name was Hashim Rehman. They engaged comfortably, enjoyed each other's company and very quickly the conversation strayed into religion and Islamic faith. Up until this point, Khuram was uninterested and lazy in his approach to his religion, but that afternoon, the easily persuadable young man went through somewhat of a spiritual awakening. He and Hashim became good friends and it wasn't long before Khuram's family noticed a change in his behaviour, as he became more observant of the faith of Islam and its rituals, and expected others to follow suit.

Soon his thoughts turned to marriage, and Hashim's younger sister, Zahrah, seemed like the perfect match. Although well educated, she came from a culturally traditional family and therefore had an expectation that she would marry through arrangement rather than love. And so, on Christmas Day, in 2013, the nineteen-year-old Zahrah Rehman married Khuram Butt, four years her senior. Eager to start a family, it wasn't long before she became pregnant, and their first child, a little boy, was born in October, to the delight of everyone.

However, the next few years saw Khuram lurch further into Islamic doctrine, taking on a strict and extreme interpretation of sharia law, and enforcing it on his household and especially on his wife. His behaviour was becoming erratic and his work life dysfunctional, to the point where he was unable to hold down employment for any length of time. He secured a job with the London Underground but after a couple of weeks he called in sick, complaining that his company-issued footwear was affecting his feet, this to the utter dismay of Zahrah;

'You must think of your family, Khuram, we need a wage to pay our rent and put food on the table.'

'How can I work when those crap boots have injured my foot, anyway I'll get sick pay from them, don't worry, we'll be fine.'

'But you've just started with them Khuram, they won't be happy when you're calling in sick already.'

'Everybody does it, Zahrah, it's a huge company, there are thousands working there, anyway, they're lucky that I don't sue them for the injury to my foot, trust me, I know what I'm doing.'

Although there was nothing that she could do about it, the last thing his wife was prepared to do at that stage was to trust him. She had watched in horror as he uncompromisingly took on his strict interpretation of Islam. In the earlier days of her marriage, he had been a kind and caring husband but now he had reduced her to an almost invisible being. She was forced to cover her face with a niqab, so that only her eyes were visible, and forced to wear a loose black abaya from head to toe. And when any of his friends or associates called to their home, which they did regularly, she was made to hide away behind a curtain, which he had installed, so she would not be seen.

Not one to do things by halves, Khuram shouted his new-found faith from the rooftops. He shaved his head and grew his beard long and untrimmed. He attended mosques and shouted down the Imam for preaching the wrong interpretation of the Koran. And as he continued to expand and espouse more extreme views, he became marginalised from his community; rifts and cracks began to appear in his relationships. He developed an obsessive interest in the war in Syria and he developed a hatred for what he considered the loose and immoral habits of Westernised society.

He was quick to anger and he regularly argued about Islamic ideology with his family, or with Hashim, his friend and brother-in-law.

'Have you not heard of the old saying, Khuram; "When in Rome, do what the Romans do."' Hashim advised one day in a heated argument.

'Of course, I have, but that was before the Prophet Mohammed disseminated the sacred Koran. The laws of Mohammed are above local laws.'

'So, you think that you can break the laws of England because sharia law is above them?'

'Of course, they are. England's laws are made by man, sharia law is handed down by Allah through the Prophet Mohammed. How can man-made laws be superior to Allah's laws?'

'But if you ignore the laws of the land then you're left only with chaos, civil unrest, with every religion doing its own thing in the name of their God. Society becomes dysfunctional, it leads to total mayhem.'

'Yes Hashim, you're right, that's what we must do, create mayhem, civil unrest.'

'But why for god's sake, to what end?' cried Hashim, in exasperation.

‘Because this country is morally bankrupt, my friend, and America too. The West is corrupt, evil, and it needs to change. And you need to change, Hashim, and my family too, it has corrupted all of you.’

Hashim had heard enough. He decided that he would need to distance himself from this dangerous radical, this fanatic, this fantasist. But he worried for his sister, Zahrah, and her little boy. He had a feeling that this wasn’t going to end well, that it would end in tears. The only question was, whose tears would be shed?

14

After the initial shock and the necessary and ineluctable outbursts, when Freddie actually thought about it, he really wasn't particularly put out about the fact that Rob wasn't his natural father. Besides the fact that they didn't have a whole lot in common, he believed Rob to be controlling, ungenerous and embittered, but the bottom line was that he just didn't like him very much. They fought regularly, sometimes over silly issues and always over important ones. He did feel really bad for Rob when his mother broke the news, and he did think that she had been dreadfully deceitful and that she lacked moral courage when it happened way back then. He was the same age now as she had been when she became pregnant and he knew that if something like that happened to him, he would be brave enough to face the truth, to 'do the right thing'. Of course, it's always easy to do the right thing when you actually don't have to do anything, and the easiest thing in the world to do is to judge, particularly from a distance of twenty-two years, the distance of a generation. And not just any generation, the most changed generation in Ireland since very probably the time of the Great Famine and the mass emigration of its youth.

And so, Freddie got over the episode fairly quickly, and anyway his mind was on bigger things; friends; motorbikes; girls, college, and not in any particular order (except college, college was always last). In fact, the order changed regularly depending on how his hormones were working at any given time. After his mother's grand announcement and once she had moved out of their home, there was no way that he was going to stay in the house with Rob who then displayed a permanent hang-dog look. So, he took up student accommodation on Trinity college campus fully sponsored by his guilty parents. Unlike many students in second year law who had to work extremely hard to get good results, Freddie was one of those who did very well without having to over-apply himself. And it seemed the same went for making friends and meeting girls. With his easy-going personality and his shock of untamed red hair and piercing blue eyes, he was considered to be extremely attractive. But most of his female friends agreed that the most attractive feature about him was that he didn't seem to know it.

One evening, when asked by his then-girlfriend how he felt about the whole father screw-up, he said that it didn't bother him at all that Rob wasn't his natural father, but neither was he bothered to find out who his birth father was.

'But aren't you dying to find out who he is?' she asked him as they were making out in his room.

'No, not particularly.'

'Wouldn't you like to solve the mystery?'

'It's not a mystery, Carrie; loads of people don't know who their birth parents are. They made a bloody export industry out of it in Ireland, and anyway, I at least know *one* of mine.'

'You poor baby, imagine being told that your dad wasn't really your dad after all.' She seemed to find this quite sad but also quite endearing and she wanted to reach out and mind him, succour him. Freddie could feel something change in her, feel her get a little more nurturing, and he thought that this was an interesting perspective. He hadn't come across this neediness in his girlfriend before, but he warmed to the theme.

'Yeah,' he said, 'I suppose it is a little disconcerting.'

'Of course, it must be, baby, you poor thing.' She wanted to mind him more.

Warming further to the theme, he vulnerably offered: 'Like one minute you've a dad and the next minute you haven't, it's kinda sad really.'

'Oh, you're hurting inside baby; I can feel it, come here to me.' As she pulled him closer, he felt that she was close to tears. 'I'm gonna be strong for my man,' she whispered in his ear. But as her strength seemed to crumble, Freddie could feel a heightened urgency to her passion and he wondered that maybe if he just shed a tear that all hell might break loose and he could get a whole new dimension to this fucking business. But hard as he tried, he couldn't manufacture a single tear, not even a little one. But it didn't particularly matter because she was all over him anyway like a rash, entreating him, 'fuck me, my poor, poor vulnerable baby, I'm so fucking hot for you now.'

And so, without the need to shed a single tear, Freddie stumbled on a new truth about life - new to him at least - and that was that sometimes the opposites of the same continuum unexpectedly produce the same outcomes. As in this case for instance, strength at one extreme and vulnerability at the other, both seemed to produce the same intense orgasmic response in his lover, which of course lent a correspondingly heightened prize for him. And he made this insightful discovery while he was being minded savagely by his girlfriend, and yes indeed, all hell did break loose. *Hm, interesting insight*, he thought!

His mother also seemed to be obsessed about his feelings for his birth father:

'Do you wonder what he's like, darling?'

'Nope.'

'Even a little?'

'No, not really.'

'How's your studying going, are you able to study in your rooms?'

'Yeah, of course.'

'And are you eating properly? You look a little thinner, you know.'

'I'm eating fine, Mum. You don't need to worry about me.'

'You look like him, you know.'

'I look like whom?'

'Your father, you've always looked like him, and your mannerisms, how you hold yourself.'

'Mum, stop it with this please, I told you I've no interest in what he looks like or how he holds himself.'

'Well, maybe he'd like to meet you, have you thought of that?'

'Mum, how the fuck would he like to meet me when he doesn't even know that I exist? And I'd imagine the last thing he'd want right now, whatever he's doing with his life, is for me to turn up.'

'How's Carrie, do you see much of each other?'

'Yeah she's fine, she told me to say hi to you.'

'Ah, that's lovely, she's such a nice girl, and I miss seeing her, miss seeing both of you together.'

'Well, I told you that she was busy tonight, she could have made it last night or tomorrow night, but you insisted on this evening.'

'Yes, of course, I know. Listen Freddie, I'm sorry about bringing up your father earlier but I just needed to know how you felt about him, that's all. That's why I wanted us to be able to chat on our own for a change.'

'Yeah, well you know how I feel about him, Mum, which is the same as how I felt about him the last time you asked me, and I promise if I ever change my mind you'll be the first to know, ok? Now, let's eat cause I'm famished.'

A few months later, on a Saturday afternoon, Freddie was playing for Trinity in the college's rugby league, and towards the end of the game he noticed Rob standing at the side-lines amongst a scattering of other parents and friends and supporters. Rob was animatedly shouting for Trinity and when Freddie took a pass out on the wing Rob was shouting for him to *go go go*, and get to the try line. But he only got a few metres when he got hammered by his opposite number and was unceremoniously dumped on his arse on the grass, without the ball and without much idea where he was. He was helped into the changing rooms and after a very cursory check for concussion, which he passed (by remembering his name and his age, very scientific), he headed for the showers. Once out of the clubhouse he was surprised to see Rob waiting outside for him.

'You ok, Freddie? You took some hammering there.'

'Yeah yeah, I'm fine thanks, Dad, never saw him coming.'

'But you were having a great game, that try you got in the first half was a peach.'

'Oh, you saw it? I didn't see you there.'

'Yeah, I was a little further back watching. Hey, do you wanna get a pint or something? That's if you have time, of course.'

Freddie hesitated; he had plenty of time, he wasn't meeting up with the lads until that evening, but he wasn't sure that he wanted to spend the time with Rob.

'Hey, if you haven't got the time, no problem, we can do a rain check, catch up next time.'

'No, no, I'm ok, I'm meeting the lads later but sure, let's grab a pint, I could use one now actually.'

They headed down the road to The Ginger Man and Freddie found a table by the window while Rob ordered the Guinness.

'So, how're you doing in your new place, well settled in, I presume?'

'Yeah, it's great actually, the problem is that you could live on the campus and never leave, everything is around you.'

'Fat chance of that happening to you of all people, I'd say you hardly know the inside of your rooms.'

'Ha, yeah, you're probably right, there's no fear of me. And how're you doing at home with Ellen?'

'Yeah, good, good. Sure, Ellen is hardly ever around; she's hopping between your mother's place and home. I just know she's playing both of us. She tells each of us that she's broke, and of course we're both forking out. Ah, there's no fear of Ellen either. How's Carrie doing?'

'Well, I don't know actually, because it's not Carrie anymore, it's Linda.'

'Ah, Linda, must remember that. So, what does Linda do with herself?'

'She's in college with me, not in law, in meds. So, have you spoken to Mum recently?'

'No, not for a while, I must give her a buzz soon though. But listen Freddie, I just wanted us to catch up, I know we haven't always seen eye to eye …'

'You mean never.' Freddie laughed.

Rob smiled. 'Yeah, ok, well let's say nearly never. And anyway, I know that a lot of that was down to me, as they say, I was the adult in the relationship. But we never really discussed how either of us felt after your mother dropped the bomb, I mean how we felt about our relationship, you and me … and don't worry I'm not here to have that discussion now but I just wanted to say it, to put it out there.'

'Hey Dad, in case you're worried, I'm doing fine, seriously, ok? And I'm not sure that there's a whole lot to discuss. It hasn't really affected me at all, like I don't go around wondering who my birth father is. I'm sorry to say, like it or not you're stuck with me. By the way, you're not gonna believe this, but they do a concussion protocol as you know once you've been taken off with a head bang and after asking me the usual questions, my coach asked me who was the crazy guy shouting at me from the side-line, and I told him it was my dad, and he said that that was cool.'

Rob seemed stuck for words, and then he shook his head and smiled. 'You know what Freddie, we write narratives about ourselves and our relationships, but we're rarely on the money.'

'How do you mean?'

'Listen, no matter what happens, like between us or in the future, you know that I love you. I know you're thinking that I've a strange way of showing it sometimes, but I love you and I'm always here for you. I just need to say that, so you know.'

'Ok, Dad, let's not get too mushy for fucks sake,' he said humorously. 'I hear what you're saying, and it works both ways by the way. Now I still think it's your call for the pints, after all I'm just a poor student.'

Later, as they were leaving, the two men embraced outside the door of the pub, and as they were parting to go their separate ways, Freddie suggested: 'Hey Dad, I enjoyed the catch-up, don't be a stranger on the side-lines, we need all the support we can get.'

Freddie qualified with a 2.1. Law degree and interviewed for the top four law firms in Dublin. To his surprise (but, it seemed, to no one else's) he was offered a place in each of the company's and he chose Arthur Cox, as he was keen to specialise in mergers and acquisitions, and they were handling a number of major international clients at that time. He spent five formative years learning his trade in Dublin while excelling within the firm. Together with his technical expertise he was highly regarded for his personal interactive manner, balancing a professional approach and an informal style which endeared him to clients. Then, when he was twenty-nine, the company asked him to move to their expanding business at their London office, and, as was his nature, Freddie willingly grabbed the opportunity.

And during those heady years in Dublin, he enjoyed life to the fullest, always skirting the edges of propriety and conventions and, with a touch of recklessness, savouring the chaotic Dublin scene and regularly tasting the more exotic capitals of Europe. He sought out adventures and believed that the best adventures were made in the moment and in Freddie's head, the moment was always now. He loved life and he lived every day with energy and vitality and a confidence which seemed to represent the zeitgeist and unique spirit of *his* age, of *his* modern Ireland.

But once he moved to London life took on a more serious dimension. The office was highly competitive in both chasing clients and in internal promotions. And although he was well used to working long hours in Dublin, it was brought to a new level in the smaller office on Fleet Street, and his opportunities for socialising were seriously constrained. But Freddie loved the London scene and London loved him, and it seemed that the London females especially loved him. Being

Irish was a very tradable currency and Freddie was the personification of Irishness. After a few short-lived romances, he met the love of his life, Saahira Jalal and after a hapless first start; they tumbled head over heels in love. It was one of those chance encounters that tests the faith of the deniers of fate. He was having dinner with a few friends in the Borough Market and they were sitting outside in the warmth of the evening sun when he jumped up from his chair to order drinks. As he turned around from his table, Saahira was walking towards him and talking to her friend and (he argued later) not looking where she was going. She bumped into him, spilling her own wine on her top and jeans.

'Ah, you clown, look what you've done. Didn't you look where you were going?'

'Sorry, really sorry, but I think you walked into me.' Freddie pleaded.

'What am I, a fool? Why would I walk into you, you rushed at me, and look at my clothes you idiot, they're ruined.'

'Hey, hey calm down, no need to be like that; here let me see if I can clean it.' Freddie grabbed a napkin and on one knee started to rub the wine stain from her jeans.

'My god, get away from me you animal, he's attacking me,' She screeched to her friend and pushed him away. He stumbled backwards to the ground. His friends thought this was hilarious and jeered and cheered him. Then Saahira turned her ire on them.

'You buffoons, you idiots, you bloody juveniles, do you men ever grow up?' This of course only caused further derision from them.

Freddie pleaded with her friend to help him out, 'Listen, if it was my fault then I am really sorry, let me replace your drink.'

'It's not my drink I'm worried about, you idiot, it's my clothes, my night is ruined now.'

'Well, let me get you a drink and I promise I'll get your clothes cleaned tomorrow.'

'You bloody bet your life you will.'

Eventually her friend calmed her down as one of his mates refreshed her drink. She sulkily took Freddie's number and was still mumbling and muttering as she walked away.

'Wow, that's some woman, Freddie, she had you by the balls.'

'Nah, I was always in control,' he lied, 'but she's feisty all right, and gorgeous, and she's got my number.'

'Oh, you poor bugger, she's got your number all right.'

It became a running joke between them much later when they became lovers and they both accused the other of having contrived the incident in order to create the opportunity for them to meet, and therefore fate really hadn't played its part. They each strenuously denied this of course.

Saahira was a first-generation Syrian Londoner. Her parents, who were both doctors, had fled Damascus in 1995, as the country under the increasingly ailing President Hafez al-Assad, lurched towards tyranny, with the emergence of newspaper censorship, human rights abuse and even political executions. They were accepted in the UK as political refugees and they settled in East London, setting up their own medical care centre. They encouraged Saahira to follow them in a career in medicine and on the evening that she and Freddie first met, she had been celebrating her graduation from St. Mary's hospital in Paddington; she was now ready to start out on her own medical journey.

Five years after they met, Saahira gave birth to a beautiful baby girl who they named Fabeena-Marianne, and that's when Freddie came face to face with his biological ancestral question-mark for the first time. And it came from two fronts; firstly, Saahira was insistent that they know the hereditary risks passed down from both sets of parents and grandparents. And secondly, Freddie had a revelation, not quite a Damascene conversion, but something close to it. From the moment that he first put his hand on Saahira's tummy and felt the foetus move inside her, an unnatural (or maybe natural) need to understand his own lineage took hold. Once the prospect of becoming a parent became real, he fiercely needed to know the identity of his birth father.

One evening in the middle of May, Saahira arrived home exhausted after a long day at the medical centre. Her practice was in a working-class area in the heart of Barking, East London, and the majority of her patients were first and second generation Middle Eastern families. For the last couple of weeks, a vomiting bug had been sweeping through the local community, and no matter how many hours she put in, it just wasn't enough. Freddie had put Fabeena to bed before his wife came home and the front door was hardly shut when she flopped on the sofa and closed her eyes. 'Christ, what a day,' she sighed. Freddie poured them both a glass of Sauvignon and he joined her on the sofa, and with his arm around her shoulder he pulled her to his chest.

'You're working too hard there, Saa, you need to pull back a bit, darling.'

'Hm, wish to God I could.'

'Well, do as I keep telling you, get more staff, the clinic can well afford it.'

'More staff just means more patients, Freddie, you know that's the way the system works. Anyway, once this bug has worked its way out, things will ease off.'

'You know you could move your practice to a different area, less demanding, more private.'

'Ha, you're so bourgeois my love, you think private patients have nicer health issues, or they don't complain as much. And who's gonna take care of the people who really need it the most, Eh? Riddle me that.'

'But you don't need to expend all your energy saving the whole of East London, darling, you need to save some for yourself, you need to take care of yourself.'

'Listen up everyone, my husband's philosophy: save yourself at the expense of everyone else,' she jibed.

'Ha, you're twisting my words, Saa, you know that's not what I'm saying. I'm just saying that you need to take better care of yourself.'

'Well, *you'd* better take better care of me, husband, because today I got a very serious offer of marriage.'

'Wow, I hope you told him that you were happily wedded to a wonderful Irishman.'

'Of course, I did, but it didn't seem to bother him. I wouldn't mind but he's already married with a child and another on the way ... a child that is, or maybe it's another wife on the way.' She laughed at her own wordplay.

'Funny girl.'

'And it didn't seem to bother him that I'm his wife's doctor too.'

'Jaysas, some joker.'

'Well, that's the thing Freddie, he was deadly serious. He told me that he was a TV star and surely I must recognise him. And he knew that I was Syrian, which seemed to obsess him. Asking me, have I been back to the old country often. Like I mean, in the middle of a war?'

'Hm, sounds like he's after spooking you a little, Saa, and you say you know his wife?'

'Course, she was only in with me last week, she's nearly her full term. Ah she's lovely, but doesn't seem very happy, seems like she's very much under his control. You know, extreme Islamic values, that sort of thing.'

'I know I don't have to tell you, darling, but you need to be careful. There are some real weirdos out there. Anyway, what makes him think that he's a TV star?'

'Well, I didn't ask him, did I? I didn't want to indulge him or encourage him any further; it was enough to refuse his offer of marriage.'

Freddie laughed and said, 'C'mon, let's eat, I'm starving.' He went to the window to close the blinds against the evening chill. As he did, he noticed a car parked by the footpath across the road. Something caught his attention, maybe it was the lonely silhouette of the figure in the driver's seat. Suddenly the darkness inside the cabin exploded with light as the driver lit a cigarette and, for a couple of seconds, Freddie got a glimpse of his face, his shaved head and long black beard. The driver looked directly at him as if he wanted Freddie to see his face, before extinguishing the flame. Then the car accelerated from the kerb and sped down the road and into the darkness. Freddie watched as the lights disappeared, and suddenly shivered as a dark chill washed through him, and he quickly closed the blinds to the hostile night. He didn't mention the incident to Saahira that evening, but instead waited until the following morning, in the knowledge that daylight diffuses fear. They agreed that he would notify the local police, which he did that morning, but, as he relayed to his wife later, they seemed more interested in the complainant than the complained.

*****

Khuram Butt was a TV star. Well, a star in his own head at least. But he had good reason to believe it as he had only the previous year featured in a BBC documentary: *The Jihadis Next Door.* The programme profiled a group of Muslims who were linked to the proscribed international terrorist organisation, al-Muhajiroun and who were cheerleaders for Isis. Butt's fellow-travellers who featured in the documentary included the occasional spiritual leader, Mohammed Shamsuddin, who preached; '*The real life is the life of the akhirah, the afterlife, and not this life. This is not the real life, my dear brothers. This is a passing time for us, so this is a type of jihad for you.*'

Khuram Butt liked that phrase; he often repeated it to himself, like a mantra. And whenever he was having a bad day, when things weren't going well, when people pissed him off, particularly the unbelieving kafirs, he'd remind them that '*the real life is the life of the akhirah, not this life.*' And in recent times he was heard to say it frequently, because these days, life really pissed him off quite a lot.

But his appearance in the 2016 BBC documentary meant that he now enjoyed a level of local recognition and notoriety, particularly among the Muslim clientele of the Ilford Fitness Centre in East London, where he hung out and occasionally worked as a receptionist. It was here too that he met fellow sympathisers in the war against westernised beliefs.

But today should have been a special day. Because today he had asked the beautiful doctor at the medical centre to marry him. Although this was the first time that he had actually met her, he had seen her come and go from the clinic many times as it was close to the fitness centre. One evening he watched as she left her practice and he decided to follow her to find out where she lived. Once he'd established her address, he made a habit of driving there at night, and parking across the road in the hope of catching a glimpse of her in her home. On one occasion he saw her embracing her kafir husband in the front room and he imagined that it was his own arms that were wrapped around her waist, and it was his mouth covering hers. Initially he had been annoyed and disappointed that she seemed fully westernised and contaminated, a sign of weakness, but he reasoned that of course it wasn't her fault. She had been coerced and manipulated and conditioned, yes, brainwashed into infidel customs and practices. But he knew that just below the surface, there slept an Arab woman, a Muslim, a Syrian. And he was sure that once she became his wife he wouldn't have any difficulty in liberating her from her infidel husband and child, freeing her from her westernised behaviours, allowing her to conform to Islamic ways, to his ways. In fact, once they were married, the family could move to Syria and fight in the civil war where, unfortunately, events were going badly. Yes, he would join in the good fight, he would offer the Isis rebels his courage and skills; he would be the bravest of soldiers, prepared to fight to the death for Allah, to be a martyr of this Holy War. She of course could no longer be a doctor, she would leave all that silliness behind her and she would need to understand *her* place in *his* world; serving him and his household, bearing him children. To this end he had even told Zahrah, his own woman, that he intended taking a second wife, it was only becoming of a man of his stature and ambition.

Yes, that at least had been his plan until now, and today *should* have been a special day but the stupid doctor had declined his offer of marriage. She didn't take him seriously. She'd laughed at him. He'd felt humiliated. It was a deep and constant frustration of his that a lot of people didn't take him seriously, a lot of people weren't listening.

However, that would all change. A new plan was already taking shape in his mind, a masterplan. Soon the name of Khuram Butt would be known and honoured throughout the Islamic world. If he could not go to Syria, then, so to speak, the mountain would come to Mohammed … to London. He smiled at his cleverness, his ingenuity. He now knew this to be his real destiny, his true kismet.

15

Jessica Mason was born into old Bostonian stock. They were quintessential WASP and rabid Republicans. It was said (mind you, mostly by the Masons themselves) that their lineage could be traced back to the Founding Fathers, to that tentative first foothold on the Plymouth Rock.

The original of the Mason species owned vast tracts of rich Virginian land and were steeped in the cattle business. However, the immediate years following the civil war saw significant change in the social and human fabric of southern American society and like many other land and slave owners, the Masons were witnesses to the burning crosses, the scorched harvests and the changing of the guard. And so, in the spring of 1873 they upped sticks and migrated north to the fast-growing city of Boston, New England. There they started one of the first meat processing and meatpacking plants and built a wealthy dynasty, under the brand *Mr. Mason Meats*, which prospered until the 1960s. However, following years of mismanagement, primarily by Jessica's father, Theodore Mason, the family were reduced to a fraction of the empire they once owned. Yes indeed, if the Masons were heritage rich, they were now very much wealth distressed.

Anthony Castelletto first met Jessica Mason in the summer of 1984, the year of Orwell's dystopian prophecy, and at twenty-five years old Anthony was two years her senior.

They had been invited separately to a garden party by a mutual friend, and in the haze of a hot afternoon sun he saw her standing by the pool chatting to another guest. She was different. Unlike the Abbaesque fashions on display she was dressed in 70's hippie flared jeans and a cheesecloth top and she reminded him of Ali MacGraw in *Love Story*. She looked beautiful … and bored. She seemed to be half listening and half scrutinising the party crowd. Smoke from the barbecue drifted over in their direction and she moved away to avoid it. *Ah, separated from the herd.* He moved quickly and introduced himself.

'Ah, so you're Castelletto the shoe makers?' she said confidently.

'Well, we're the footwear design people actually, but the question is academic because I'm not *you're*, I'm *me*' he answered.

'And you're Mister Mason Meats,' he ventured, 'or in your case, is it Miss Mason Meats?'

'Yes' she said proudly, 'producers of the highest quality beef in the whole US of A.'

'Ah, interesting, so what's a lady like you doing in a place like this?'

'Looking for a husband of course,' she laughed.

As they moved away from the noisy barbeque party crowd, he offered her his reefer. She took it and pulled a long drag, inhaling deeply.

'Wow, good stuff,' she said.

'Only the best. Imported. Columbian.'

She took another drag and returned it to him. Her head felt lighter, unencumbered.

'So, you're looking for a husband. How big is the dowry?'

'Aha, clever boy, you've hit the nail on the head.'

Over lunch with her parents, a few weeks after meeting Anthony, Jessica casually dropped her new relationship into the conversation:

'I met a nice guy recently.'

'Oh, that's lovely darling, do we know him?' By that, her mother Winnie meant did his family belong to their circle.

'Probably not, he's one of the Castelletto's.'

Her father, Theodore Mason, asked from behind his newspaper:

'The Italians?'

'Well, he's about as Italian as you're Virginian, Daddy'

Winnie asked: 'Castelletto's the shoe makers?'

'That's so reductionist, Mummy, they're not shoe makers, they're footwear design people actually,' she said without a hint of irony.

Her father looked around the newspaper with growing interest: 'I know his father, Sylvester, I met him a few times at the Chambers meetings, seems like an ok kind of guy.'

'That's not his father, Daddy, that's his uncle, his father died years ago.'

'Ah, but he's working in the business I presume, what's he doing there?'

'No, he's not in the business, he's doing his own thing, he's travelling and experiencing.'

'Aha, travelling and experiencing … What a joke. Sounds just like your uncle William, a disaster, look what happened to him. Went away to find himself and got lost, not only couldn't find himself but couldn't even find his own way back, aha. He hasn't been seen in years, a blessing.'

'He's not like Uncle William, Daddy, he's a very together guy and very serious about his career.'

'My advice, stay away from him, Jessica, find one of the merchant princes of Boston, there are plenty of them around, and they'll value the Mason name.' And losing interest, her father resumed reading his newspaper. Winnie reached over and squeezed her daughter's hand. 'Don't listen to your father Jess, you meet whomever you want, too many unhappy marriages come from covenants of convenience rather than of love.' It was no secret that her marriage to Theodore had been concocted to strengthen two business families, and two families' businesses. Jessica jumped up from the table and hugged her mother, 'I *so* knew you'd say that Mummy; you're the best mother in the whole world.'

As she was leaving the luncheon room, she overheard her father - being indiscreet and loud as ever - scolding his wife, 'You should know better than to encourage that girl, Winifred, you know as well as I do that it'll end in tears.'

'It may well do, Theo,' she heard her mother reply; 'but unlike me, maybe she'll at least know love along the way.'

But it seemed like her father had long ago stopped listening to his wife, and hence, heard nothing of her wisdom.

Nonetheless, in spite of his misgivings the wedding took place, but *because* of his misgivings the reception was a catastrophe. Having consumed far too much brandy between them, Theodore Mason and Sylvester Castelletto, Anthony's uncle, had been verbally sparring all afternoon, while disappearing under a dark cloud of Cuban smoke. Both bragging about their respective social standings, their political contacts and their superior business acumen. Each argumentative cut-and-thrust raised the temperature a few degrees until, finally, it reached boiling point. Theodore had had enough and took exception to a perceived slur in reference to the mismanagement of his beleaguered Mason Meats:

'How dare you, sir, talk to a Mason like that.' And he hit the table hard with his fist, knocking and spilling glasses; 'we who have fed the American people for hundreds of years, through depressions and wars …'

Sylvester broke in: 'It was people *like you* who caused the depression for fucks sake …'

'My god, how dare you, sir … and you, you little Italian cobbler, you just-off-the boat wop, it's a wonder you didn't get seasick getting to the wedding'

Sylvester jumped to his feet, angrily pushed his chair back and knocked it to the ground with a noisy clatter.

'Who the fuck do you think you are, Mason. How dare you disrespect the Castelletto name like that and I fucking paying for everything at *your* daughter's wedding.' Theodore slowly rose to his feet and, defensively, and a little sheepishly, said; 'I paid for the meat'

Sylvester shouted exasperatedly; 'What're you talking about you idiot, you're in the fucking meat business, it didn't cost you anything. Now apologise for disrespecting the Castelletto name or I'll fucking have you right here and now.' And with that he raised both his fists and took a boxer's stance. Theodore leapt from his chair, whipped off his jacket, and he too took up a boxers pose and barked; 'Hold me back, hold me back or I'll kill him'

Then, from somewhere, a shattering roar: 'Stop. Stop. Stop this at once!'

Silence, and everyone froze.

'How dare you, you selfish animals, you're ruining my daughter's wedding. How dare you behave like this on the biggest day of these kid's lives. You should be ashamed of yourselves. You're both a disgrace.' And Winnie moved to her daughter's side and held and hugged her in her arms.

Silence.

Sylvester's arms went limp and fell to his side. Then he grabbed his jacket from the ground and, addressing the newlyweds he mumbled: 'I'm sorry Anthony, and I'm terribly sorry Jessica. Com'n Lucille let's get the fuck away from here.' And he grabbed his wife's hand and with heads held high they made their way from the reception room.

And so, the great expectation of the coming together of two old Bostonian families never materialised. Anthony and Jessie moved away from the city, away from their kin, first to Medford and then to their beautiful log house in Framingham. And yes, occasionally they visited Syl and Lucille, and other times they visited Theo and Winnie, but the Mason and the Castelletto families were never to meet again. However, the chaos of the wedding reception brought Jessie and he even closer together, made them more determined to protect their independence, and they swore to each other that they'd never let outside forces interfere in their lives or their marriage. Jessie used to joke that their log house was their impenetrable little castle, their *Castelletto.*

But now external forces had breached their fortress, and the most depressing aspect of it all for Anthony was that it was self-inflicted.

Jessie had lowered the drawbridge and simply invited the enemy into their home, their bedroom, their lives.

*****

It was noon Wednesday, the day after Anthony received the file from the private investigator, and as he drove up Eucalyptus Avenue towards his house he suddenly felt very sad. He parked in his driveway and noticed that Jessie was standing in the open front doorway.

He had given some thought as to where they should meet and, although at first he favoured some place outside of their home, neutral ground, after weighing up the pros and cons he settled on the house. Here he felt more comfortable and privacy wouldn't be an issue, plus he also needed to get clean clothes and other personal bits and pieces.

'Hello, Anthony.'

'Hello, Jessica.'

'I've made some fresh coffee, would you like a cup?'

He'd never seen her so nervous before, but then again, he'd never seen her in many other different guises before he so dramatically interupted her affair.

'Yes, I'll have a cup please.'

He had prepared a plan in advance of their meeting and central to it was civility; there would be no hysterics, no drama - at least not from him. He soaked up the familiar wood smells of the log house and looked around the hallway, where everything was in its place. He then went into the living room, the comfortable space in the house, with its high-pitched roof and big open fireplace with logs stacked on one side, and the large stone chimney climbing the wall and disappearing out through the roof. He stood by his leather chair and waited for her to return from the kitchen with the coffee. He thought that if he willed himself really hard, maybe he could make the dossier in his hand disappear and cause the recent events to un-happen.

Jessie came in with the coffee mugs and was barely able to keep them from spilling as her hands shook so nervously. He took the mug from her and he sat down on his chair. She sat across from him.

'What I want to do, Jessie, is talk about the future, where we go from here, but first I need to know a few things, and whatever else we do, let's try and keep this civil, no hysterics.'

'Yes, of course.'

'And truthful, it's really important that we protect the truth here, Jessie, you understand?'

'Yes, yes of course, Anthony.'

'So, who is he and how long have you known him?'

'Well, he's just some guy from the city, Anthony, he means nothing to me. I only met him recently. It's just a stupid fling thing. I'm so sorry that it ever happened, I guess I just felt very lonely recently and you've been traveling a lot and I guess I needed some attention, but it was stupid and it should never have happened. And I'm so, so sorry that it did, and if I could turn back the clock, I promise you I would.'

'Ok, so when did you say you met him?'

'Oh, I don't know, maybe four or six weeks ago, I bumped into him in Faneuil Hall when I was up in the city and we just got talking and … well, that's how it happened.'

There followed a silence then his wife continued: 'I love you, Anthony, you must believe me, and Maria and Julian, our beautiful family. I swear to you, our family is the only important thing to me.'

Anthony decided to bring the charade to a halt as there was nothing more to be gained from her further incriminating herself.

'Ok Jessie, enough of the bullshit, here, take a look through this.' He slid the dossier across the glass-topped table toward her. 'You should recognise what's in there.'

She didn't know what it was but from her husband's tone she knew that it was radioactive.

'Pick it up, open it,' he ordered.

She tentatively reached for it and picked it up. She opened it at the first page. At first it was a blur and she didn't recognise anything. She had to concentrate to read a few lines of the transcription of her first digital conversation with her lover, two and a half years ago. But she still didn't understand its meaning and she looked at him with a quizzical look.

'What's this?'

'It's what you think it is. Look through it, look at the pictures.'

She turned over a bunch of pages and read more transcripts, more of their texts to each other, and then the full impact of it slowly began to dawn on her. Then she flicked further through until she found the pages with the images. Her face visibly changed colour, as if someone had suddenly opened a valve and let the blood drain away. Her mouth fell open as she turned a page or two and she seemed hypnotised by the enormity of what was in front of her and she was stuck in the moment, unable to function. He leaned over and took the folder from her hands.

'No more lies, Jessica, it's really important now that I hear the truth from you.'

'But how … how did you get those?' The expression on her face was one of incomprehension as she tried to make sense of the evidence in front of her.

'It doesn't matter how I have these; the important thing is that you now tell me the truth. Trust me, nothing else matters at this stage except that you're truthful.'

Her stomach lurched and she leapt from her chair and, with her hand covering her mouth, ran to the bathroom behind the kitchen. Anthony heard her throw up violently and then continue to retch for a few minutes. He went into the kitchen and poured them fresh coffees in fresh mugs and waited there for her to return. When she eventually came out, she had done a little to tidy herself, to compose herself. He offered her the coffee, which she took and sat on a kitchen chair while he remained standing, leaning against the cupboards.

'It looks like you have everything, what more do you want?' she said bitterly.

'The truth Jessie, I want to hear it from you.'

She sipped some coffee, rested her arm on the table, and wiped her hand back and forth as if clearing invisible crumbs, or brushing away the lies. Nothing for a few minutes, then:

'I was out with Andrea one day for lunch, oh, two or three years ago, we were having coffee or wine or something. I was telling her how brain-deadening bored I was with my life. Bored with the tennis club and the golf club and the children, and you, everything, bored shitless with my life. She was laughing at me and told me that I needed to get some real excitement and she started telling me about this adult dating site. She said that you can meet these gorgeous guys on this site and it's perfectly safe and legal. She said she does it all the time, and she has lots of regular guys who she chats to and they have amazing conversations, really explicit, really horny. So, I signed up for it. I was really nervous and scared at first but then I got braver and started chatting with guys, random guys from God only knows where. Then one day I met Bill in the chatroom, and we started chatting, fairly innocently at first but then kinda serious. Our lives were similar. He has a wife and kids, but he doesn't love her anymore, he's just staying in the marriage for the kids. I told him I still loved you but you're away an awful lot and, and … and the excitement is gone from our marriage. Most guys on the site are from all over the US or even the rest of the world, but Bill lives just up the road in Hopkinton. And so, we agreed to meet this one afternoon for a drink over in Worcester. You were away somewhere. In any event, one martini led to another and another and Bill booked us into a local motel. It was his first time too and, well, that was it; that was the start of it … that's it, Anthony.'

'Do you love him?'

She thought about it for a little while. 'Yes, I think I do. I do know that he loves me, and he'd leave his wife except for the kids. But - and I know you won't believe me when I say this - but I love you too.'

A troubled silence followed. Anthony was thinking about the last piece of information that the investigator had given him and wondered at what point he should tell Jessie, and now just didn't seem to be the right time. Or was it?

'In case you're worried, I'm not going to contact this guy, I'm not in the business of messing with other people's lives, I've enough of a mess on my own to be getting on with.'

She looked relieved. 'So, you're telling me that you're not going to contact him? Or his wife?'

'Yes. Listen, I don't ever want to come across that prick again, and if I do, I'll probably kill him. You might pass that on to him next time you meet. And in relation to his wife, why would I screw with her?'

Jessie was relieved.

'Ok, we need to talk about the future, the kids, this house, our home. I'm seeing my attorney on Friday and I'd suggest you do the same. I can stay where I am until the weekend but I'm going to need to lease a place fairly quickly until we decide what to do with this place. You can stay here in the meantime.'

'Why don't you stay here Anthony, I can move to one of the other bedrooms, it would save you lots of hassle.'

'After what happened here? Seriously? Nope, that certainly won't work. This house will never be the same for me again, Jessie.'

She started crying for the first time. 'Of course, I'm so sorry, Anthony.'

'Well, there's gonna be plenty of collateral damage, what did you expect? And speaking of which, what have you told the kids?'

'Nothing, I just told them that we had a bad argument and that you were staying away for a little while.'

'Well, you'd better tell them something soon cause I'm meeting both of them tomorrow evening and they need to know.'

He could tell that she wasn't up for that and it wasn't going to get done. 'Listen, if you're not up to it I can let them know that we're separating temporarily without saying anything about the affair, for the time being at least.'

'Yes, ok, I suppose so … thanks.'

'Ok. Well, I need to get some clothes and things.'

Anthony brought his packed case down to the hall where Jessie was waiting for him. She had been sitting on a chair by the hall table and she got up when she saw him.

'Before you go Anthony, I just want to say that I never ever wanted to hurt you and it's breaking my heart to see the damage I've done and the hurt I've caused, I'm so so sorry.' Her voice faltered and it seemed that what little strength she had mustered dissolved and now she was crying again. She made a gesture, a move towards him, as if to embrace him, but she stopped, and her arms fell to her sides.

Anthony thought that this had to be the time to tell her. In knowing what he knew he couldn't just walk away and let her get more hurt down the road. But she'd think that it was vindictiveness on his part, crap!

'Listen Jessie, it is what it is with us now. But just be careful with this guy, he may not be giving you the full story.'

'Why are you saying that? You don't know anything about him, you're being spiteful.'

'I promise you I'm not, I'm just looking out for you, Jessie, that's all. Now I gotta go, I'll be in touch about sorting stuff out, take care of yourself.'

Anthony walked briskly down the driveway to his car and threw his case in the back. He climbed into the driver's seat, started the ignition, reversed from the driveway and headed east towards Framingham.

He never once looked back at the woman crying in his doorway.

16

London, Monday 22nd May *(12 days to Nadir)*

I had to read the text for a second time: *'Hi Jack, you can advise your client that the DNAs are a match'*. 'Fuck!' I thought. Well, I thought I'd thought it, but I wasn't aware that I had actually said it out loud and the people around the table had stopped talking and were looking at me. I was chairing an afternoon meeting in the London office and when I looked up from my mobile, I saw a dozen sets of eyes staring at me.

'Everything ok, Jack?'

'Yeah, sure, sure, sorry, just got the wrong answer to something. Ok, where were we, who's got the intel on their due diligence?'

I guess the text shocked me, but it didn't surprise me too much as I had had an impending dread of the DNA outcome. Deep in my gut I had this feeling that it was true, it was too bizarre to be made up. *So, it's confirmed then, I do have a son and a granddaughter, and they're here in London, somewhere*. I could have passed him on the street this morning on my way to the office. I wondered if I'd know him or would he know me? What did Marianne say again, that he knows I exist but he doesn't know who I am? I wondered if that was true, though. There was obviously an awful lot more she hadn't told me, and of course I still had a decision to make. Embrace it, like Lizzie says, or invoke the 'do nothing' principle as Al says. But I knew my own mind and I wasn't the kind of person who could actually just walk away, not because I cared too much, but because I was too curious. I knew I couldn't resist the urge to find out. I left the office and walked back to my hotel with my head reeling.

But I had to tell someone and as always, Lizzie picked up within a few rings;

'I got the DNA results back and there's a match.'

'Wow bro, you've got an extra kid.'

'I've got an extra kid and an extra grandkid, sis.'

'That's so fucking exciting Jack, are you excited?'

'Excited doesn't quite describe it, Lizzie, more like scared shitless. What am I going to do, for crying out loud?'

'Reach out and grab it with both hands, darling. Consider yourself lucky, a whole new chapter has opened up in your life.'

'Ah Lizzie, come on, even you know that it's a little more complicated than that.'

'Why? Why is it so complicated?'

'Well, for a start, Bea. She'll be apoplectic.'

'But why, Jack, it's not like that you even knew Bea when this happened. Sure it's gonna be a shock to her but she'll get over it, she'll have to get over it. Anyway, she needs to be a little less precious.'

'Hm, there was never any love lost between you two.'

'Ok then, so what *are* you actually gonna do?'

'Dunno, I just got confirmation this afternoon, you're the first person I rang.'

'Oh Jack, that's so sweet that you rang me first. By the way, what're their names?'

'Freddie and Fabeena, I think. Freddie I'm sure of and I think she said that Fabeena is the baby's name. Oh, and you met Marianne at least twice, according to Alex anyway. Do you remember her? He said we met her over on Aran, and he said that you had the hots for her.'

'Jaysas Jack, I had the hots for anything in a skirt back then, but I've been thinking about it since you told me last week, and I think I have a vague memory of her. If she's the one I'm thinking of, she was beautiful; tall, hippish, blond. You were punching way above your weight there, bro.'

'I'm so glad that I called you sis, you do soooo much for my confidence.'

'Your confidence is bulletproof Jack, 'bye, love you.'

I didn't bother calling Alex as I'd only get his negative philosophy and I knew that realistically it wasn't an option, and anyway, that's not what I wanted to hear.

I started imagining the conversation with Bea, but it ran into a brick wall very quickly. This would surely throw her completely off course. Everything would be questioned with this other woman back in my life. No, worse than that, this other woman who is the mother of my son. In other words, she and I now have a significant shared interest and will have for the rest of our lives.

And then what about the kids, what will they think? Will their noses be put out of joint? Maybe Ben more than Sean or Sadie. Right now, he's the eldest, but of course he won't be any longer when Freddie enters the fray. And no matter what anyone says to the contrary, we always encumber the eldest with greater responsibilities and expectations … fuck! Maybe I will call Alex after all.

Or maybe I live two lives. Keep the families separate. Have a relationship with Freddie and his family but never say anything to Bea and the kids. I mean, why mess up their lives? They haven't asked for this and it's not like we'd all be living in Spiddal.

It reminded me of a story my mother told us when we were younger, about a cousin of hers who went away to Kilkenny to become a priest. After he was ordained he was moved to a parish in Dublin. Fr. Kevin was his name. While he was busy carrying out his priestly duties, he was busier carrying out his procreative duties with this woman he met, which resulted in her having two children by him. But that wasn't the end of it. He was then moved to a parish in Cork, but the woman and his children stayed in Dublin. And then what did Fr. Kevin do? He met another woman in Cork and had two more kids with her, for fucks sake. So, not only is he a parish priest but he's got families in two parishes, Dublin and Cork, and no one was ever the wiser. That is until he dropped dead suddenly one day on the Cork to Dublin train while having a full Irish breakfast in first class, just after Limerick Junction.

Seems like he made the journey regularly as the rail staff attested to; *Ah yes, Fr. Kevin, sure we knew him very well, lovely man, so holy, a great priest*. And at the graveside, the bishop wondered who the two distraught women and children were, almost throwing themselves onto the coffin. He didn't have long to wait though, because the next day the two women, sporting very dissimilar accents, presented themselves to his Palace seeking child maintenance. The two families, who hadn't known that the other existed until they met at the bishop's front door, apparently became great friends and visited each other regularly thanks to the Bishop of Cork. The sly bishop agreed, in return for their silence, to pay for amongst other privileges, a yearly return family train ticket for the Cork to Dublin service. They soon discovered that they fared much better with Fr. Kevin dead than alive, which appears sometimes to be one of life's little quirks. You couldn't make it up.

*****

I ordered a flat white and found a seat by the window in the little café across the road from the offices of Arthur Cox, just off Fleet Street. It was Monday evening at 7.15pm and the offices in the legal district were emptying of staff, some heading for home, others making their way to meet colleagues and friends and lovers for an evening drink or dinner. Marianne had told me that Freddie worked for Cox's in London and I had rung their reception earlier to confirm that he was in the office. I watched as some staff left the building, chatting and waving their goodbyes, and going their various ways. A little later another group came out and chatted for a while before dispersing. About 7.30pm the café guy who had served me was making a nuisance of himself cleaning tables and noisily moving chairs, obviously in an attempt to get us, the last few customers, to leave so that he could close up. I was about to give up when the door of the offices opened again and it looked like the last of the staff came out, a group of three, but Freddie wasn't there. Crap, I thought, I must have missed him earlier, and what the fuck am I doing here anyway. Just as I got up to leave, the door opened again and he emerged. Jesus, my heart missed a beat and, panicking a little, I quickly sat down again out of sight of the window as if (stupidly) I could be seen. I looked again and yes, it was definitely him, at least from what I could remember from the image that Marianne had shown me. It was his build and his fair red hair that gave him away.

Freddie joined the other three and they started walking together down Fleet Street. I waited until they were well advanced before I left the café and crossed the road to their side. I followed them until they came to the junction of Farringdon Street and they turned down toward the river and Blackfriars Bridge. They had split into two couples and I could see that Freddie was chatting animatedly to a female colleague. They crossed over Blackfriars and turned left down the Embankment towards the Tate and a few minutes later turned up Southwark Street. I knew this area fairly well as I often went there with friends or colleagues, and I guessed that they were heading for the Borough Market. They eventually stopped at Hoopers on Stoney Street and sat outside at a table with high stools. One of them ordered drinks from the bar. I found a table outside Porters, the bar next door, and ordered a beer, and I sat slightly back but was close enough to pick out Freddie's Irish accent amongst his colleagues and I could see him in profile. Except for his hair and maybe his posture, I couldn't see too much of myself in him, but even from a distance his bonhomie and expressiveness screamed Sommers, and in particular Lizzie - at least someone will be happy, I thought.

I realised that I was grinning.

I continued to sip my beer, mesmerised by the surreal and extraordinary situation in which I found myself. The excitement and intensity of the moment, this game of stalking and hide and seek had my adrenals pumping and my heart pounding, so hard in fact that I thought that maybe others around me must be able to hear it. I even surreptitiously looked around to see if anyone was looking at me. Then it dawned on me that there sat my son just a couple of metres away and close enough to almost reach out and tap him on the shoulder, or if I chose, to embrace him. My thoughts were interrupted when I saw Freddie gesticulating toward the notice board on the pavement outside the pub and he seemed to be quite irate. His colleagues were laughing and attempting to mollify him, but he was obviously upset over something. I watched as he went into the bar and a few minutes later he arrived back with one of the restaurant staff who I presumed to be the manager, and he led him to the sandwich notice board. Freddie was pointing at it and arguing quite intently with the manager and I had to lean sideways quite a bit to make out the 'Thought for the Day' chalked on the slate board. I was more than a little surprised to read:

"What do the Irish use as a sunblock? The pub of course!"

Although voices weren't raised, I heard the occasional words from Freddie: 'disappointed … racial slurs … anti-Irish … wrong message …' I watched, enthralled, in fascination and admiration. Then the manager went back into the bar and returned with a cloth and wiped the board clean. Both men shook hands and Freddie turned to return to his stool amid his laughing and jeering colleagues. Then something strange occurred. Although I could see my son by looking around and between other customers who were standing or sitting at tables, I knew that I wasn't in his direct line of sight. But just as he was about to resume his seat with his back to me, and for no apparent reason, he turned around quickly and looked in my direction, almost as if he knew that I was there. *Jesus, did our eyes meet? But he doesn't know me, I'm obviously being paranoid.* I froze. But then I realised that he actually wasn't looking at me, he was looking beyond me. I turned my head to see what caught his attention. Three men were pushing their way through the evening crowd, and it seemed like they were deliberately trying not to avoid people, not caring that they were bumping into them. They were looking around, surveying the area, and they looked like trouble. There was a real aura of danger about them; no one challenged them as they progressed through the evening crowd. They appeared to be of Middle Eastern origin. One was ahead of the other two and he seemed to be the leader. He was taller than the others, his head was shaved, and he wore a long black beard. The three of them were dressed in Arab garb. They shuffled past my table and, as they got to where Freddie was sitting, the tallest stopped suddenly when he saw him; he seemed to recognise Freddie, but was surprised to see him, taken aback. I looked immediately to see Freddie's reaction, and he too seemed to recognise the leader, and he too looked surprised. He had that expression of '*where do I know him from*?' The leader shouted in Freddie's direction, 'Allahu Akbar,' and then, with his colleagues, continued to push their way through the crowd, looking from left to right, and on up the street until they were out of sight. Freddie seemed a little shaken, pale, rooted to the spot. One of his colleagues grabbed his arm, pulled him to the table and handed him a beer. They started talking again, laughing, and the banter started up with vigour. But from where I was sitting, and from what I could see, the fun had stopped for Freddie. The mood had changed.

I was intrigued by what I had witnessed. *Who were these guys, did Freddie know them? And if so, how?* It was clear that he definitely recognised the tall guy, who seemed to startle him. And why did they shout at him, at Freddie specifically? And what were they up to anyway? They looked like they were sussing out the place. But for what? Well, whatever they were up to, they were trouble, and Freddie looked like he felt it too.

I finished my beer; I had outstayed my little game of hide and seek. My mood too had changed. I took one last look at my son and as

I slipped away from my table, and melted into the evening crowd, I determined there and then that I would have to meet him, and meet him soon.

17

Boston, Tuesday 23rd May *(11 days to Nadir)*

Maxine hadn't made any plans to see Anthony that day, indeed they hadn't made any plans to see each other again, but she did expect to hear from him over the next few days. Or maybe it was more hope than expectation. But she liked the guy, liked him a lot in fact. She didn't know where he had come from or what kind of trouble he was in, knew nothing about him other than what he had told her, and there was no earthly reason to believe any of it. As she knew from experience, and as Patsy her friend would say: as men breathe, they lie. And even if what he told her about his background was true, none of it was current. Everything he said about himself and his family was said in the past tense, and there was an unexplained lag between the then and now. No explanation as to why he was staying in a motel or what had happened that he turned up in the bar just over a week ago, badly bruised. She didn't even have his surname. But he was definitely running away from something; she knew that for sure. She'd seen it all before. Men turn up out of the blue and as fast as they appear, they disappear. They do something wrong, something bad, workwise or home-wise. Mostly with their wives or girlfriends - or worse still, their kids. A bit of violence here or caught with their dicks out there. And they exit quickly, get the fuck out fast, or get kicked out and stay away long enough for the dust to settle. And then they crawl back home with their tails between their legs, promising they'll never do it again, on their mother's and father's graves, they'll never do it again. Until the next time that is.

As she sometimes did, Maxine reflected on her own life, her own relationships, her compulsive need to fall in love, her craving to be loved. Even as a child, wanting to be heard above the noise, the poverty of love and intimacy.

Back then in the seventies they lived in Detroit, Michigan. The city was still making cars, but the writing was on the factory wall, at least for those who could read the signs. Her father and mother worked for Chryslers, working shifts, as much overtime as they wanted and taking home real good incomes. But they must have believed the Union's rhetoric, believed that the gravy train would always keep running through their town and through their lives. And if her parents earned big, they spent just as big. Maxine was the middle of five kids, kids who wanted for nothing, except the company of their parents. Then the Union's bluff was called, and the gravy train pulled up one day and didn't get going again. The auto manufacturers moved their production facilities to Mexico or Brazil, or sometimes to another State closer to the customer. Detroit died in the seventies and eighties. Maxine's parents soon burnt through the little savings they had. The kids now wanted for everything except the company of their parents, who continuously quarrelled and fought. Maxine left home when she was eighteen and no one seemed to notice, or care.

She moved west to California for a few years and married the first guy who told her that he loved her. But he only loved her for a little while and they separated, without too many memories and without acrimony (except for the fight over the precious vinyl collection, she lost). Not long after the divorce, she fell hopelessly in love with a Canadian musician and followed him and his sax to the jazz scene in New Orleans. There, in the Big Easy, they rented a cabin at the back of the city where Lake Pontchartrain laps its backyard. They made a beautiful child together; they seemed so happy and content. Then one morning, she woke to an empty bed and baby Judy crying in her cot. Not a signal, not a word, not a note, not a dollar bill. He'd just walked out in the middle of the night, in the middle of their lives, not even the courage to say goodbye. She discovered the next day that the tall long-legged black singer in the five-piece jazz band had also done a bunk. She spent the next few weeks alternating between sobbing and screaming, 'What a prick, I fucking hate him,' and then she'd urgently cover baby Judy's ears with her hands so that the child wouldn't be hurt by the anger and disappointment of life. Well, at least not yet anyway. There was nothing for her in New Orleans, so she moved north to Massachusetts and she and Judy settled in Framingham and came to love their new little family at the Black Cat Club.

However, with Anthony she felt that there was something different. He didn't fit *that* kind of profile, and she'd meant it when she'd told him that he was one of the good guys. He just felt right. It was hard to explain, but she couldn't see him doing real harm, well, not deliberately anyway.

But, as he hadn't texted her, she hadn't made any arrangements to get cover for work, so she arrived as usual at 8.00pm. The place was virtually empty, and she dreaded the shift ahead. Because it was midweek, only herself and Patsy were working the tables. Things must have been quieter next door in the Delta because Venus herself was sitting at the end of the bar having a beer. She blew Venus a kiss and then couldn't avoid looking at the large television screen above her head. The big fat orange face of Trump spouting something or other. 'Jesus Christ, I hate him Pats, what the fuck have we done to deserve him. And we've three and a half more years of this. What are we doing to ourselves? Make America Great Again, you mean make Trump great again.' Patsy saw the pain in her face.

'Calm down Max, don't get yourself all riled up, you'll do yourself a brain injury.'

'I fucking hate him Pats, how, tell me how the fuck did we do this to ourselves?'

'And you think Clinton would be any better, do you actually believe anything that comes out of that woman's mouth?'

'Well, at least she's a woman, which would've been something different.'

'They're all the same Max, trust me. You thought Obama was going to change the world and what did he do, nothing, nothing for the likes of you and me at least.'

'That's not true Patsy, what about health care? And now this asshole is talking about getting rid of it, give me a break.'

'Anyway, don't mind The Donald, what about your new friend, eh, eh?'

'What new friend?'

'Don't play all little miss innocent with me Maxi darling, its Anthony, isn't it, isn't that his name? What's his story then, what's he hiding from, eh?'

'Don't know what you mean, Pats, he's not hiding from anything as far as I know. But anyway, how would I know, I only met him once, on Friday night.'

'And once on Saturday night and once on Sunday night and once on Monday night, c'mon girl, that's not your MO, you obviously fancy him, it's written all over your face. You've checked your phone a dozen times since you came in, and you're only in the door.'

'Well, so what if I like him? Don't I deserve to like someone, or be liked by someone?'

'Course you do honey, but you don't deserve to be hurt by some asshole again, so be careful is all I'm saying.'

By 10.00pm Maxine had given up any hope of seeing Anthony that night and went to the bathroom to refresh herself. She was only there a few minutes when Patsy came bursting in, breathless and whispering loudly, 'He's here; he's outside, quick for fuck's sake before he goes away.'

'Ok, ok, I'm coming, keep your voice down or he'll hear you, go back and keep him busy until I get out, I need to fix my hair.'

'Yeah, and push your tits out too, the little you have.'

Anthony was sitting at the same table in the corner as the first night, and Patsy was bordering on kidnapping him, virtually sitting on his lap. He was edging away from her, or attempting to, to put a distance between them both, and when he saw Maxine, he pleaded with his eyes to be rescued.

'Ah, I see Patsy has been keeping you busy, Anthony, she's such a good friend. Ok Pats, now down girl, down!' But Patsy had swapped loyalty for lust, was locking in and had no intention of giving up this prey and this tip.

In the meantime, Dolly was belting out *'Cowgirls don't cry"* and Venus, who hadn't worked thirty minutes all night, decided that this could be her one and only chance of a live customer, and so she wandered over from her bar perch. 'Well, introduce me girls, ah never mind, I'll introduce myself. Hello darlin', you look like you could do with a massage, my name is Venus, personally trained in the Orient, and I give the finest massage this side of Bangkok, satisfaction guaranteed.'

'Sweet Jesus, I don't believe it,' fumed Maxine.

Candy the waitress, who had little to do all night, thought, *hang on a minute, he's my customer,* and pushed her way between Patsy and Venus. Meanwhile Dolly started up another song. *"What's a sweetheart like you doing in a dump like this"* and as she sang she moved around the small stage to get a better look at her co-workers apparently fighting over the cowboy in the corner. But she leaned too far at one point and was about to fall off the stage when the drummer leapt forward and caught her arm, just in time to avoid a disaster, but knocking cymbals in the process. Dolly got such a fright that she shouted, *'Fuck,'* very un-girly-like (but probably very cow-girly-like) into her microphone.

Everyone froze and looked at her, except Venus, who whispered *sotto voce* to Anthony. 'The happy ending is on the house tonight, honey.'

Maxine couldn't contain herself. 'What the fuck are you all up to, did I miss a full moon or something? You're all like bitches in fucking heat … c'mon Anthony, grab your coat, we're getting outta here.' She grabbed him by the arm and literally pulled him from his seat and across the floor to the office door and without letting go of him, opened the door, stretched in, and grabbed her bag and coat, then half-pulled and half-steam-rolled him back across the floor to the door, pushed him out ahead of her, turned around to face the startled audience and barked, 'You're all a fucking disgrace.' Then she stormed out and slammed the door as hard as she could behind her.

They stood outside in the parking lot. 'I'm so, so sorry for those animals, Anthony, I'm so embarrassed, you must think we're an awful lot, I really don't know what got into them.'

'Hey, it's not a problem, I promise. It was funny, hilarious actually.'

'And it was so nice of you to drop by, to be honest I was hoping all night that you would.'

'Well, I'm glad that I did, I wouldn't have missed that drama for the world, ha-ha.'

'That's silly, you *were* the drama, they all want to get their claws into you.' And she reached up and kissed him on the lips. 'And so do I,' she said, smiling. 'Do you want to get a drink? We can go to Mulligans down the street. It's an Irish bar, you'll like it.'

'No no, please, no pretend Irish bars.'

'Oh, why?'

'Well, one day if you see the real thing you'll know why. Do you want to get a drink back in the hotel room?'

'Hey, do I what? Would love to, c'mon cowboy.' She linked arms with him and rested against him as they walked back to the cabin.

Maxine didn't stand on ceremony when they reached his room. As soon as she was past the doorway, she stripped until she was down to her sexiest bra and panties ensemble *(Thank Christ I'm an optimist,* she thought). She was about to go further when he said, 'Wait, don't take them off, that's a job for a man.'

He sat on the edge of the bed and pulled her to him until she was standing between his thighs and he buried his face in the heat of her breasts and cupped her ass with his hands, pulling her as close as he could until he could feel her against his hardening prick. She held his head between her hands and in turn lost her face in his hair and breathed in the strong scent of man. Then she grabbed his hair and roughly pulled his head back and brought her lips to his. They kissed passionately while he worked his hands inside her panties and between her thighs, which she parted eagerly with a little whimper. 'Oh, my sexy fucking cowboy,' she rasped and breathed hard and discarded her bra and flung her head back and pulled his face into her breasts. As he worked his fingers into her wet hot sex and sucked greedily on her swollen nipples, she ground herself against him, forcing a rhythm to his fingers to match her own she groaned louder and bit his ear and licked his cheeks and gorged on his lips and tongue. She exploded in shuddering spasms as her legs buckled and she clung to his body until the last ripples subsided.

Maxine fell on the bed, spread-eagled and sated; 'Jesus Christ Anthony, you're a fucking angel.' Anthony laughed. 'Well, I'd better get my clothes and wings off then before you fall asleep.' She leaned over and pulled him down to her and she kissed him and whispered, 'Hurry, hang your wings behind the door, I think I feel a second coming.'

Afterwards they lay resting against the bed board propped up by pillows, the bed covers pulled down to their waists, sipping homemade gin and tonics on the rocks with roughly cut slices of lemons. 'Hm, a man of many talents it seems, a great fuck and quite the little barman, we must get you a job at the Black Cat, honey.'

Anthony was quiet, thinking.

'A penny for your thoughts?' she asked.

'Ah, I was just thinking about us, you and me, and how fate brought us together.'

'You think it was fate and not my irresistible beauty and bountiful tits?'

'Aha, well there's certainly no denying your irresistible beauty and indeed your bountiful tits, but fate had to play its part first.'

'You think that fate runs our lives?'

'Hm, not sure about that, but there's been a few times in my life when it certainly played a major role.'

'Really? Tell me, tell me, tell me.'

'Well, lots of times. Like the time a couple of years ago when I was in Paris on an assignment with my colleague, Jack, and if it wasn't for fate we probably wouldn't be around now.'

'Hmm, sounds mysterious, tell me, what happened? And who's this Jack?'

'Jack is, as you might say, one of the good guys. I've known him for over ten years, he hails from Ireland.'

'Ah, Irish Jack.'

'Well, just Jack actually. Anyway, we were in Paris to kick off this deal with a company called Trudeau, it was January of 2015. We arrived as usual the day before, which was a Tuesday, and to kill some time and do some prep we checked out the Trudeau offices. You know, so we'd be oriented the next morning.'

'Ah, clever boys.'

'So anyway, we got a cab and found their place on Rue Nicolas-Appert. But you know what else is on Rue Nicolas-Appert, in fact right alongside it?'

'No, but you're going to tell me, right?'

'Well, only the offices of Charlie Hebdo, of course.'

'Charlie Hebdo? Ok, I know the name, remind me?'

'Well, they're the French magazine that publishes cartoons about everything sacred and un-sacred, no one's spared, but it's all satirical stuff.'

'Yeah, yeah, I remember, they did the Mohammed stuff.'

'Exactly, and they paid a price for it. They were attacked by a couple of Islamic terrorists. Twelve people were killed, but it spilled over onto the street. Some people were killed outside the Trudeau offices. But here's the thing, it was the exact time, 11.30am, when we were supposed to be at those offices.'

'But why weren't you at the office?'

'Because of fate, Max, fate. We got a call that evening from one of their senior guys to say that their CEO had got ill or something and the meeting would have to be rescheduled. We were really pissed off until, of course, we watched the news the next morning and saw the whole attack unfold, it was unreal.'

'Wow, you could have been right in the middle of it darling.' She leaned into him and kissed his shoulder. They were quiet for a while, comfortable, enjoying their silence, their naked bodies, the smells of being satisfied, and their own random thoughts. But of course, like all good mysteries that need to be unpicked and solved, Maxine couldn't live with her one, couldn't wait for the mystery to reveal itself. And thinking of Patsy's warning, '*you don't need to be hurt again by some asshole*', she said in her bed voice:

'OK, so can I tell you a story now?'

'Of course, I love stories.'

'So, for the whole of my grandma's life, well at least for as long as I remember, she was an avid reader. She'd devour five or six books a week, especially thrillers or mysteries, the local library couldn't keep up. And after finishing each book she'd say with the greatest of satisfaction, '*Well, that's another one read cover to cover.*' We always wondered why she made a point of saying it until we discovered later on in her life that she never ever fully read a book. She'd start every one with the best of intentions, but after maybe thirty or forty pages she couldn't bear the tension and couldn't wait until the plot lines were weaved together, so you know what she did?'

'Go on, go for it.'

'With every book she'd jump to the last chapter and read the ending.'

'Every book?'

'Every single book.'

'But how did you find out?'

'She told us, of course. Why? Because, for the same reason that she couldn't wait for the ending, she couldn't keep the mystery from us any longer. She had to tell us.'

'Ha, your granny was a little she-devil I imagine.'

'So?'

'So, so what?'

'So, what's the ending?'

'The ending? What ending?'

'To the story of us, of course.'

'Aaaahh, clever girl, a little devil like your granny, methinks.'

She turned towards him, put her arm around him and rested her head against his shoulder; 'I love this Anthony, I love you and me together and I promise I'm not looking to have your babies or anything, ha, even if it was possible at forty-eight. But I hate not knowing where you've come from. I've met enough guys who've done bad things and I've ended up feeling like an accomplice to their stuff and feeling used when one day they just up and disappear.'

He put his arm under her head and shoulders and pulled her closer to him.

'Ok, well what do you want to know?'

'Well, why are you here, out of the blue, what happened? You say you travel a lot, is it illegal stuff, drugs or contraband, is that what happened? Are you hiding out or something?'

Anthony gave a great laugh and pulled her closer and kissed her hair. 'You silly girl Max, you beautiful, sexy, silly girl. Yeah, I'm on the run from the FBI and the CIA and Interpol, oh, and the KGB is after my tail too. Darling, if I was hiding out, I'd hardly be doing it in broad daylight. No, unfortunately it's a little more mundane than that. Yes, I travel with my work quite a bit, like that time in Paris, but it's all very legal, very corporate, all very moral and responsible. Well, I suppose it depends on which side of the human divide you're on.'

'How do you mean?'

'Well, I guess if you think it's morally acceptable to generate wealth for the few on the basis that eventually everybody gains because wealth flows down anyway, then what I do is perfectly morally acceptable, and I'm a hero.'

'Hm, now I'm really getting worried.'

'However, on the other hand, if you believe that wealth should be spread amongst everyone equally and that free markets have failed the majority then you'd probably want a nationalistic approach, and you may not fully appreciate what I do. In which case, I'm a villain.'

'Jesus Anthony, why couldn't you have been just a normal down-to-earth regular kinda criminal?'

'Ha-ha, I'm not a criminal darling, I'm just a businessman. I work in the world of mergers and acquisitions. We buy businesses, mostly when they're struggling, and we might asset strip them and then sell them on or merge them.'

'Sounds a bit like a second-hand car dealer to me.' But Maxine understood very well the business world that Anthony occupied, and capitalist or socialist didn't matter a fuck to her once some of life's wealth flowed her way, which unfortunately it hadn't now for a long time.

'Well, I'm not after your wealth, honey, I'm only after your sexy body. Ok, so you're not an international criminal, but what are you doing here? What are you running away from?'

'I'm not running away from anything, Max, but I will tell you why I'm here. So, you know that I'm married and with two kids. Well, the week before last when I was coming back from Europe and I arrived home early …'

And Anthony told Maxine the story fairly accurately as it happened but omitted the more sordid and salacious details.

'Oh, my poor baby. Jesus, that must have been awful, really traumatic for you, poor, poor baby. I'd fucking kill him.'

'Him? And not her?'

'Of course, him. Well. The two of them I suppose, but I'd mostly kill him. Patsy says that as men breathe, they lie.'

'And women don't?'

'Oh honey, you're so fucking naïve. Women scheme, men lie.' And then a scary thought struck her, and she jumped away from him. 'Jesus, you didn't kill her, did you?'

'No, for Christ's sake, but I tried to kill him.'

'Really? Seriously? You tried to kill him? How?'

'With roses, I tried to stab him to death with roses.' Maxine cracked up at the picture of Anthony laying into this naked cuckoo with a bunch of flowers, and her laughter was infectious and he couldn't stop himself from joining in. If the moment for Anthony was a cathartic one, it was downright erotic for his lover, and she grabbed his face and kissed him passionately and pulled him over on top of her, saying, 'Oh you poor lovely innocent silly baby, come here, I need you inside me *now*, I want to fuck your brains out.'

It was 9.00am the next morning and Maxine sat in the only armchair in the cabin, sipping a coffee and biting into a pastry. She was wearing her bra and panties. She had woken early and walked to the corner diner down the street and made her purchase. She sat in the chair and looked over at the sleeping man in the bed. *So, how does the story end*, she mulled, *what the fuck do I do now? Decision time, Max.* Anthony stirred and like a sleeping dog, opened one eye and liked what he saw, so he opened the other one and sleepily made a *hmmm* sound. She leaned over towards the bed and handed him a coffee and a croissant. 'It's a cappuccino; I think you said that you liked cappuccinos. The croissant has chocolate in it, you need to keep your energy levels up, an old man like you.'

'They must have been surprised in the café when you walked in dressed like that.'

'I wasn't dressed like this, I was naked. I just put these on now because I didn't want you to see my bare tits and get all hot and horny again.'

'Well then, they must have been *really* surprised, and where did you pull your money from then?'

'Oh, that would be telling, it's a cowgirl's secret.'

'Ok, well best keep them secrets secret. What're your plans for the day?'

'Once I've finished this five-star breakfast I'm outta here, busy day ahead, and you?'

'I'm in the office for the day. Do you want to meet for dinner later?'

'Well, I'm actually off this evening, but I'm supposed to be meeting a friend - a girlfriend by the way before you ask - but she's notoriously unreliable, she'll likely cancel. I'll buzz you later if that's ok?'

Anthony nodded and sipped his coffee and took a bite from his pastry and as he chewed, he said, 'I want to ask you something.'

'Yep.'

'I'm in Europe the week after next, I'd love it if you came with me?'

Maxine looked at him closely and sipped some more coffee. 'I've never been to Europe. I've hardly been outside Massachusetts in years.'

'Well, now's your chance.'

'I can't go. Where in Europe?'

'At this stage it looks like London.'

'Anyway, I can't go.'

'Why not? Are you on a wanted list too?'

'I don't have any clothes for Europe, sorry.'

'What? What are you talking about?'

'I told you Anthony, I don't have any clothes for London, or anywhere else in Europe.'

'Ah come on Max, stop joking around, you'll love it, and you'll meet my Irish friend, Jack.'

'Yes of course, Irish Jack. Thanks, but no thanks.'

'What? What's got into you? I thought you'd love the idea, and your flights are free because I've got enough air miles to take me around the planet ten times. And the hotel is paid for, and we can go into Boston over the next few days and I can buy you some clothes.'

'I don't need you to buy me clothes, Anthony.'

'But you said that you have no clothes for Europe, even though that's completely ridiculous.'

'Well, it might be ridiculous to you, but it's not to me and I'm not taking your money.'

'I tell you what, will you at least think about it?'

'I have thought about it, and thanks but no thanks.'

'Jesus, Max, you're bloody stubborn.'

'People say so.'

'Ok, do me a favour and please think about it, just today, that's all I ask.'

'Ok, I will. Now let me ask you a question. Did you love your wife before you found her in bed with this prick?' Anthony thought about it for a minute and answered honestly: 'Yes.'

And at that moment, Maxine knew how the story would end. She made her decision.

'Ok, now you think about something for the day, Anthony. She fucked up, partly because she was bored out of her head, mindless days on her own, mindless conversations with mindless airhead friends. You said it yourself, partly your fault. You were off living the dream, sauntering around Europe while your marriage was getting stranded in the doldrums. Stuck. Going-fucking-nowhere-stuck. And your idea of adding a little spice was a bunch of flowers that smelt of aircraft fuel from the fucking airport. Do yourself a favour, Anthony, go back to her. I'm sure she's a good woman, everyone deserves to fuck up at least once in a stuck marriage.'

Anthony was speechless. Where the hell had this come from? He felt like he'd been hit across the head by the proverbial four-by-two. Maxine gathered her clothes and got dressed.

'I gotta go hon, busy day ahead. I'll buzz you later about tonight.' She blew him a kiss as she pulled the door closed behind her.

But she never rang that day, or the next day. Anthony texted and called her phone half a dozen times but there was no return text and she didn't pick up. A couple of nights later he went to the Black Cat, but even before he had a chance to sit down, Patsy came over to him and said that Maxine had taken a few days off and she wasn't sure when she'd be rostered back on again. He was confused and disappointed but mostly just very sad, racking his brains to see what he'd said or done to piss her off. *Maybe she's got some family emergency, maybe she'll call next week,* he thought, unable even to convince himself. His ringing phone startled him. It was Jack calling to confirm the schedule for the Boston meetings later in the week and asking if he and Jessie would join him for dinner some evening as he hadn't seen her in almost six months. Anthony told him briefly that he and Jessie were on a break from each other, he didn't want to go into it over the phone, but he'd fill him in over dinner on one of the evenings.

* * * * *

Framingham was like a steam room that last week in May, with temperatures soaring to over 100 degrees and low thick clouds making for impossibly high humidity. Anthony came back from the office in sweat-soaked clothes. He stripped off the minute he got into the cabin and lay on his bed naked, and cooling in the noisy but barely effective air-conditioning. He'd spent the last couple of days between his office and his cabin, mooching around, lost, and failing miserably to keep himself interested or even occupied. Now he lay on the bed staring at a stain on the ceiling, and the more he concentrated on it, the more it seemed to be growing and moving and sneering down at him and he thought, *Christ I'm going off my game here, what the Christ am I doing with myself anyway, and what am I like.*

He flicked on the television and a guy from CNN was interviewing some arms expert who was warning about a catastrophe if Korea's nuclear-tipped missiles, capable of reaching the U.S., were commissioned. '*Jesus,*' Anthony barked, and he jabbed the TV control and switched channels and it landed on the BBC World News. A guy was doing a piece about world-wide Isis-sponsored terrorism. He detailed a couple of recent terrorist attacks in London and a recent one at a concert in Manchester. Anthony shouted, '*Christ,*' again and once more jabbed at the control. To his horror, he landed on Fox News and Trump was still mouthing off about how many people turned up to his inauguration, followed by mouthfuls of patriotic rhetorical nonsense, building walls and pulling up the drawbridges and blocking immigrants. And in the unbearable heat of the day, compounded by the toxicity on his TV, he swore louder: *'Jesus Christ!'* Suddenly, there was silence. Something stopped making noise, and for a second, he couldn't figure it out. Why has it gone all quiet so suddenly?

Then he realised that the air-conditioning had stopped and he immediately felt its effect as the room began to heat up quite quickly. He grabbed the phone by his bed and when Reception picked up he said his air-con had packed up, and asked if someone could come and fix it immediately. The woman apologised but said that the main central cooling unit had overheated and they were working on it but it would probably take a few hours to repair.

He said, 'But I'm bloody melting in here!'

She said, 'There's no need to take that tone with me, sir. We're all feeling the same and the technicians are working as hard as they can' and he slammed the receiver back on its cradle and shouted '*fuuuck!*' And he slumped back on his bed like a defeated man. And then, as if on cue, he heard Trump incredibly say that humans aren't causing global warming and that he wouldn't be going to the Paris Climate Accord in a couple of weeks. And as Anthony's room heated to boiling point, so did its defeated occupant and he caught the control and fired it as hard as he could against the man with the orange face on the TV. When the control simply bounced off the screen, he grabbed the glass on his bedside locker and, with greater anger and determination, he fired it too at the screen, which eventually stopped Trump talking. Anthony didn't realise that he had been screaming obscenities at the TV until a knock on his door interrupted him. *It's Max,* he thought, *thank Christ*. He jumped off the bed and rushed to the door and opened it in one move, but Maxine wasn't standing there. Instead, the hotel receptionist and a security guard stood there, and the receptionist blushed at the sight of a very naked but clearly distressed man. 'We've received complaints from other hotel guests about a disturbance, Mr. Castelletto, is everything all right?' The security guard was trying to look around the naked man to see if there was any problem in the room and then inquired, 'Is your TV damaged, sir?' When there was no response, the receptionist warned him that he needed to keep the noise level down and then emphasised gravely, 'And if we receive another complaint, sir, then we will have to escalate this to the next level.' But Anthony was gutted that it wasn't Max and so he just stood, stood and slumped, slumped in his sweating nakedness and simply said. 'Ok.' He quietly closed the door. It took a few seconds for the receptionist and the security officer to grasp that the audience was terminated.

Anthony turned around and walked into the shower cubicle, switched the control to cold, and, when the spray hit him, he slid down the tiled wall and sat on the tiled floor and stayed there for a long time with his head resting on his pulled-up knees, held together by his wrapped arms. Eventually the water stopped flowing and he was left shivering uncontrollably, paradoxically, in the heat of the day.

18

Boston, Thursday 25th May *(9 days to Nadir)*

Jessie was distraught. No, way beyond distraught, hysterical, unable to control her feelings, her emotions, crying, screaming, rocking back and forth on the ground, pulling at her hair like someone demented, rushing to the bathroom to be sick, talking out loud to herself, calling herself hideous names; you stupid bitch, you whore, cunt, fucking idiot, you dumb fuck, how could you be so stupid. At one point she had tried to be sick again but there was nothing left in her stomach and she just dry-retched and coughed and spat, with her head in the toilet bowl. Then, with great effort, and in an act of final resignation, she got up from her knees and went to the medicine cabinet and looked at the half dozen bottles lined up on the shelf. She reached for one in particular, her jar of Halcion with its active ingredient of benzodiazepine. There were maybe twenty or so tablets in the jar. *This would surely be enough,* she thought. She filled a glass with tap water and opened the lid of the jar and shook out half a dozen of the little blue tablets. She looked at herself in the mirror; *Christ you look shit girl, old, a hag, how did you think anyone could love you, you old delusional fool.* She threw the handful of tablets into her mouth and took a large swallow from the glass and in one action washed the pills down. As they were making their way down her oesophagus, she felt an urgent nausea building from her stomach as her abdominal muscles first contracted and then expanded to project the invaders back out of her system, and with such force and alacrity that she couldn't even make it to the toilet bowl, but instead spewed the tablets across the bathroom. She slumped to the floor again, bent over, kneeling, one arm hanging over the bath. She rested her face on the edge of the porcelain and absorbed its coolness. She was crying, sniffling, shaking.

Eventually, she found the strength to push herself up to her feet and made her way back into the bedroom. She sat at her dressing table facing her bed and on it, the scattered photographs. They had arrived earlier in a brown A4 envelope with her name and address hand-printed with thick black marker ink and she had taken the envelope with the rest of the post and a coffee to her bedroom to relax before she started her day proper. She opened the brown envelope first as it looked the most interesting. There was no note with it, just the four glossy photographs. The pictures were very similar: close-ups of the interior of a blue car with two people kissing in the front seats. The angles were slightly different in each picture and in one of them the whole car was in the frame. A date was imprinted on each, three days previously, and it was obvious that the date had been digitally embedded by the camera. On the back of each print was a single name handwritten in thick marker: Clara Goldberg.

She recognised Bill immediately, but she didn't recognise the blond woman with him. She knew that it wasn't his wife, as she had seen images of her on a number of occasions and anyway, Bill didn't love his wife, especially not that way. She looked at the date again, and she counted on her fingers three days back, Thursday, Wednesday, Tuesday. Just below the date in smaller print was the time, with a few minutes separating each photograph. One read 15.37.15. But she was talking to Bill on Tuesday afternoon, it must have been around two o'clock, pleading with him to meet her, but he'd said that he was in the city for the day. And then she looked at the photograph showing the image of the whole car again and she recognised where it had been taken. It was the Hopkinton State Park, where they had been together a number of times in the past, even as recently as last week. She picked up her cell phone and hit Bill's number, but he didn't answer. That was normal. Within a few minutes her phone buzzed and Bill said;

'Everything all right, honey? You know we talked about this before, it's probably not a good idea to call out of the blue like that.'

'Can I ask you a question and will you give me an honest answer, Bill?'

'Course honey, you know I'll always give you an honest answer.'

'Who is Clara Goldberg and why were you kissing her out in Hopkinton Park on Tuesday?'

Except for a little heightened breathing there was silence at the other end for a few seconds and then the line went dead. She rang his number again and again but all she got was an engaged signal. She felt her stomach turn and just made it to the toilet bowl.

Now she sat at the dressing table, her head resting on her arms. She felt humiliated and ashamed that she had actually tried to end her life. And she felt sad and bitter, but at no one except herself. She lifted her head and looked in the mirror and mumbled: 'What a horrible and selfish woman you are, and you didn't even think of the kids.' She let her head fall again on her arms and cried and cried, and then, when she stopped crying, she cried some more. Obviously, Anthony had sent the pictures, or most probably had them sent by one of his minions. She climbed onto the bed and lay back over the covers. She picked up one of the pictures and with obsessive care tore it in half and then quarters and so on until she couldn't tear it any smaller. Then she gathered the pieces in her clenched hand and fired them across her bedroom and they burst like confetti over her bed and on the floor, and she methodically did the same with each of the remaining photographs. And then she climbed under the covers and fell asleep.

Jessie slept through the morning and stirred at 12.30, awakened by her phone buzzing. It was her friend Andrea whom she was supposed to meet for coffee at noon at *Roma*. She didn't pick up; she'd call her later. There were also two missed calls from her lawyer's office. Crap, she'd missed her 10.00am appointment. 'Ah, fuck him … fuck 'em all.'

But after a little while she did rouse herself and made it through the confetti of tattered dreams to the shower. She felt a little more human after twenty minutes under the spray. When she came out, she noticed the opened bottle of Halcion and thought again about the kids. She thanked Christ for her delicate stomach and nausea. She went downstairs in her dressing gown and made herself a coffee, called Andrea and pleaded with her to meet later in the afternoon at *Roma*.

'I hate to be the one to tell you darling, but you look fucked.'

'Thanks friend, I've worked very hard to look this bad actually.'

Andrea had been up to date with the events so far and Jessie filled her in on the postman's present this morning.

'Ouch, that's horrible, what a prick.'

'Yeah, I can't believe it that he's seeing another woman.'

'No, I'm talking about Anthony, what a prick to do that to you.'

'Well, I'm only guessing that it was Anthony.'

'Of course it was the prick, who else would or could do it? He had all the other pictures and emails too.'

'Anyway, Andrea, I'm not talking about Anthony here, I actually believe that he did it to protect me. I'm talking about Bill, I loved him, for God's sake. I've jeopardised everything for him and now I find out that he's cheating with another woman.'

'Ah honey, listen to yourself. First of all, you didn't jeopardise everything for him, you jeopardised it for yourself. Secondly it's all just a game, there's no love in this stuff.'

'How do you mean it's just a game?'

'I mean that it's all just a fabrication, Jess, me and Jeff from the club, you and Bill. Sandra and her tennis coach, whatever his name is. It's just a game, honey, and the rules are clear. Rule number one: it's not real, rule two: nobody takes it seriously, rule three: don't confuse it with real life, and rule four, and this is the most important rule, don't confuse fucking with love.'

'Jesus Andrea, you're so fucking cynical.'

'I might be, darling, but right now I'm not the one with a broken heart, or the one who looks like something that the cat just dragged in. Tell me Jess, if Bill wasn't faithful to his wife, why in the name of everything that's holy would he be faithful to you?'

'Because he said that he loved me, and when we did make love I could feel it in his passion, his honesty. We're not all like you and Jeff, you know.'

'Oh, you poor delusional baby, come here to me.' Andrea reached over and gave her friend a long warm embrace. 'It's a game, Jess, and Bill knew the rules and his only fault was that he assumed that you knew them too.'

'But there's gotta be more to it than that, Andrea. There's gotta be some meaning to it.'

'Think of it like a Hollywood film set, darling. On the facade there's all this fantastic detail, magnificent colour, the picture of perfection. But around the back it's just sheets of chipboard held up by screws and planks, there's nothing.'

'Hang on; are you talking about the affair or about the marriage?'

'Both, actually. I mean I guess when we get married first, we're idealistic, and we have every intention of making it work and to not make the same mistakes our parents made. But then the kids come along and the drudgery kicks in and we inevitably grow into our parents, because we were always them anyway. And the good and exciting stuff like making a home and a family eventually morphs its way into the film set.'

'So, have I lost them both for good, do you think? I mean Anthony and Bill?'

'You never had Bill, that was the illusion. So, he's gone, forget about him, put it down to experience. He was a bit of excitement and a good fuck and that's it.'

'And Anthony?'

'Hm, that's different. Even though your marriage has become stale and something of a façade too you can probably rescue it. I couldn't be bothered rescuing mine, I'm quite happy playing the game, as is Jonathon. He's happy to keep the marriage intact, turn a blind eye, he knows the rules too and it suits us both. But you're different from me,

Jess. And so is Anthony, so go after him honey, chase him, start again, fuck him like you fucked Bill.'

'And the infidelity?'

'Your infidelity wasn't the problem, girl, it's just a symptom of those other things that weren't working in your marriage. Like I say, go after him, get him back, and prove all of us cynics wrong.'

* * * * *

That very same evening, less than twenty miles away in downtown Boston, Anthony was hosting Jack at the *Lafayette* restaurant on Beacon Hill. Jack had flown in on Wednesday afternoon, but this was the first chance that the two friends had had the opportunity to have some time alone. The waiter served them their dinners and topped up their wine glasses and, as soon as he left, Jack continued with the conversation. 'I can't believe that it was only this day two weeks ago that Marianne walked back into my life, it seems like a very long time ago.'

'Yeah, I know what you mean, time seems to have warped or something since I left you in Dublin and look at the shit-storm that I walked into.'

'Both of us, my friend, both of us.'

They had brought each other up to date on their respective dramas of the intervening weeks and now that they were both in the trenches, albeit in different war zones, there was a freedom to their conversation. There were no taboo subjects, a new openness prevailed, anything and everything was up for discussion.

'You know, I'm always fascinated by the vagaries of life, Jack. Like the idea of the sliding doors moment when an inconsequential decision turns out to totally change your future. For instance, because I decided to take an earlier flight my life has been altered irrevocably.'

'Yeah, you mean like our Charlie Hebdo moment. I know what you mean but I'm not convinced. These little so-called sliding door things can happen a dozen times every day of our lives, or, to put it another way, maybe that's just how our lives work. Maybe they're the little nudges that keep us between the ditches. It's how we stay on our chosen path.'

'You surely don't mean that I chose a path which included me walking in on Jessie?'

'No, of course not, what I mean is that maybe it was always going to happen, and changing flights was just one of the sliding door moments to get there, one of the little nudges.'

'So, you think that it was fate then, and not chance? I wouldn't have put you down as a fatalist.'

'Well, not really fate. I suppose I believe that we chart our own destinies. That's not to say that shit doesn't happen from out of the blue. You know what they say, if you want to give God a good laugh, just tell him your plans. Look, what I mean is that maybe the groundwork for what happened was laid by yourself and Jessie and how you treated your relationship, like maybe it was inevitable that there was going to be an implosion.'

'So, you're suggesting that the only unknown was *when* and not *if* it was going to happen?'

'Listen Anthony, I believe that, in the main, we control our lives and our own destiny. Sometimes we get surprised when something comes out of the blue but then when we actually put it under the microscope, we see that we should have seen it coming a long way off.'

'Then we're the architects of our own misfortune? Ok, well how does that theory work in your case, with your son, are you saying that you should have seen this coming?'

'Well, yes, I guess I am. Not specifically the deliverance of a child whom I knew nothing about, but some kind of deliverance, some reckoning. If I had been a bit more honest with myself when I was younger things might have turned out differently. I'm recently realising that my memories of key events are somewhat different to what I now actually know to be true, and I don't know why that is. But I presume that I've filtered my memory files to suit the narrative that I've written for myself. I've deleted or hidden stuff away. Like, why did I hide from Marianne when she came looking for me in Galway?'

'But you didn't know that she was looking for you, did you?'

'My memory says that I didn't, but the facts say that I went underground, disappeared, and my gut tells me that I did hide from her.'

'But why, why would you hide from her?'

'Dunno my friend, maybe deep down I knew that I'd fucked up. But because she couldn't find me, she consequently told the big lie and she sowed the seeds of her own destiny, to which of course I was inextricably tied, and which inevitably led to this moment. It's cause and effect. Like when we humans first realised that we existed, we very quickly woke up to our mortality.'

'Wow, not sure that I agree, Jack. You can talk about destiny and everything but at the end of the day, it will have been Jessie's infidelity that ends our relationship.'

'Well, I wonder about that, Anthony. Let me play the devil's advocate for a sec; have you ever strayed, ever been unfaithful?'

'Uh, not really.'

'Oh dear, that sounds ominous, how do you mean not really?'

'Well, there was this one-night stand a long time ago.'

'Go on.'

'You want me to tell you?'

'Of course, I want to understand your motivation.'

'Well, it was before you and I met so it must have been about twelve, thirteen years ago. I was in Berlin for a few days on business and I remember on the second day when I'd finished work I went to the hotel lounge for my usual poison before dinner. The place was fairly quiet and I was sitting at the bar for a while when this woman came in and sat just a few stools from me. As she was ordering her drink, I looked at her in the display mirror behind the bar and she just happened to look at me and I kinda stupidly raised my hand and said 'hi' to the mirror. She laughed and turned to me and introduced herself and said that she'd seen me at breakfast that morning. Anyway, we got chatting. Her name was Sylvia and she was a professor of mathematics from the Stuttgart University. She was in Berlin on business and due to leave the next day. She was stunning, Jack. Sophisticated, funny, intelligent, her English was impeccable, better than mine. After a couple of drinks, we moved to the restaurant and had dinner together and it was as exciting as a first date. I was flirting shamelessly with her, but it was like kicking an open door. Anyway, after dinner we left the restaurant to go to our rooms, but once the elevator doors closed, we were all over each other. I don't know who made the first move, it seemed to happen naturally, without any awkwardness. We went to her room and virtually ripped each other's clothes off. It was intensely erotic and incredibly sexual, no preamble, very few words were spoken, no terms of endearment. Later, I left her room sometime around four or five. She was asleep, I didn't wake her.

I got a few hours' sleep myself and when I went down for breakfast in the morning I was praying that she wouldn't be there, and at the same time hoping that I'd see her. But there was no sign of her. We'd swapped email addresses the previous evening and after a few days I sent her an email, just to touch base. She sent me back an mail with just 'Hi' and attached a picture of her family; herself, her husband and her child. Even I didn't need to read between the lines, I got the message. For months afterwards I felt guilty and horrible that it had happened. I hated myself for betraying Jessie. I had always sworn that something like that would never happen to me, other men yes, but not me. But what annoyed me the most, Jack was that I knew in my heart and soul that all through dinner, all through the evening, I wanted it to happen, I wanted her. I had premeditated it.'

'And what made you do it?'

'Christ, I don't know; drink, horniness, opportunity, my ego was massaged? Maybe I thought I deserved some attention, maybe I was lonely … I don't bloody know, Jack.'

'So, isn't that the same as what Jessie did?'

'Christ man, she's been screwing a guy for over two years, and she says she loves him. That's a bit different than a one-night stand, don't you think?'

'Hey bud, trust me I'm not judging here. I'm certainly not one to judge. But let's face it, infidelity is infidelity, it's kind of binary. I don't think that the definition includes a 'how often' or a 'how long' clause, does it? I'm just saying that maybe you need to cut both of yourselves some slack, the reasons why you both strayed aren't very dissimilar.'

'So, you say that you're not one to judge, what does that mean?'

'It means exactly what it says. Bea and I have been apart on two occasions, only for a few months each time, and I met someone very briefly the second time we were separated.'

'But if you were apart then surely, you're entitled to meet someone?'

'No, no. The reason we were apart was that Bea was unwell. She went through periods of clinical depression with a sprinkling of paranoia thrown in for good measure. She's been afflicted with it for most of her adult life, certainly as long as I've known her, it comes and goes. But back then she had lots of dark and negative thoughts about me and the kids and her work partner and her friends, and bouts of melancholy. It was she who left the nest. She went back to Paris, stayed with her mother both times and, in fairness to her mother, she contacted me every other day, keeping me updated. And of course, credit to herself, she worked her way out of it each time with the help of a very good psychiatrist in Paris, and of course meds. It's fairly full-on when it happens, everything gets dysfunctional, fucked up. The second time it happened I was going through some crap myself. Anyway, about a month after she left I met this woman in London. She was an exec with a company we were going to acquire but which we never did in the end and I called her up and asked her out. We dated for a few weeks. She was a lovely woman and I enjoyed the fling while it lasted but, to be honest, I wasn't exactly crying when it finished.'

'And who finished it, you or her?'

'Oh, she did. She told me over lunch one day that although I was a nice guy, she kinda would prefer to date someone who was fully present all the times when we were together. Present in the moment I think is what she said. Well, I thought that I was, but clearly not. Anyway, that was that. Bea never knew, and until now, no one else knew.'

'And why did you do it?'

'Ah, purely selfish reasons, Anthony. I told myself that I needed it. I was lonely, and I deserved it and anyway, what harm was I doing. But of course, even though Bea never knew, I was still doing harm, harm to myself and to our relationship.'

'Hm, don't know, bud, and I'm certainly not quite sure if I'd call that infidelity. Maybe you need to take your own advice and cut *yourself* some slack.'

The conversation was interrupted when the waiter arrived and cleared their plates and topped up their glasses. When he left Jack picked up the chat:

'Yeah well, anyway, enough of philosophising. Tell me, this Maxine, she sounds amazing, and you haven't seen her since when?'

'A full week, this day last week actually. But you're right, she's fantastic, so down to earth, clever, funny, no demands, no veneer, honest, sexy. I even asked her to travel to London with me next week, but she said no.'

'Why not?'

'Oh, I've no idea, she said that she doesn't have the clothes for London, but obviously it's something else.'

'Know what we should do, Anthony? We should get a cab right now to Framingham, go to her bar and surprise her.'

'Christ, no, Jack, are you mad, no way, man. I'm never ever gonna surprise anyone again for the rest of my life. Anyway, the ball is in her court now. If she wants to contact me, she knows where I am.'

'Yeah, ok, just kidding. Listen, I got a call from Marianne earlier in the week and she's in London next week visiting her son and grandchild …'

Anthony cut in, 'You mean *your* son and grandchild, you'd better get used to it, buddy.'

'Yeah, yeah, ok, my son and grandchild. Anyway, she wondered on the off chance if I was there too and if so, could we meet for dinner. Well, I don't want to meet her on my own so would you mind if you and I had dinner with her one evening?'

'An attractive woman for dinner? Go for it, my friend. But by the way, please no drama, I've had enough drama in the last two weeks to last me a lifetime.'

* * * * *

At that same time, but three thousand miles east of Boston, Marianne lay curled up on her bed in South Dublin, wide awake in the small hours of the morning and listening to Puccini, who was competing with the noise playing havoc in her head. It felt like her tinnitus had notched up another octave and moved to a higher frequency. But although she was denied sleep, she virtually purred like Romeo, her tomcat, at what she had achieved over the last few months. Firstly, she'd had to find Jack, track him down. In reality, this wasn't too difficult considering she knew where he had lived in Galway, and she knew some of his old friends. A casual browsing on social and business media and a few contrived calls to unsuspecting people gave her most of Jack's post-college life, including his early professional career with Accenture and his move to Lyon. It was Uncle Marty in fact who brought her right up to date and gave her Jack's whereabouts in Spiddal when she rang, claiming to be from the central statistics office. And with a little gentle prodding he also gave her Jack's family circumstances, his wife's name, and the names and ages of their three children (he got all three ages wrong). Then Marianne struck lucky one day when she stumbled on a photograph in *The Times* of Jack with some colleagues, as they were announcing the successful completion of an international business deal. That trail led to his Dublin offices on the Grand Canal Docks and, after a few calls to some of the better hotels in Dublin, she discovered where he stayed when he was in town. But the *piece de resistance* was when her friend Susan was approaching her fiftieth birthday. Marianne offered to organise her party and suggested the Westin Hotel as an ideal venue. She obviously couldn't be sure if Jack was going to be there that evening, but the way she figured, she probably had about a twenty percent chance of bumping into him. As luck would have it, he turned up, unaware of what lay in store for him.

Yes indeed, it's true to say that Marianne did keep an open file on Jack, a very open and active file (aka stalking), and not for her own benefit of course, as she convinced herself, *only for the benefit of my son*. A couple of weeks after meeting Jack in the Westin, she made a few calls to his Dublin and London offices and very easily ascertained that he was, in fact, due in London the following week. She then called Freddie and virtually invited herself to their home for three nights, to arrive Tuesday and leave on Friday. She also mentioned to him that she was meeting Jack for dinner on one of the nights and that he *might* also be in a position to meet Freddie at some point during the week. Next she called Jack and told him that she was in London for a few nights the following week and, on the very off chance that he might be working from the London office, that it would be lovely if they could meet for a coffee or even dinner some evening, obviously just to chat about Freddie and Fabeena. Jack gave no commitment, but Marianne could sense his interest in the potential opportunity.

As Puccini faded into the small hours of the morning, Marianne purred again in self-satisfaction, uncurled herself, and loving that her eyelids were beginning to feel luxuriously heavy, she slipped into a deep and satisfying slumber.

* * * * *

While Marianne was asleep in her south Dublin home, Freddie, Saahira and little Fabeena slept soundly in their modest terraced house in east London, unaware of the danger lurking outside their windows. It was 2.30am, and as he sat in his old red car parked across the road, Khuram Butt continued to mentally construct the pieces of his plan. Earlier that evening, once the last of the gym members had left and he had locked up the Ilford Fitness Centre for the night, he had met with his two associates in the alleyway behind the Centre. There they had discussed the various elements of his plan, especially the timing and the list of equipment that was needed. They decided that it should happen over a weekend, a time when it would be most busy. As this was Thursday, this upcoming weekend would be too soon - they weren't yet fully prepared. Possibly the following weekend, and so the first Saturday in June was pencilled in. They made a list of the various items that each needed to acquire the week ahead, and then, as always, they knelt together and prayed to Allah for a successful outcome to their holy mission.

He now slouched in his car, in the moonlight, looking up at the doctor's darkened bedroom window. He said her name out loud; *Saahira Butt*. He liked the sound of her name attached to his. And although he might have been a fantasist, he wasn't a stupid man. He knew that they might never be together but he still occasionally liked to spend a little time outside her home at night-time, and always with the possibility of stealing a glimpse of her through the windows - anyway, it meant spending less time in his own home, his prison.

19

London, Thursday 01st June *(2 days to Nadir)*

I looked at Anthony pleadingly; 'c'mon bud, , let's get out of here, I've a pain in my brain from looking at figures. Anyway, I need a drink and some food.'

'Ok, ok, let me just try and finish this page, Jack, these numbers are bugging the crap out of me, what these guys are saying about the margins just isn't adding up.'

'But you've been saying that from the start my friend. C'mon, *please,* it's half seven, we can pick it up in the morning.'

'Yeah, ok.'

We closed our laptops and bagged them and headed out onto the busy street still buzzing with commuters. It was a balmy, dusty evening and we walked the short distance to the Tower Bridge Hilton. Although my apartment was in Holborn I had decided to stay in the Hilton for convenience as Anthony was in town. He had flown in on Monday morning and we'd worked flat out over the last few days and evenings to cover every thread of the due diligence. Despite what we were led to believe from HQ, this project was turning into a ball-breaker and we had extended our stay in town to Friday night, including an option on Saturday if it was needed. I gave Bea a quick call from my room while I changed and met Anthony in the bar for an aperitif.

'So, what do you think?'

He didn't have to give it much thought. 'What do I think? I think we'll be lucky if we're getting out on Sunday.'

'Fuck, that's what I was afraid you were gonna say, and unfortunately I agree.'

'How's Bea and the kids?'

'Yeah, she's good, they're all good. She sends her love.'

'You're a lucky man, Jack.'

'Yeah, I guess I am, bud, if I could just figure out how to deal with this new-found family of mine.'

'You haven't met him yet, have you?'

'No, no. I told you that I saw him one evening, or more accurately I stalked him one evening. Once I saw him, that was it, I was a goner. But I really don't know how to deal with it, I mean home-wise with Bea and the kids.'

'Yeah, but sometimes you just gotta go for these things, you know. Throw it all up in the air and let the pieces fall wherever they will. I know you're a bit of a control freak, Jack, but you can't control everything all of the time, that's one thing I'm learning.'

'And so, how're you coping, any contact with Jessie? It must be what, three weeks ago at this stage, is it?'

'Yep, three weeks tomorrow. No contact really, except through our attorneys, but not much more. I did meet her last weekend as I was getting some stuff from the house. It wasn't planned, and it was my own fault, she was supposed to be out of the house while I was there but I arrived early and so we shared an awkward fifteen minutes.

'And the kids, how are they taking it?'

'Yeah, they're ok. They don't know the gory details, but they have a fair idea about what happened. I think that they see it as a temporary little blip.'

'And have you decided what you're gonna do - with Jessie, I mean - can you see yourself getting back with her?'

'Ah, I don't know, Jack, if you were to push me on it right now, I'd say no, but sometimes I really miss her. Funny thing is, it was nice to see her last week, you know.'

'And what about Maxine, any more contact from her?'

'Nah, nothing. Man, she was so good and easy to be with, I sometimes wonder if that's the future for me, a woman like Maxine.'

'When you say a woman *like* Maxine, well you've found her, she's Maxine. But maybe you're just on the bounce Anthony, reacting from what happened, looking for the opposite of what you had and possibly

Maxine gives you all that right now. Maybe she's looking for something too, like a commitment or something. Does she know your situation at this stage?'

'Yep, she knows exactly what happened and how it happened. And, believe it or not, she says that I should take Jessie back.'

'Wow, like turkeys voting for Christmas. She's some woman, my friend.'

'Yeah, I know, but we're living in different worlds. Anyway, enough already, so, are we still meeting your ex tomorrow night?'

'She's not my ex, ya chancer. Surely there's a statute of limitations on when an ex is no longer an ex.'

'Nope buddy, by the very definition of the word an ex is always an ex. Bit of a coincidence that she's in London the same week as you, no?'

'Hm, not really. Apparently, she comes over regularly. You can get very cheap flights from Dublin to London these days, thanks to Ryanair. It's probably cheaper to get from Dublin to London than it is to go from Dublin to Galway.'

'And what about the Brexit factor, will it change all that?'

'Ah, I've no idea. It certainly won't make it cheaper or easier anyway. I still can't believe that they're gonna go through with it. But you know what Anthony, you can almost feel it in the air over here, something's changed. I never thought I'd say this, but even having lived here years ago I'm slightly more conscious of being a Johnny Foreigner these days, although it's probably all in my own head. You know, I remember the first time we came to London when I was a teenager; there was my mother, Lizzie, and me. We were visiting an uncle of my dad's family in Dagenham, Uncle Jimmy. He worked at the Ford Plant like a lot of Irish emigrants in London, the lucky ones. We used to call them the Dagenham Yanks because when they visited their relatives in Ireland they'd be splashing around cash and telling us how good their lives were in London.'

'Aha, just like the Irish Americans you mean?'

'Exactly. Anyway, we were only here for a week, but I remember being very self-conscious of being Irish. Me and Lizzie would put on English accents in the shops for the craic, but deep down we felt kinda ashamed or something about being Irish, certainly felt inferior. But I think it said more about us than it did them. I don't know; being Irish in London back then wasn't comfortable. It was the times of the IRA bombings in England, and I suppose that's what the Irish accent represented. But now I get a chill when I listen to May or Johnson or that fucking Dickensian Rees-Mogg, and their right-wing cronies bristling with their patriotic rhetoric rants. I tell you Anthony, this is a good country, one of the best in the world, and it'd be a shame if Brexit made it a less welcoming place.'

'Yeah, you're right, I agree.'

They were thoughtful for a while, then Anthony broke the silence.

'Listen, apropos of nothing, remember last week in Boston at dinner and we were talking about destiny and fate and everything?'

'Yes, of course.'

'Well, there's something that I never told you about before.'

'Yeah, go on.'

'Remember our Charlie Hebdo narrow escape in Paris?'

'Eh, of course I remember, how could I forget?'

'Well, for me it was *déjà vu*. The same thing had happened to me before.'

'Seriously? Go on, tell me.'

'It was really weird, like spooky you know. So, a number of years ago I was due to fly to L.A., to the head office of the company I worked with at the time. I had my ticket and everything, but - and this never happened to me before or since - I missed the flight. I never miss flights, Jack. I was driving through the Tunnel on the way to Logan airport and there was a crash ahead of me, literally only about four cars ahead and it was at least an hour before I drove free from the accident. I remember looking at my watch when I got to the airport carpark and it was 7.15, which still gave me thirty minutes to get my flight.

I thought I'd be able to make it so I literally ran to the ticket desk to get a boarding pass. Back then, and you'll remember this, they might even hold the flights for you if you were delayed. Anyway, in spite of, or maybe because of, me haranguing the lady behind the desk, she wouldn't issue me with a boarding pass; she said the departure gate was closed. I remember that the flight was even running late so she could easily have let me through. She was being a bitch; she said the gate was closed and that was it. I stood there, boiling over, you know my temper sometimes, but there was nothing I could do about it. So, I missed the flight.'

'So, you missed a flight, happens to people all the time, Anthony, what was the big deal?'

'Yeah, I know, but the big deal was that it just wasn't any flight. It was American Airlines Flight 11, and it was Tuesday morning, Sept 11th, 2001. It was the first hijacked flight that day and it was the one they crashed into the North Tower.'

'Jesus Christ Anthony, I never knew, why haven't you told me this before?'

'Oh, I don't know Jack, I rarely if ever talk about it, it had a profound effect on me, even to this day. I still sometimes get these nightmares, crazy dreams, waking up in a state, sweating, distressed. At the time it took me a couple of months to get back on a plane again.'

'But I've flown with you loads of times and I've never sensed anything?'

'Yeah, yeah I know, I've no problem whatsoever flying these days. But unfortunately, it doesn't stop the nightmares.'

'What kind of nightmares?'

'Well, it's the same mad one, Jack. I'm in the plane and the hijackers have taken over the cabin, and they're beating passengers and stabbing them and they're trying to get into the cockpit. I'm in my seat and I've taken off my seatbelt and I want to attack them, but my body won't move. I can't get out of my seat; my legs feel paralysed or something. And no matter how hard I try, no matter how hard I struggle, I can't move off my seat. And the hijackers are laughing at me, "come and get us you kafir coward, you got no balls, you Americans are weak," and the other passengers are shouting at me to get up, get up, do something … but I can't, I can't move … or maybe I won't move. Maybe I'm afraid to get up.'

'Wow, I'm so sorry, my friend, I didn't know, I never guessed. Christ, that's awful. And how does the dream end?'

'Well, even though it's a little different every time, it ends mostly with one of the terrorists coming at me with a knife or a gun, and he's laughing at me, and I know I'm helpless and I'm gonna die. And just at that point, every time, I wake up. I wake up in a sweat, sometimes shouting, the sheets are soaked. If I'm at home, Jessie is calming me; I've obviously woken her with my hysterics.'

'Christ Anthony, that's a tough ride. And did you ever get counselling or anything?'

'Yeah, I went to a couple of sessions at the time. The guy said that it's probably some kind of guilt complex; that I believe that I should've died too, I shouldn't have survived, and in my subconscious I'm still trying to fight my guilt, fight my demons.'

'But why would you have guilt? You didn't choose to miss the flight, and anyway, even if you were on the plane, there's nothing you could have done, there's nothing anyone could have done. And that's not hypothetical, unfortunately we know the actual outcome.'

'But that's exactly the point, Jack. If I *had* been on the flight, would I *actually* have done anything? Would I have had the courage to take on the hijackers, to put my life in danger, the courage to stand up and fight? And I think my subconscious is telling me that I wouldn't.'

'But that's ridiculous, Anthony. First of all, you weren't on the flight, and secondly, what would any of us do in the same situation? None of us knows how we'd react. We might like to think that we'd do the right thing, but no one ever knows until we come face to face with it, and anyway, who the fuck knows what's the right thing to do.'

'Hm, maybe, maybe. The guys at my company, and Jessie of course, thought that I was on the flight, they assumed that I was dead until I was eventually able to get through to them.'

'Jaysas, that must have been dreadful on Jessie.'

'It was of course. You know, I haven't had the nightmare in a while, Jack, but I had it last night. I woke up in a state, in a sweat, looking for Jessie, reaching for her in the bed, calling her. And then the whole screw-up of our marriage sank in … *again*.'

Jack put his hand on his friend's shoulder and empathically offered; 'that's tough Anthony, I'm truly sorry, sorry for you, and sorry for Jessie. But it's early days my friend. And things change. One thing is guaranteed, things always change'

'Yeah, you're right, I guess.'

They sipped their drinks and then, a little more light-heartedly, Anthony said; 'I've got an uncle, Uncle Syl, you met him actually, Jack, a great guy. He lives out on the seafront and even though he's ninety-two he still keeps his hand in the family business. When I was in my thirties, maybe thirty-four or five or something, we were chatting over a beer one evening about life and stuff. My dad had died when I was young and Syl kinda became my father-figure, my mentor. So, this day I'm asking him about when does life all work out. You know when you're in your thirties and you've a lotta shit going on and somewhere in your subconscious you kinda believe maybe that at some stage in life there'll be a landing, things will get sorted, get resolved. And you know what he said? He said: "Some things never get resolved, some things never get worked out, we die with some shit unresolved, and you know why? Because we die in the middle of our lives. Even when we're old, we die in the middle of our lives and we still have a lot of unresolved stuff going on." And then he said; "the truth is messy, Anthony, and that's why life is messy."'

'Hm, interesting. Smart guy, your uncle Syl, he's as smart as you're lucky I think, considering that missed 9/11 flight, someone must have been praying for you, bud.'

'Yeah, I guess. But when you add it to the Charlie Hebdo get-out-of-jail card, you kinda start believing in destiny, with a capital D. Like when it's not your time to die, it just ain't your time to die.'

'Hm, that's a little too fatalistic for me, Anthony. But on a positive note, it seems to me like you're a pretty safe guy to be hanging around with.'

'Yeah, I guess, well until it's my time anyway.'

'Well then at that point,' Jack said humorously, 'I'll just get the fuck away from you.'

20

London, Friday 02nd June *(1 day to Nadir)*

The next day in the office was, to use a technical term, brutal. Anthony was frustrated that he couldn't nail the discrepancies. He was convinced that they were hiding something, not quite a second set of books, but the margins were too fat for a business like this. *They're making components for fucks sake, high volumes, low margins, and the margins here are too big.* Naturally the value of the business was set not just on their volume sales but as a multiple of their profits. And with these numbers, this acquisition would cost almost twice the value that it was worth, at least according to Anthony, who had a nose for these things. So, while he was interrogating the books, I was interrogating senior management, who seemed intent to obscure and obfuscate at every turn.

At lunchtime I got a call from Marianne to confirm the dinner that evening.

'It's not too late to invite Freddie along.'

'I told you, Marianne, I'm not ready to meet Freddie yet, and anyway when I meet him, I'll want to meet him on my own.'

'Yeah, ok, well if you change your mind just give me a call.'

'Listen; see you at the Humble Grape at eight. By the way, you know I'll be with Anthony.'

'Yep, you told me, I'm looking forward to seeing him again, looking forward to seeing you again too, Jack.'

The afternoon went much like the morning, Anthony and his financial advisors in the boardroom poring over printouts and financial analysis, and me and my team interviewing company executives. Depending on the agreed market value, the executives were looking at a major pay-day, and so naturally it was in their interests that the worth of the Enterprise be maximised. But even though the discussions were generally cordial, there seemed as if there was some underlying energy. It wasn't what was being said, it was what was left unsaid, what was being held back. Towards the end of the day, I wandered in to Anthony in the boardroom with two coffees and we chatted and reviewed our notes and the day's progress. We were both weary and stressed from the tension and the drudgery of the day.

'They're like smiling assassins, Anthony, all grins to my face but my back is feeling very unloved.'

'Yeah I agree. I just know that we're not getting everything.'

'And do you feel the underlying tension around the place or am I imagining it?'

'Yep it's weird, there's definitely an agenda at play but we've another few days. Hopefully it'll be enough to get completely under the bonnet.'

'Anyway, enough for today, we'd better get moving or we'll invite the ire of the temperamental Marianne … and that's not a pretty sight, I'd imagine.'

We arrived at the Humble Grape on Fleet St. at 7.00 and ordered drinks at the bar while we waited for our guest to arrive.

'You know that this is my last one, Jack.'

'Presumably we're not talking about your gins and tonic.'

'My last assignment, asshole.'

'Yeah, just kidding, but I was hoping that you'd push back the decision until you get some clarity on Jessie. Like two life-changing decisions at one time isn't recommended, as you well know.'

'I don't need any clarity on Jessica. I can't unsee what I saw, and anyway, I'm only making one decision, the other one was made for me.'

'And what about the firm? I presume you haven't given them a whisper, or they'd have probably been on to me to get you to change your mind.'

'No, not a word. As far as they're concerned, I'm over in Chicago next month, assuming we get this finalised this week.'

'And what about the shoe business, did you have any thoughts about joining them? From what I gather they'd welcome you there with open arms.'

'Eh, I keep telling you, it's not the *shoe* business, it's the *footwear design* business,' he corrected me. 'Ah sure Uncle Syl would die a happy man even at the thought of me working there, but no, I'm definitely not looking at that as an option. But listen, I'm in no rush to get into anything for a while, I don't need the income, I'll take my time and maybe do something very different. And you know what, Jack, there's something about Maxine that has given me a whole different perspective on things, a kind of a new freedom of thinking.'

As he was talking, I noticed Marianne entering, and whispered, 'Well, speaking of a different perspective, our guest has just arrived.' I waved over to her.

'Hi guys, sorry I'm a little late.'

She offered her cheek for Anthony to kiss and then did so similarly to me.

'Great to meet you again Anthony, you're both looking very smart.'

'Likewise, Marianne, you're looking very lovely yourself.' Anthony gushed.

I quipped, 'Ok boys and girls, enough of the mutual adoration. It's good to see you, Marianne, what's your poison?'

'A dry martini please, Jack. So, how is your trip going, Anthony, are you always away? Does your wife ever get to see you?'

Ouch, I thought.

'Ah, well yes, occasionally, I guess …' Anthony mumbled, as he studied his shoes.

'And what about you, Jack, you must be travelling a lot too, are you ever home?'

'Hm, probably travelling about three weeks in four, same as this guy. But the one week at home is actually in Dublin. But it's ok, it'd be very rare that I wouldn't be home for the weekend. Mind you, this could be one of them. So how about you, how often are you in London?'

'As often as they'll have me aha, maybe once every two months. I'd come more often except I don't want to outstay my welcome.'

After we were shown to our table and we'd ordered our meals, we dispensed with the small talk carcass and went straight for the big beasts. Anthony, either provocatively or innocently, threw the bait to snare the elephant in the room.

'So, you guys have a son together, that must be interesting?'

I had just sipped some wine, and I actually spluttered it. What the fuck was Anthony doing, especially after I had warned him earlier to stay miles away from any subject of a 'sensitive' nature, like, Freddie. Marianne couldn't believe her luck, and not one to let an opportunity go, she dived straight in.

'Ah, Jack told you, that's great Anthony. It's really good that we can chat about it openly. In fact, this is the first real conversation about our son and granddaughter that Jack and I have had. It's quite liberating.'

Anthony gulped as he felt his instep being crushed by my heel.

'Well, yes, of course Anthony knows about our son, and he knows the circumstances of when it happened, and he also knows the sensitivity around it.'

I could actually hear Anthony gulp a second time.

'And which sensitivity is that, Jack?' Marianne asked me with a faux innocence.

'Well, let's be honest, Marianne, every sensitivity in the book for fuck's sake. Like my wife and my own kids, like me myself, like the lad and his daughter.'

'You mean *your* son and *your* granddaughter surely, Jack. The only sensitivity is the anxiety in your own head. I had it for over twenty years before I told anyone and trust me, people get used to the idea very quickly. Don't you think so, Anthony?'

Anthony gulped a third time and was about to say something when I cut across him.

'Yeah, Marianne, you did, and when you did tell everyone, your family fell to pieces. Correct me if I'm wrong, but I believe that your husband left you, your home was broken up, your relationship with your parents and your kids changed and half your friends stopped talking to you. That's the sensitivity that I'm talking about and the collateral damage that it causes, particularly to people who are completely fucking innocent.'

'Well, that's not true Jack, and by the way, the so-called friends that don't talk to me anymore mustn't have been very good friends in the first place, so good *fucking* riddance to them.'

The sound of Marianne emphasising the vernacular actually jolted Anthony, not that he wasn't used to the female expletive, but the way she pronounced the word 'fucking' had a kind of guttural and arresting feel to it, almost poetic.

'Ok guys, I know that this is an interesting conversation, but everyone else in the restaurant probably doesn't need to be part of it.'

We glanced around at the other tables and mumbled apologies to Anthony, and with that our tempers were interrupted as our meals arrived.

Anthony was not about to start the next conversation but neither did Marianne want to let this one drop.

'I don't know if you know, Anthony, but Jack hasn't met his son yet, or obviously his granddaughter.'

Anthony said nothing, pretended instead in fact that he hadn't been addressed. And then she addressed me directly.

'Freddie was telling me earlier that he, Saahira, and Fabeena are going to be away in Europe for the next few weeks, they won't be in London again for some time, in fact.'

'And?' I asked tetchily.

'Well, they're leaving next Monday but they're here for the rest of this week. I mean it'd be an opportunity for you to see Freddie, you know, before you go back to Ireland.'

It had in fact been in my head to possibly see Freddie on this trip but I just didn't want to be bounced into it by Marianne; I was now getting a better understanding of her prowess for manipulation.

'And you're here until tomorrow, is it?' I asked her.

'Oh, I'm away in the morning; I'm on the noon Ryanair flight.'

'Well, I'll see. We're up against it on this project so I'm not quite sure what spare time I'll have.' I looked at Anthony for some reaction but, as he had no idea if I wanted him to suggest that we'd have time or that there wouldn't be a minute to spare, he just kept eating as if he were on a table on his own.

'Let me look at it, Marianne, I'll let you know before tomorrow is out. I could possibly meet him some time Saturday, as it looks like we might be here until Saturday night or even Sunday. But please don't say anything to him until I get back to you tomorrow.'

'That'd be fantastic, Jack, of course I won't, I'll wait until you contact me.'

After a breather in the conversation, which only lasted a few seconds but seemed like an age, Anthony offered, 'Phew, good, so we can move on then.'

We all laughed a little nervously and were a little relieved, and on the strength of him getting the moment right Anthony summoned the courage to suggest a toast. 'To father and son.' To his evident relief, we raised our glasses, and as we toasted, Marianne added, 'To father and son and granddaughter.' *Never one to miss a trick,* I thought.

'So, tell me Anthony, how *does* your wife survive without you?'

I shot a look at Anthony who seemed to be considering the question at length, as if various responses were competing in his brain, and then he candidly offered:

'Well, it seems she survives by screwing other men.'

For the second time that evening I spluttered my wine. Marianne was left speechless and with her glass in mid-air. She looked at me, her whole face a question mark. I looked at Anthony who very casually lifted his glass of Chardonnay, took a sip, and just as casually placed it back on the table, then picked his fork up in his right hand and continued to dissect the sea bass on his plate.

'What Anthony means is that he and his wife, Jessie, are in the middle of a temporary separation,' I offered. But Anthony didn't seem to hear anything I said and carried on explaining almost disinterestedly:

'Three weeks ago, in fact, the day after I met you in Dublin, if you remember I was flying back the next day. Well, I arrived home a little earlier than expected, which by the way I now realise is a very dangerous thing to do - take my advice and always arrive on time, or better yet, late - and I walked in on my wife being screwed by a stranger, and in my own bed for good measure.'

'Jesus, Anthony, I'm so sorry, that's awful.' Marianne instinctively put her hand over her mouth and her other hand on his arm and gently squeezed it while she looked to me to say something, any fucking thing. But I was in the middle of realising that this had been the worst idea I'd *ever* had, possibly in my whole life. And all I could think of was, *why the fuck don't I take Al's advice more often*. Then Marianne moved her hand from his arm to his resting hand and gently squeezed it.

'So, needless to say, we've split up, it's over, our attorneys are agreeing on the details as we speak.'

'Oh God, I'm so sorry Anthony, I didn't know.' She threw a dagger-look at me, which screamed, '*why the fuck didn't you tell me.*'

'Ah, it's ok, maybe not the nicest way to find out, but it certainly deals with any ambiguity.'

I jumped in. 'But there's nothing final yet, Anthony, and from what you've told me and in spite of what happened you still have feelings for Jessie, isn't that true?'

'Well, yes of course, Jack, you can't simply erase nearly thirty years of being with someone without missing that life, no matter what the circumstances.'

'Well yes exactly, and we all make mistakes, there's none of us around this table who hasn't fucked up royally at some point.'

'Are you talking about me, Jack?' Marianne charged.

'I'm talking about all of us, Marianne, yes you, and me and Anthony I'm sure.'

'But you're really talking about me, right? You really can't get over my fuck-up can you, you really haven't forgiven me have you, Jack? You judge me, you blame me, that's why you won't see your son, because you can't get beyond the fact that I did the wrong thing thirty-five years ago, when you were nineteen by the way, nine-fucking-teen, and I was twenty-one. Yes, I fucked up when I was twenty-one and in deep shit at the time, but you, of all people, can't accept it … and yes, it was my fuck-up, but you were bloody involved too, boy.'

'Wow wow, take it easy, I didn't mean that, and you know it.'

'No, I won't take it easy. You fucking men are all the same, we make one mistake with our bodies and we get to pay for it the rest of our lives while you assholes can do what you fucking like and walk away with your dicks between your legs, give me a fucking break for Christ's sake.'

'But with respect, Marianne,' Anthony intervened - and I thought, *holy fuck* - 'you didn't make a mistake with your body; you made a mistake with your decision.'

'My decision? Ah, you mean my lie, go on say it, you mean my lie.'

'Actually no, I'm not talking about your lie, I'm talking about your decision; the decision you made to come clean ten years ago.'

Marianne looked thrown. 'You're saying that that was the mistake? That I should have lived with it for the rest of my life?'

'Well, I'm just saying that the decision had consequences for everyone, including yourself, and you made that decision knowing the consequences. Even now, ten years later, the fall-out is still being felt.'

'Ah, so you're suggesting that I should have lived with the lie and then everyone else's life would be unaffected? Take one for the team, is it, is that what you clowns call it, Anthony?'

'Well Marianne, I suppose what I'm asking is, what actually has been achieved? I mean besides the obvious destruction of your marriage, and the pain caused to your husband and your family, your friends.

The most important outcome should be what difference has it made to your son, knowing that his father was not his birth father. I would say it hasn't improved his lot one iota. It's more than likely injected uncertainty and doubt into his head. Maybe you've given him a burden to carry that he doesn't need, a quest to find his father, which must be like an unquenchable thirst. So yes, what have you achieved?'

Marianne went to answer but I lifted my hand slightly and cut her off and said firmly but gently, 'What has been achieved, Anthony, is the truth. But I think surely you're missing the bigger point, it's the lie that was the cancer, not the truth. The truth was the cure. Their marriage was based on a lie and not on honesty. Freddie's parentage was based on a lie and if the truth fucks with his head, or my head for that matter, then so be it. We're big boys, shit happens. I've got a friend, Alex, who you've both met. You, thirty-five years ago Marianne, and you last year, Anthony, and he's got this very simple philosophy which is to 'do nothing'. He calls it - rather unimaginatively actually - the principle of 'do nothing'. Ten years ago, had Marianne gone to him for advice he would have told her to invoke the principle; leave well alone, don't rock the boat, let sleeping dogs lie. But of course, he would have been tragically wrong, because their lives weren't well, and the boat was being rocked and the dogs weren't sleeping. What has been achieved, my friend, is the outing of the truth and I have the greatest respect for this lady who, knowing the consequences, had the courage to go through with it and do the right thing.'

I could see that Marianne was close to tears and she reached over and kissed me on my cheek and said, 'Thanks Jack, you have no idea how much that means to me.' Then she turned to Anthony and kissed him on his cheek and said, 'I respect your view completely, Anthony, I've often doubted the decision I made in coming clean but I've never regretted it, and although I don't agree with your view, I thank you for your honesty.'

Anthony smiled, turned to me and said, 'I got a bigger kiss than you, Jack, now tell me who's right or wrong.'

We finished our dinner and kept the rest of the conversation to so-called safer subjects like kids and Brexit and Trump, all of which drew loud groans (kids), disbelief (Brexit), and derision (Trump) from all three of us, but lots of laughter as well. At one point I excused myself to check in with Bea and on my return, I found my co-diners in the middle of a very obvious conspiratorial chat.

'What's the scoop, you two? Fill me in.'

'Nothing Jack, I was just telling Marianne about our problem at the office.'

I laughed. 'You're really an awful liar bud, I know that that's certainly not what you were talking about. Never mind, keep your little secrets, I'm not bothered.'

As we left the restaurant Anthony suggested that Marianne come back to our hotel for a nightcap. Ah, I thought, I never saw that coming, I really am blind to signals sometimes. To make up for lost ground when we got back to the hotel, I said that I needed to finish some bits and pieces in my room and bid them both goodnight. It was 11.00pm and I was happy to be in my own company for the last hour of the day. Once in my room I poured myself a Jameson, diluted with a little water, and listened to Elvis Costello and laid back on my bed. I closed my eyes, but not to sleep.

Well, it's decision time Jack, are you gonna meet your son or not?

Eh, 'course I'm gonna meet him.

I have to meet him; I have no option, especially after seeing him in the Market.

It's too irresistible for me; there isn't a force in the world that can stop me.

Part 3

* * * * *

Saturday 03rd June

There's nowhere you can be that isn't where you're meant to be ...
John Lennon

21

07.00am (14 hours to Nadir)

I didn't expect to see Anthony at breakfast the next morning at our usual 7.00am time, but when I arrived at the restaurant I found him with a half-finished breakfast, a cup of coffee in one hand, and the Times in the other. I caught the heading on the front page:

'*UK's Terror Threat Level Increased from Severe to Critical*'

'*Hm, that's not very comforting*' I thought, as I read the next line, '*UK bracing itself for further terrorist attacks.*'

'Ah, morning Jack, nice of you to eventually join me.'

'It's only seven, man, you're up early.'

'Been to the gym and everything Jack. You can't keep a good man down, you know.'

'Wow, I'm impressed. And how come you're not spilling crumbs on the bed sheets this morning instead of down here with me?'

'Hey, you're letting yourself down there, Jacko my friend.'

'Well, tell me, c'mon stop playing hard to get, cause you certainly weren't playing hard to get last night.'

'It's not what you think, we never left the lounge, and Marianne left a short while after you because she had to get up early this morning to get ready for her flight.'

'She left a short while after me? How short a while?'

'Oh, Jacko, now that'd be telling. That's all the information you're gonna get, my friend, except that I've been doing a lot of thinking … Now order your breakfast cause we have a busy day ahead.'

We spent much of that day as we had the previous few days, Anthony and his team poring over spreadsheets and looking for ways to discount the value of the enterprise and price-in risks, and me and my people talking to executives and the senior team and reviewing all aspects of the business. As before, the conversations were cordial, but we were both convinced that there was an underlying current at play, an agenda, and this was slowing up the valuation process considerably, and it meant that we would now most certainly be there all day today. We both had to be on planes on Sunday morning at the latest but we also needed to make a recommendation to our own Executive by Monday morning; whether to buy, and if so at what price, or not to buy, and if so why not. Therefore, we set an absolute deadline to have concluded our analysis and have our decisions made by 6.00pm.

During the morning, I called Marianne to tell her, to her absolute delight, that I'd decided to meet Freddie for dinner that evening, and she gave me Freddie's number. Then in the early afternoon Anthony caught up with me with two coffees.

'Ah, be wary of Americans bearing gifts. Everything all right?'

'Yeah, I guess. Well actually, I came in to tell you something.'

'Go on.'

'I've made a decision'

'Oh, should I be sitting down?'

'Yep, probably best … I'm gonna go back to Jessie.'

'*What*, my God, Anthony, when did this all come about?'

'Well, after we finished up last night and I eventually got to bed, I couldn't sleep. And I thought about everything, about Marianne and her lifetime secret, about you and Freddie, and having to tell Bea. And Maxine, and of course Jessie and the kids. And I thought that deep down, Jessie and I love each other but we've never really had an honest relationship. We've hidden behind being busy, behind the kids, work, golf clubs, bad sex, friends. And as we've kept ourselves occupied with stuff, we've mostly been avoiding talking about ourselves and our needs. Then the penny dropped with me, Jack. I'm not married to the woman who I interrupted screwing some guy a few weeks ago. I don't recognise that woman; she's not the Jessie who I've spent the last thirty-one years with. She's a different woman. What the hell have we been doing, Jessie and me? Well, I'll tell you: we've been playing games, smoke and mirrors, hide and seek and we don't actually know who the other person really is. But I want to get to know the woman who was having the affair, and I want her to get to know me. And I share the responsibility for what Jessie did. So, I rang her and I asked her if she wanted to start again, her and me, sell the house, move out of town, out of State even, or whatever. And after a few tears from both of us, thankfully she agreed.'

'Jesus, Anthony, that's fantastic.'

'So, from Monday we're going to find ourselves an apartment where we can live for a while and basically start again.'

'I'm so, so happy for you, Anthony, for you and Jessie. My God, that takes so much courage my friend, you're my hero.' I jumped up and embraced him.

'Well, let's not go over the top, I just wanted to tell you now because I probably won't get a chance later seeing as you're meeting Freddie and we've both got early starts tomorrow.'

'I'm so glad you have told me, and really delighted for you, but we'll get some time later or definitely before we split up, I promise.'

'Ok, well then back to this shit, we're together anyway at 6.00pm at the team meeting. It's decision time, my friend.'

Before I went back to my group, I called Freddie, my very first conversation with him. The call was answered after one ring.

'Hi, Freddie, it's Jack.'

I heard a sharp intake of breath. 'Hi, Jack, great to hear from you.' His voice was warm, friendly and encouraging, if a little nervous.

'Yeah, you too. So, I'm sure your mum told you that I might give you a call, are you ok to meet up this evening, get a munch and a beer?'

'Totally, I was hoping that we were still on.'

'Good, good, I was thinking somewhere casual, like the Borough Market maybe, is that ok with you?'

'Hey that's perfect, man.'

'Great, well why don't we say half seven at Hooper's on Stoney St., do you know it?'

'Course, a favourite of mine.'

'Good, good. Well see you then, Freddie, looking forward to it.'

'Me too Jack, see you then … hey Jack, Jack?'

'Yep still here, go on?'

'Thanks for making contact.'

'Course, see you later, Freddie.'

At 6.00pm Anthony and I met a very weary team in the boardroom to review the valuation. Each of the five work-stream leads gave their summary, and in each case the recommendation was that this acquisition made for very good value and exceeded the industry sector benchmarks. At 6.30pm the team dispersed to the four corners and Anthony and I were left alone.

'Decision time, Jack.'

'You first, what do you think?'

'The numbers say that only a fool would walk away from this. If we don't close tonight, we lose our preferred bidder position and the three other bidders are queuing up to grab it.'

'Tell me something I don't know, Anthony. Ok then, let me argue for the 'buy' position. We've done an intensive week's due diligence, all the metrics are positive, we'd be professionally reckless not to recommend this, so the answer is that we tell the board on Monday to buy.'

'But you don't believe that any more than I do, Jack.'

'Listen, we've done everything we can do to find hidden agendas and conspiracies. At the end of the day if it walks like a duck, etcetera, etcetera, chances are it's a fucking duck.'

'Yeah, maybe you're right, but it feels like a rat to me. My gut is rarely wrong, Jack, and by the way, neither is yours.'

'Ok, so what do we do? We've loaded the maximum delayed-payments against future earnings. If the earnings don't happen then we've mitigated our losses considerably.'

'Yeah, yeah I know, but that's not the point.'

'Well, what is the bloody point then?'

‘I just hate being taken for a fucking ride, Jack. I’ll tell you what; you head off to meet Freddie. I’m going to hang on here for a little while longer and chew the cud. The clock doesn’t run out anyway until midnight, but let’s both agree now that unless anything changes, we recommend the acquisition and I’ll send the email to the stakeholders before I leave later on.’

‘You sure you don’t want me to hang on with you, I can push Freddie back an hour or so?’

‘No, no, I’d actually prefer a little time on my own. You head off and meet your son, it’s long overdue.’

‘Ok, no problem, we’re gonna be in Hooper’s in the Borough Market and you’re welcome to join us for a pint later on after dinner.’

‘Go, go, go, my friend. I can tell that you’re nervous, so relax and enjoy it.’

‘Ok, ok, I’m out of here.’

We shook hands and I dumped my laptop and notes into my briefcase and, with my jacket over my arm, made my way to the street.

22

14.00pm (8 hours to Nadir)

As soon as Freddie had closed the call with Jack, he rang Marianne. 'I'm meeting him at half-seven.'

'Oh my God, Freddie, that's fantastic. I'm delighted for you, how are you feeling?'

'I'm not too bad now but I know I'm going to be as nervous as hell when I meet him.'

'Ah relax, he's lovely, you'll get on great together. What did he say when he rang? Tell me every word.'

'Not much really, just that he was looking forward to meeting up.'

'Ah come on, Freddie, give me more than that; tell me exactly what he said.'

'No, seriously, that's about it, we're meeting in Hoopers at the Borough Market, you've been there a few times with me and Saahira.'

'Yes, of course, I know it, but that's a bit casual, isn't it?' Marianne sounded disappointed.

'It's perfect, Mum. It's exactly where I'd want to meet him. Now I have to go. I was just ringing to fill you in, and I'll buzz you tomorrow.'

'Jesus, Freddie, tomorrow? And why can't you call me later tonight?'

'Ah, Mum c'mon. I'll buzz you early in the morning, I promise. Now I really gotta go here, love you.'

'Ok, love you Freddie and good luck.'

23

19.00pm (3 hours to Nadir)

I left the Hilton at seven o'clock after finishing a Jameson in my room in an effort to settle my nerves. However, as I made my way up Tooley Street, my nerves definitely weren't settled. It was only a twenty-minute walk to the Market, so I strolled casually to calm myself. I arrived at Hooper's ten minutes early and, as luck would have it, a young couple were just vacating the best table in the house, which was the one just inside the floor-to-ceiling window and which was open wide to the street. I grabbed the vacated table. Chuffed with myself, I ordered a beer and relaxed with a perfect view of Stoney Street in both directions and across to the Market entrance. But half-seven arrived and there was no sign of Freddie. *Hm, I'd probably have expected him to be on time considering the occasion.* Seven forty and there was still no sign of him, and at seven forty-five, I began to think that maybe I'd got the time wrong myself, maybe I'd said eight o'clock. Five minutes later I noticed someone, Freddie, jostling through the evening people traffic in a panic, in the direction of the pub. He was making for the pub entrance when I called him from my table, and Freddie, startled, just sidestepped a waiter carrying drinks.

'Jack?'

'Yep, that's me, hiding here in the window.'

'Jack, I'm so sorry I'm late, teething problems with Fabeena, I'll tell you later.'

'Hey, not a problem, Freddie.' I jumped from my stool and offered a gesture of embrace. Freddie didn't have to be asked twice and we hugged warmly, if a little awkwardly.

'What's your poison?'

'I'll have what you're having, I need a beer to calm and cool me down. Christ, I was afraid that you'd be gone, and I didn't even want to stop to call you.'

'Course I was never going to be gone, I thought that maybe I had the wrong time but I assumed alright that it was a female that delayed you. They have all the control, you know, even at that age.'

'Ha, I think you're right there, but I wouldn't be saying that out loud with Mum or Saa around.'

We sipped our fresh beers. 'So, Freddie, we finally meet, and you're all grown up and everything, fully formed and house-trained and with your own little family. Who would have thought, for God's sake?' He was smiling broadly. 'Tell me about this little family of yours, show me pictures. How did you and Saahira meet?'

Freddie relaxed and told his story, and I was truly surprised when the tale revealed that they had actually met here for the first time, outside these two pubs. 'When Saa heard that you suggested that I meet you here she said; "This is a good omen."' He continued with his story, describing his little girl Fabeena-Marianne, and it was clear that he doted on the child. He showed me lots of photographs and I suggested that, in spite of her colouring, I thought she had a Sommers look about her. Freddie laughed, saying, 'Sorry, but she's the head of her mother, even I didn't get a look in.' I listened intently to everything my son was saying, marvelling at the fact that we were actually having a beer and sharing a plate of tapas when only just over a month ago I didn't even know that he existed. *The curveballs that life throws at you,* I thought, *just when you think that you have it all figured out - well, nearly anyway - from nowhere comes this. If only Lizzie was here now, she'd be proud of me. "Embrace it bro." Well, I am embracing it, sis, and I'm loving it.*

Freddie asked about his half-siblings and I described each of them as best as I could, showing him pictures from my mobile. Ben's fierce independence, living now in Lyon, so determined to plough his own furrow; Sean's casual, almost lazy way about him, but very endearing, everyone loves Sean; and Sadie, well, what can you say about Sadie, a ball of energy, probably spoilt, and has me wrapped around her little finger, and she and her mother spend most of their time competing with each other probably because they're so very alike. *The funny thing is,* I thought, *I've never tried to describe them before, particularly their personalities.* And as I sketched them out as individuals, I was taken by how difficult I found it to capture their unique characters. *Christ, I need to spend more time with them!*

'Presume you haven't told them yet?'

'Jaysas no, I've only this week just told myself, Freddie.'

'And do you see it as a difficulty?'

'No, no … Well actually, yes! Maybe not your half-sibs but certainly their mother, Bea.' I explained how we had met in Lyon, and talked about our relationship over the years, which I found myself happily describing as very loving and positive and good. I talked a little about her propensity to stress, describing her gallery business and the issue with her current business partner as an example.

'Yes, I'll need to approach this with care, but approach it I will. Maybe the biggest challenge will be the fact that I've a granddaughter, which by the way I'm having difficulty even getting my head around. Not the fact that Fabeena exists but that I'm a grandad, a Papi, ha, and if I didn't see you coming from left field, I certainly didn't see the Papi bit coming.'

'And what about Ben and Sean and Sadie? How will they take it?'

'Christ, Freddie, I've no idea. I think that Sean and Sadie will probably be good with it but I'm not too sure how Ben will see it, him being the eldest. He might think that his position is being usurped or something. He's so bloody independent, but that might be a good thing too.'

'Can I tell you something Jack?'

'Yeah, sure, fire ahead.'

'I can't wait to meet them, especially now that I've met you. I was so nervous meeting you earlier. Yeah, Fabeena is teething, but to be honest that's not what delayed me. I could have been here in plenty of time but at the last minute, as I got closer to the Market, my courage deserted me. It's never happened to me before. I got so nervous I actually got sick, I thought about turning back and I had to pull myself together, talk to myself.'

'Hey, I was as nervous as hell too, Freddie, but I'm really glad that you didn't turn back, and don't worry, you'll get to meet your brothers and sister and …'

Just then, my mobile rang. It was Anthony. I checked my watch to see it was 9.25 and excused myself to take the call.

'Anthony, what's up bud?'

Anthony sounded wound-up, hyper.

'Jack, I found it, I found the problem. It's a bloody scam.' Anthony sounded so excited that he struggled to contain himself.

'Wow wow, calm down, are you sure, where are you?'

'I'm still here, I knew that they were up to something, Jack, and you knew it too, and I found it. Thank Christ I found it because we'd have been screwed.'

'Ok ok, what's the scam, what are they up to?'

'I'll explain when I see you, but essentially they're selling about 10% of their output to a third-party company who they actually own, and so the stuff is really being traded twice, which is inflating their margins, but the problem is that it's bloody quasi-legal. I'll have to explain later, but the bottom line is we can't recommend it, Jack.'

'The bastards, jaysas, Anthony, well done, my friend, you're a genius. Course we can't recommend it - have you emailed our guys yet?'

'No, not yet. I've written the memo, I just wanted to confirm with you before I push the button.'

'Well, go for it and then get your ass down here for a pint when you're out of there.'

24

21.30pm (30 minutes to Nadir)

Anthony reread the email and satisfied himself that it covered all the conditions for a 'Do Not Recommend' position, pressed 'send', and with a whoosh it was on its way. He knew that he and Jack would need to prepare a more detailed report on Monday, which would bring the curtain down on his career with the firm, and he smiled as he said out loud; 'And I can't bloody wait.' Then he packed his notes and his laptop into his case, slipped on his jacket, and said good night as he passed the doorman in the lobby. He checked his watch: 9.40, and, with a bounce in his step, he turned in the direction of the Borough Market.

25

21.40pm (20 minutes to Nadir)

At that very same moment, a white Renault van was driving west, down Mile End Road and also in the direction of the Borough Market. It had come from Barking in East London and its destination was anarchy. Its three occupants were a mix of nationalities, but they had one thing in common: they were radicalised Islamic extremists and each was well-known to the police and MI5. Their leader was Khuram Butt and he had enlisted the other members into the banned extremist group al-Muhajiroun. The driver of the van was Youssef Zaghba and, as he negotiated the relatively light Saturday evening traffic, they were quietly focussed on their destination. Khuram Butt thought back to the events of the last few months and weeks and days. He thought of the detailed planning that went into their mission, their mission for Allah. He thought about his wife, his three-year-old little boy, and his new-born baby girl who was just a few weeks old. He hadn't bothered to say goodbye to them. Remembering what his spiritual leader had said: 'The real life is the life of the akhirah, the afterlife, not this life.' So, in this life there was no room for sentiment. Sentiment was for other days, for other people, weak people. And those other people didn't understand him, even his own family, his own flesh and blood didn't understand him or his cause. They were not pure, they were westernised, contaminated by the kafir trappings. He fumed at the thought of it. Even his own wife didn't understand him. He had told her that he wanted to go to Syria and fight in the holy war and she had laughed at him. And later he told her that he was going to take a second wife, the Syrian doctor, as was his right, and she laughed louder at him, shouted at him, took their child and left. But she couldn't stay away, and she came crawling back after a few weeks.

In fact, it would have been better if the misguided woman had left forever. Oh, the disappointment and frustration of everything, of life, of hopes and dreams unfulfilled, of rejection. One minute you're a TV star and the next, rejection. And by your own people. By the Mosque. By Saahira the Syrian doctor, and her stupid husband, who he had seen only recently in the Market when they were carrying out their reconnaissance. *I should have killed him then*, he thought. No, this was not a time for sentiment, this was a time for action, for retribution.

Then he did a mental summary of the elements of his plan. Earlier that afternoon he had walked into the rental reception hall in Harold Hill, in Havering, East London and rented the Renault Master van for just twenty-four hours. He was actually looking for something bigger but he was satisfied with the large functional van and so he drove back towards Barking to meet up with his two friends and accomplices, Rachid Radouane and the youngest of the trio, Youssef Zaghba.

Once he had them together, he supervised the assembly of the tools for their mission, their mission for Allah, their mission of death and destruction. First, the bags of gravel which he had purchased in a neighbourhood B&Q. These, he believed, would give the van ballast and weight and that added unstoppability. Next, the fake explosive vests, simple water bottles duct-taped to three waist belts, one for each of them. This he knew would make the police nervous and therefore it should give them maximum time to carry out their holy mission. Then the firebombs. They had filled thirteen wine bottles with petrol and then stuffed rags into the necks of each one and shook each bottle so that the rags became infused with the flammable liquid. Next, he checked the blow torch, igniting it to make sure that it was functional. Carefully placing the petrol bombs and the blow torch in a crate, he had them loaded into the back of the van. They then dressed in the terrorist clothes that they had specially selected. Finally, the knives. They each had a twelve-inch kitchen knife with a ceramic blade which they had purchased in their local Lidl, and they strapped them to their wrists using leather ties, which gave their weapons added leverage and guaranteed that they could not be disarmed. Satisfied that all was in readiness, Butt and his associates knelt and prayed to Allah to keep their hands sure, steady, and strong, and for a quick deliverance to His arms as soon as they imparted maximum carnage.

Just before 9.45pm they reached London Bridge and travelled south across it. They carried out their reconnaissance along the bridge and also at the other side down Borough High Street, then a few minutes later returned and crossed back over the Thames northbound. At the northern end, they made a U-turn and then once again drove southbound across the bridge. As they progressed, Khuram Butt signalled the driver, who jammed his foot on the accelerator and swung the steering wheel hard to the right, directing the van towards the pavement, mounting it three times at high speed. A young French couple, Xavier Thomas and Christine Delcros, were walking hand-in-hand, sightseeing, when the van mounted the pavement and struck Xavier Thomas from behind and catapulted him into the Thames. He was the first person to die. His body wouldn't be found for three days.

Zaghba continued steering the van across the pavement of the bridge and then drove onto the central reservation at Borough High Street, destroying the tyres and crashing into the railings. The three killers abandoned the vehicle and, armed with their knives, sought out their next victims. They didn't have to look very far. In her attempt to escape, a young woman had slipped in her heels and an onlooker, who saw the impending danger, selflessly ran to help her to her feet. But they were easy prey for Butt and his accomplices who surrounded them and attacked them, stabbing both to death. They never stood a chance.

The killers then ran down the steps to Green Dragon Court. Here they set upon a group of customers and pedestrians by the Boro Bistro pub, stabbing and wounding them. They then went back up the steps to Borough High Street and randomly attacked, killed, and injured bystanders and patrons as they made their way through the eateries and cafes of the Borough Market. They were shouting, '*this is for Allah … this is for Allah*,' as they headed in the general direction of Stoney Street. And, although they were in turn attacked by bystanders, sometimes in arm-to-arm mortal combat, using whatever means at hand, the terrorists could not be stopped.

26

21.56pm (3 minutes to Nadir)

I was unaware of the maelstrom of deathly energy enveloping the Market and moving inexorably toward us, as Freddie and I were engrossed in our own intimate world of exploration and inquiry, chatting about everything and anything; our families, our jobs, our taste in music, and of course, football. Then I saw the familiar figure of Anthony making his way up Stoney Street and I hopped off my stool and stepped out onto the pavement and waved to get his attention.

27

21.58pm (1 minute to Nadir)

Anthony was happy, no, beyond happy, ebullient. His head was buzzing, having just solved the most frustrating and difficult business challenge, in spite of the company's executives' best efforts to obstruct him. And now also his mind was settled about Jessie, he knew that it would work, work better than ever before, and he was so excited at the prospects of their new and uncharted journey together. Added, of course, to the fact that just now he was meeting his good friend, Jack, the best company any man could have. As his senses tingled with life, soaking up the rich and varied culinary aromas of the Market, he caught sight of his friend, animatedly waving to him, and in acknowledgement he raised his hand. And as he made his way towards Hoopers, he couldn't help himself from grinning broadly.

Just then, as he got to within twenty metres of the bar, his line of sight was attracted to some activity at the top of the street, behind where Jack was standing. There was some disturbance, some fracas developing, and it was moving in their direction. His antenna went on high alert. The scene looked weird, wild, violent, out of control, men in hunting mode, flailing their arms erratically, people running to escape. His gut seized with anxiety, with fear, as he realised the extent of the horror unfolding and the impending danger to his friend. He picked up his pace and started shouting, '*Jack, Jack, behind you.*' As he got closer, he could see that there were possibly three attackers moving threateningly down the street, almost casually jogging from side to side. Just then he had a fearful thought, a terrible realisation. *Sweet Jesus,* this is it, *my nightmares weren't about events of the past, they were premonitions, warnings of what was to come. This is what my nightmares have been trying to prepare me for.* Even as the thought crystalized, one of the killers broke off, and unprovoked, attacked a man who was coming from a laneway. The man fell to the ground, motionless.

28

21.59pm (Nadir)

Khuram Butt saw someone waving his arms ahead of him up the street. The man was wearing a blue shirt and had his back to him. Waving like a fool, begging attention, pinning an irresistible target on his back. Butt made his way towards him, *like lambs to the slaughter* he thought. Then his attention was distracted by someone screaming; 'Behind you Jack, behind you,' trying to warn his unsuspecting dupe. *Ah, an American, definitely an American accent,* and he saw this big man running towards them. Just a few seconds before Butt reached his target, the American screamed abuse at him; '*Hey asshole, you fucking animal.*'

In a moment of indecision, Butt stopped short, and triggered by a hatred in his heart for all Americans, he reacted involuntarily and changed direction, and with his weapon poised he lurched instead at his abuser, shouting, 'Allahu Akbar.' He only struck him once, but the lethal shaft went deep to the hilt. He felt it vibrate against hard bone and deflect into soft, unresisting organs. As he extracted the blade, he knew that the American was finished and so he turned his attention to his original target, the man in the blue shirt. For a moment their eyes met.

29

22.00pm (Nadir)

The whole incident, which took just a few seconds, was viewed in horror by Freddie, who was blocked by the bar table and was momentarily unable to intervene. He struggled to get free, kicking stools and pushing over the table, aware that Jack had rushed toward his fallen friend but also seeing that the killer wasn't yet finished.

Freddie screamed at Butt; 'Y*ou fucking cunt, I'll fucking kill you*.' Butt turned in the direction of the verbal abuse, and then an extraordinary moment of recognition occurred. Freddie recognised the face of evil, the face in the car outside his house, and just recently, the face in the Market. The killer smiled at his luck; 'I don't believe it' he laughed, 'Praise be Allah, you have delivered the husband of my Syrian doctor.' and he theatrically wiped the bloody blade on his beard, and grinning, he mocked, 'I clean this just for you, kafir.' Freddie picked up a fallen bar stool and swung it violently, like a man possessed, as he launched himself toward the killer. The force of the stool knocked Butt to the ground and, although a little dazed, he swung the knife wildly, barely missing his target. Freddie backed back toward Jack, putting himself between the killer and his father, holding the stool in front as a shield, or if necessary, a weapon. Suddenly there was the sound of sirens from somewhere nearby, and Butt's two associates, who had become separated from him, ran back to their leader and shepherded him away, saying; 'We must go Khuram, come, there are bigger fish this way.' And the three terrorists made their way down the street, in the direction of the sirens.

30

22.01pm (Nadir)

I caught Anthony as he slumped to the ground, just getting my arm under his head before he hit the pavement. I knelt and cradled him in my arms, weeping. 'Jesus, Jesus, Anthony what have they done?' I kissed his forehead. 'Please, please wake up, Anthony, open your eyes. Freddie, give me your shirt quickly, for God's sake.' As Freddie ripped his shirt off, I gently lifted Anthony's polo shirt to see the severity of the wound, but even as I looked, there was a steady beat of blood pumping from the hole in his chest. I folded the shirt a few times and covered the wound, keeping pressure on it, as he began to drift in and out of consciousness. Then he seemed to get some strength and, smiling thinly, mumbled something. At first I didn't understand and so I pressed my ear to his mouth and barely heard him say in broken breaths, '*Third … time unlucky … Jack … but I didn't freeze … I love Jess … the kids.*'

'Jesus, Anthony, please stay with me, the ambulance is on the way. Don't go to sleep, my friend, *don't go to sleep*.'

Suddenly, the sound of gunshot blasts from down the street, maybe a dozen or so, followed by a second burst of gunfire. A moment of silence. Quietness. I sensed Anthony weakening in my arms, and I could feel his life slipping away. I brought my mouth to his and, although I felt frantic, I tried to quell my panic and with steady breaths, I pushed air into his lungs, again, and again; *keep them working, keep them fucking working*. I now lived only in the intensity of the moment, in the minutiae of the act, counting every breath, feeling dry lips and the warmth of our mouths, and sensing my friend's faltering grasp on life, slipping,

slipping away. I felt someone pulling at me, separating us, and I became aware again of the outside world; shouting, screaming, weeping, sirens, people running, police barking orders, and two medics gently pulled me away from my friend and then calmly but urgently assessed his condition. I had Anthony's hand clasped in mine and I wouldn't let it go.

One of the medics touched me on my shoulder; 'We need to get him out of here, sir, we urgently need to get him to a hospital.'

I became aware of Freddie releasing Anthony's hand from mine, Freddie on his knees with his arm around me, and I realised that I was shaking uncontrollably. I watched the medics, in a well-practised manoeuvre, transfer Anthony to a trolley and slide it into the ambulance. My eyes were drawn back to the pavement where he had fallen; blood stains, so much blood, still fresh, still alive, and mockingly dancing in the reflective blue of the ambulance lights. I reached out and touched with my fingers the stain, the stain of violance, the stain of extreme intolerance. The medics wrapped a blanket around my shoulders and, with Freddie's help, encouraged me to climb into the ambulance. They sat me next to Anthony as he lay on his cot, and before the doors were closed my son embraced me and whispered, 'I'm so, so sorry, Jack, but he protected you, he protected us.' A policewoman had run over and was talking to the medics, asking them about Anthony, taking notes, and then I heard her say, 'Yeah, it's a terrorist attack, Isis more than likely. They're dead, three of them, and it looks like we have about seven or eight dead, and loads injured, some badly, maybe up to fifty. I've never seen anything like it in my life, it's bloody carnage.'

31

22.15pm (Nadir)

As I held his hand, I was distantly aware of the ambulance screaming through the London streets with its sirens blaring and it seemed like forever before we reached our destination. Then it came to a stop and the doors were flung open and hospital staff swarmed around us. 'Where are we?' I asked one of the medics.

'St. Thomas' Hospital sir, he'll get the best of care here.'

Anthony was quickly taken from the ambulance and rushed through the hospital doors as a female medic barked orders amidst a scene of controlled chaos. As I was helped from the ambulance a police car arrived carrying Freddie, with a blanket wrapped around him. We were brought to an observation room and given medical checks, and other than both of us being in a state of shock, we were otherwise given the all-clear, but we were advised to stay overnight for observation. Two Met officers stayed with us and carried out a preliminary debrief, during which I was surprised to hear Freddie inform them that in all likelihood he had come across the killer twice before. A short time later we were joined by the female doctor who had earlier taken charge of Anthony. Even before she introduced herself, I knew her tidings.

'Mr. Sommers, Jack if I may, I'm Anna Franchetti, I'm the senior doctor on duty tonight. I understand you are Anthony's friend?'

'Yes, yes I am'

'I'm very sorry, Jack …'

'Yes, I know.'

'We did everything we could, but his injuries were critical. I'm really sorry that we couldn't do more for him.'

Although I wasn't surprised, I could feel my shoulders hunch with a terrible resignation. 'Thank you, I know you did, there was nothing you could do. I knew that he had gone, I knew that when he was in my arms.'

We were given a private room for the night's observation. Freddie called Saahira and explained that he was with me in St. Thomas', and, to her utter shock, filled her in on the essence of what had happened. He later told me that he intentionally omitted to tell her that he recognised the killer as possibly her clinic patient, the crazy guy who had asked her to marry him. There would be time enough to unpick that one over the next twenty-four hours. He also called Marianne just to say that we were both safe, but that my colleague had been killed, little knowing the brief moment that she and Anthony had shared just the previous night. I made the difficult call to Bea and broke the tragic news about Anthony. Bea was hysterical, but then she quickly thought about Jessie.

'Jesus Jack, poor poor Jessie, who's going to tell her?'

'I'll tell her, once I've spoken to the police.'

'Oh Jack, this is awful, someone needs to be with you. I'll get a flight over first thing in the morning, or maybe Ben could get there faster from Lyon, you can't be alone there.'

'No, no, I'm fine, darling. The staff here are excellent and I should be home tomorrow anyway, hopefully.' As I said this, I looked at my first born sitting across from me and thought ruefully; *If you only knew, ma cherie, but you will very soon.*

And then my attention turned to Jessie. I asked the police officers if I could be allowed to break the news to her. They agreed, once they'd had time to inform their Framingham counterparts who would visit her house to be with her. And so, I scrolled my mobile contacts for Jessie's number and when I found it I just sat on the bed and stared at it for a long time. As I looked at her name

I couldn't help saying out loud; 'He saved my life, how can I tell her that he gave his life for mine?' The officer suggested kindly, 'You don't need to tell her everything now, sir, there might be some things that you'll wish to tell her at a later time, maybe face to face. For now, she just needs to understand a few details. A terrorist attack in London, unfortunately her husband is one of a number of innocent victims, and you were with him at the end.'

'And he told me to tell her that he loves her.'

'Yes of course sir, tell her that, of course tell her that he loves her. Our colleagues in Framingham will call us shortly when they're at her house and you can make the call then. We've notified the US Embassy also, so they'll coordinate everything from here.'

The night wore on. Medical staff came in every hour to monitor us both, do tests, ask us questions, and check for shock. We didn't speak to one another very much throughout the night but when we did, it was to recall once again every detail that led to the attack and every exhaustive microsecond of the attack itself. Questioning one another: Where was I standing? Where were you sitting? How far away was Anthony? Did you see the attackers? Why didn't we see the terrorists earlier? What were his last words again? What did the killer say? And so on. But nothing changed each time of the asking, or the telling. Mostly though, a silence came over us and we fell into our own thoughts, our own reveries, alone with our own demons as we questioned ourselves: *could I have done anything differently to have altered the outcome? Maybe moved here, jumped there, reacted faster, said this or that.* But other than choosing some other restaurant in some other part of town, it seemed that everything, contrived to lead us to that moment. That destination. Our date with destiny. The nadir of our lives.

On occasions during the night, my thinking became confused, muddled. I found it difficult to hold on to reality, unable to ground thoughts, battling abstracts, punching clouds.

Anthony was dead. Was he dead? I need to check his body. But why was it Anthony? Was it fate, that ultimate agency that put him right there, at that precise moment? No, it was I who put him there. He had no business being in the Market, except my business. My business killed him. He died in the middle of his life. And what about his nightmares, his dreams of paralyzing guilt? But when it mattered, he didn't freeze. Is death the only exit of nightmares?

But I froze. And Jessie, poor Jessie, screaming down the phone at me, crying and screaming, robbed of a second chance with a beautiful man, robbed of any chance. What of her guilt. What of my guilt.

32

Sunday 04th June, 6.45am (Nadir)

I awoke from a light sleep with a start. Sweating, my neck cramped from sleeping awkwardly in the chair. The clock on the wall read 6.45am. I had been asleep for only thirty minutes by my reckoning, but it was enough to momentarily erase the horror of the previous night and now I had to relive it and experience it all over again, as if for the first time. *Will this be my sleep future?* I looked over at Freddie, who was dozing in the other chair. I got up and opened a window to freshen the room. The morning had fully arrived, and everything in the outside world looked normal, surreally so. Dogs barked, cars passed, birds sang. But not in my world, my world was in turmoil, my world was fucked.

At 9.00am, Freddie and I were given a final medical check and we were cleared to leave St. Thomas'. Someone had procured an ill-fitting shirt for Freddie, and the two Met officers who had stayed close to us for the night drove us to my hotel and from there to Heathrow. Freddie stayed with me until I was safely aboard the 12.15 Aer Lingus flight to Dublin.

As the aircraft powered its way up into the clear June summer sky, shimmering in the noonday sun, I pondered the last few weeks; the last few days; the last few hours, and wondered, where to from here? Which direction would my life now take me, take my family? Where is my destiny?

One thing I knew for sure though, and knew it with the utmost of certainty; everything now was different, everything now was changed, changed utterly, and nothing could ever be the same again.

Epilogue

There's a crack, a crack in everything,
that's how the light gets in, that's how the light gets in
Leonard Cohen, Anthem

Why did he protect me? Why did he choose to save my life over his? The question haunted me as my flight took me over the Pennines and on over the Irish Sea, and then later during the two-hour drive home to Galway. *Was it instinctive, reactive, an automatic response maybe? Or did he feel that he was indestructible, incapable of death, because of 9/11 and Charlie Hebdo. What did he say? 'Third time unlucky.'* Tears welled up in my eyes every time I remembered the moment. And I went over and over it again in my head. *When I turned to see what Anthony was shouting at, I looked straight into the crazed face of the killer, and for a split second, our eyes met.* But the danger was incomprehensible to me, I didn't understand and so I just stood there for that split second, dumb, and froze. *I did nothing. I just stood there while he killed Anthony. I fucking froze.* Somewhere between Dublin and Galway, I rang Lizzie. I had already called her at 7.00am from the hospital and had filled her in on the previous night's events, just the bare facts. But now I needed to tell her what had really happened. She listened carefully. In the telling I cried, cried hard when I relayed the killer's moment of indecision because Anthony offered his life for mine. 'And I froze, Lizzie, I fucking froze while he killed Anthony.' My sis told me to get off the motorway at the next ramp and pull into the side of the road.

'You didn't freeze, darling, you're just imagining that now. It sounds like it all happened in the blink of an eye. You didn't freeze, you just didn't have time to react, there's a world of a difference between them. Anthony had time to do something and he did the only thing open to him, and I promise you that you would have done exactly the same. You're in shock bro, and you're feeling guilty now - and so am I because I should have picked you up from the fucking airport.'

'No no, I'm ok sis, I'm fine, I promise, I've had my little breakdown. I guess I needed to say it out loud, and thanks, you're the best.'

'No Jack, it's you who are the best. You've been through hell and back in the last twenty-four hours and you're not out of the woods yet. But you need to remember one thing really well - the killers are the bad guys here. Anthony did what he did probably because he loved you and wanted to protect you, but - and this is the important thing - I know you better than anyone else in the world and I promise you that you'd have done exactly the same to protect him.'

Because of investigative delays and international red tape, it took two weeks to repatriate Anthony's remains. Jessie, Maria, and Julian flew to London to bring him home, and Bea and I travelled back to Boston with them. He was buried in the Castelletto family grave in Fairview Cemetery in Boston and, even though he was in his nineties and frail, uncle Syl led the graveside eulogy, and Jessie and the kids said their chosen words also. And then Syl asked whether the Irish visitors might like to say something and I, taken by surprise, thought for a moment and offered, 'My friend Anthony is a hero. You should be so, so proud of him. And it's important you know that his final words were that he loves his family, he dearly loves Jessie and Maria and Julian. And you know something, I didn't realise how much I loved this man until it was too late, but it's a lesson I'll take with me forever.'

Bea and I stayed over in Framingham for a few days after the burial, much to Jessie's appreciation. On one of the evenings the two women went for dinner and I was left to my own devices. But I had a mission of my own. I called a cab to take me to the Black Cat Club in town and smiled to myself when I entered and heard Dolly singing *The Great Pretender.* She winked at me when she caught my eye. I found a table where I had a view of the stage and the bar and in no time a waitress appeared dressed in a cowgirl outfit.

'Hello honey, my name is Candy and I'll be your waitress for the night. Eating on our own, are we?'

'Yes indeed, thanks.'

'Ah, you're English honey, how cute. My great grandpappy was from England, and do you like what you see?' and she pushed her breasts almost into my face like I'm sure she had done with Anthony and every other male customer at the bar. 'I mean on the menu, baby.' She gave me a well-rehearsed laugh and showed her breasts even more if that were possible without them being released from their meagre and ever-suffering stays.

'Irish, actually. And I'll have a Bud please, and your deep-fried fish and fries.'

'Oh, my gawd, you're Irish, how cute. Beer and scampi coming right up darling, and would you like a bit of company with that?'

I guessed that it didn't matter whether I said yes or no, I was getting company anyway, but I said that I was ok on my own, just to see what would happen. In a couple of minutes Candy arrived with my beer, and soon after that my uninvited company arrived with my fish and chips.

'Hi honey, Candy tells me you're Irish, that's so cute, my great grandma came from Ireland,' as she shuffled in alongside me and offered her hand. 'My name is-' But I interrupted her before she had a chance to say it.

'Maxine, you're Maxine.'

'Oh, Candy told you?'

'Nope, but my name is Jack, Jack Sommers. I was a friend of Anthony's.'

I saw the shock on her face as her shoulders slumped. 'You're Jack, of course you are, you're Irish Jack, Anthony told me about you, oh my God, I can't believe you're here. I can't believe what happened to him, we saw it on the news. I cried and cried and cried, poor Anthony.'

'Yeah, it was terrible. But he told me about you too, Maxine, he told me all about you.'

'Really? He talked about me?'

'Yes, of course he did, that's why I called in to see you, to tell you that you meant a lot to him. He'd want you to know that.'

'He was my knight, you know, my knight in shining armour. He wanted me to go to Europe with him, but I couldn't. I told him that I didn't have clothes for Europe and he laughed. We had such fun together, Jack. I know it was just a short time, a few weeks only, but he was such a lovely guy. I couldn't go to Europe with him 'cause I was afraid that I'd fall in love with him, you see. No, I *knew* I'd fall in love with him, and it would break my heart, Jack, and I couldn't let my heart get broken again. It wasn't really the clothes, you see. He told me what happened with his wife - poor Anthony - but I know that deep down he loved her, so I told him to go back. You see, it was never the clothes, Jack.'

'Yes, he told me. Listen, he bought you something. Obviously his intention was to give it to you himself but, well …' I took a small gift-wrapped box from my pocket and handed it to her. She impatiently tore off the wrapping and slowly opened the box. Inside was a gold ring which had two hands holding a heart underneath a crown. There was a little note folded underneath which she opened and read aloud: *Max, you're a sweetheart, love Anthony.*

'I was with him when he bought it, he wanted to get you something nice, but he didn't know what to get and I suggested this. It's called a Claddagh ring. It represents friendship and love. It's of Irish origin, actually from Galway, where I live, and Anthony loved Galway and said that it was perfect for you.'

She put the ring on her middle finger and brought it to her lips and kissed it, then turned to me and put her arms around my neck and drew me close. She hugged me tightly and whispered, 'Anthony was right, you're a good man, Irish Jack.'

About two hours into the Airbus A321 return midnight flight from Boston to Dublin, I was sipping a Jameson, unable to sleep, unlike Bea who was sleeping soundly alongside me (Bea's big moan about flying was that she could never relax on planes, but the reality was that Bea could never stay awake on flights). She was lying on her side in her business class seat with one arm thrown over my waist. I thought about the last couple of traumatic weeks. Bea and I had flown to London to be with Jessie and the kids and it had taken an excruciatingly long time to release Anthony's remains. The grief-stricken family were hanging around the hotel for days trying to come to terms with his death and then wanting to see where the attack took place. I offered to take them there, back to the Market. It was still closed to the public, but the police escorted us up Stoney Street and we stopped outside Hoopers. I described as best I could how it happened. The five of us stayed there for a while, variously weeping, talking, asking questions, giving each other comfort. Maria and Julian wandered through the market with one of the officers and Jessie, Bea and I huddled and embraced. Although earlier I had dreaded bringing them to my ground zero, I subsequently realised that it had been a hugely cathartic experience, not only for Anthony's family, but also, surprisingly, for myself and Bea.

And then, of course, I thought about Bea's reaction when I told her about Freddie. Early on Sunday morning, the day following the attack, Bea apparently had called the three kids and asked them to come home as soon as they could so that we as a family could be together for a few days. I got home from London that Sunday evening and Bea and Sean and Sadie were waiting for me. Ben had booked himself on an afternoon flight from Lyon and was due to get in later that evening. I relished the support and closeness and comfort that I felt in the bosom of my lovely family. I went to bed early that night not long after Ben arrived home; exhaustion had finally caught up with me. But I didn't sleep well, and my mind was bubbling with procrastination about when the best time would be to tell Bea. I woke with a start just after 6.00am and, as quietly as I could, I left our bed and went to the kitchen to make myself a cup of tea.

'Here, let me, darling.' Bea's voice came from behind me. 'I'll make one for myself too. You didn't have a good sleep. I could feel you were restless all night.'

'Sorry I woke you, hon.'

'It's not a problem, Jack, I was asleep with one eye open anyway.' and she wrapped her arms around me. 'God, it's so good to have you home safely.' I sat on one of the kitchen chairs and Bea put our teas on the table and sat alongside me. 'You poor baby,' she said.

Now is as good a time as any … I hoped!

I reached out for her hand and held it in both of mine.

'Hey Bea, there's something I need to tell you and there's no easy way of saying it, but I guess now's as good a time as any.'

She looked at me and I could see by her face and the tension in her hands that her already primed senses were going on high alert. I know she feared the worst. It was as if this was the moment when all of her insecurities were about to say *I told you so.*

'It's another woman, isn't it?'

'What? Christ no, Bea, no, of course not, it's you who I love, for God's sake. Anyway darling give me a chance to talk, you couldn't guess in a million years what I'm about to tell you.' And I held her hands firmly and started. 'When I was nineteen and just out of boarding school, I met this girl …'

And I told her the story, the story that was thirty-five years old and yet strangely just four weeks new. And I omitted nothing in the telling, including meeting Freddie for the first time only thirty-six hours earlier at the pub where Anthony was slain. I told her about Freddie's wife and daughter, my granddaughter, whom I hadn't yet met. I told her about my own confusion and disbelief and the positive paternity test. And I told her about my concerns and worries about our own family, Bea and the kids. She never tried to interrupt me once while I spoke. And then I was finished.

And she said nothing for a while, and then; 'This woman, whatever her name is, did you love her back then?'

'Jaysas, Bea, I was nineteen for God's sake. I came out of the darkness; I was bumping into walls. Love? I obviously didn't even know how to have sex, girl.'

'And now? What do you feel about her?'

I leaned forward and put my hands on either side of her face, and pressed gently.

'It's you I love Bea, it's you I've always loved from the first day I saw you in the park by the Pont du Morand. I've never stopped loving you and I've never loved anyone else. Marianne may be the mother of my son but that's all she is. She means nothing to me and she will play no part in my life, in our lives, I promise you that.' I knew that she was upset, confused, trying to absorb the shock, but I felt that we were safe, and so I went further; 'There's one other thing I want to tell you, Bea. I've come to a decision, a big decision actually. I want to leave the firm, do something different with my life. Be home more, with you and the kids, help you with your business. Don't worry, I'll stay miles out of your way, but I want to be more available.'

I knew that Bea had spent years negotiating her bouts of anxiety, her troubled thoughts, fighting demons, worrying and waiting for someone to destroy her happiness - which paradoxically was the very fuel which fired her distress. She'd sometimes confide that she could actually make herself ill, anticipating, waiting … waiting for someone to break up her family, a woman to steal me away from her, or some dreadful catastrophe that would take our kids. She told me later that in her anxiety, she always knew that this moment would arrive. So, when I finished telling her my story, she said that she felt strangely calmed, soothed, and almost secure. The moment had arrived. But she still had her man, and her kids were safe upstairs in their beds, and her life wasn't broken. Most importantly, she said that the moment had passed. We both knew of course that some turbulent waters would still flow under that bridge of anxiety before Bea could fully take on board the new reality. But right then, in that moment, she felt calmness and we both felt a renewal of a fundamental trust in our relationship. It seemed to bring us back to our earlier years when we were first together.

We told the kids later that morning. And if Ben's nose was out of joint, he didn't let on. Bea opined that maybe it was because there was such an age gap between he and Freddie, but either way, the three seemed genuinely excited that something new had come into their lives, and the only question now was: how soon could they meet?

Obviously, there were the texts and calls from Marianne. I ignored them for the first few days. But it was frighteningly reminiscent of that summer of '82 when she had tried in vain to contact me. And yes, I was now certain that I had indeed avoided her back then, but now I also understood why. Of course, it wasn't because I had some knowledge or insight or premonition of Marianne's pregnancy. I now understood that I had avoided her because I was hiding from my own embarrassment, my shame, my inferiority, my ignorance. I'd acted with cowardice, but not with any malice.

On the Tuesday after Anthony's death, I went on my own for a walk up over the hills behind our house. After a while I stopped and rested on a rocky outcrop, which gave me a view overlooking our house far below, and in the distance the village of Spiddal and beyond over the ragged rocks and jagged coastline surrounding the bay. I called her then.

'I was worried about you, Jack.'

'I'm fine, Marianne.'

'Poor, poor Anthony.'

'Yeah, it's awful for his family. Bea and I are flying to London tomorrow to be with them.'

'Freddie told me how it happened. It must have been dreadful for you.'

'Well, it wasn't great I suppose.'

Silence.

'I was thinking, Jack, now that you've met our son, maybe the three of us could get a meal sometime. You know, some evening, in Dublin or in London. Whatever would work for you, what do you think?'

Fuck I thought, *straight to the point and straight to her next agenda.*

'No, Marianne, I don't think that that would be a good idea at all.'

'Oh, why not?'

'Listen, I'm delighted I've met Freddie and I intend fully embracing our relationship. I'm really looking forward to getting to know him and for him to meet my kids and Bea. And I can't wait to meet his wife and my grandchild.'

"*Our* grandchild, Jack."

Silence.

'And me, what about me, where do I fit in?' she asked.

'Well, I think you've done what you set out to do, Marianne, which was to get me and Freddie together and I fully admire your drive and your determination in achieving that.'

'But?'

'There's no but. That's it. We need to move on now, Marianne. And you must understand that there's no little family of Freddie, you, and me. There's you and Freddie, and there's me and Freddie. Be grateful for what you've achieved.'

As Bea sleepily turned closer into me now, I put my arm gently over her shoulder and with my other hand lifted the window blind and looked out into the vast blackness of the night. It felt like the plane and its quiescent occupants were hurtling into a black void, a dark emptiness. But in the far distance, far away to the east, in the direction which the jet was travelling, I could just make out a pale light on the night horizon. Red-tinged and expectant, and I marvelled at the breaking of a new dawn.

Notes on the Terrorist Attack
London Bridge and Borough Market, 3rd June 2017

The Attack

At 21:58 BST, on 3 June 2017, a terrorist vehicle ramming and stabbing took place in London. A van was deliberately driven into pedestrians on London Bridge, and then crashed on the south bank of the River Thames. Its three occupants then ran to the nearby Borough Market area and began stabbing people in and around restaurants and pubs. They were shot dead by City of London Police officers. Eight people were killed, forty-eight were injured, including members of the public and four unarmed police officers who attempted to stop the assailants. British authorities described the perpetrators as "radical Islamic terrorists".

The attack was over at 22:16

The so-called Islamic State group took responsibility for the attack.

The Victims

Chrissy Archibald, Canadian (30)

Sebastien Belanger, French (36)

Kirsty Boden, Australian (28)

Ignacio Echeverria, Spaniard (39)

James McMullan, UK (32)

Alexandre Pigeard, French (26)

Xavier Thomas, French (45)

Sara Zelenak, Australian (21)

Note: Anthony Castelletto is a fictional character

The Terrorists

Khuram Butt, Pakistani (27)

Rachid Redouane, Moroccan (21)

Youssef Zaghba, Moroccan (22)